PENGUIN BOOKS

Fools of Fortune

William Trevor was born in Mitchelstown, Co. Cork, in 1928, and spent his childhood in provincial Ireland. He attended a number of Irish schools and later Trinity College, Dublin. He is a member of the Irish Academy of Letters.

Among his books are *The Old Boys* (1964; Hawthornden Prize), *The Boarding House* (1965), *The Love Department* (1966), *The Day We Got Drunk on Cake* (1967), *Mrs Eckdorf in O'Neill's Hotel* (1969), *Miss Gomez and the Brethren* (1971), *The Ballroom of Romance* (1972), *Elizabeth Alone* (1973), *Angels at the Ritz* (1975; Royal Society of Literature Award), *The Children of Dynmouth* (1976; Whitbread Award), *Lovers of Their Time* (1978), *The Distant Past* (1979), *Other People's Worlds* (1980), *Beyond the Pale* (1981), *The News from Ireland* (1986), and *The Silence in the Garden* (1988). He has also written many plays for the stage, and for radio and television. Several of his television plays have been based on his short stories. Many of his books are published in Penguins, including an omnibus, *The Stories of William Trevor*, containing five collections of stories. In 1976 Mr Trevor received the Allied Irish Banks' Prize, and in 1977 was awarded an honorary C.B.E. in recognition of his valuable services to literature.

Fools of Fortune won the Whitbread Award for the Best Novel of 1983. It has received considerable critical acclaim: the *Daily Telegraph* called it 'a sad book . . . written with wisdom, delicate comedy, and a sweet, beguiling nostalgia for what could have been. And throughout, a sense of gentle, philosophical resignation eases the sadness'; Philip Howard in *The Times* wrote, 'a beautiful, affectionate and humorous, as well as a terrible story . . . William Trevor at his best'; the *New Statesman* commented, 'a fine piece of work . . . it communicates something authentic: a sense of melancholy; yet a complicated one, not without hope – a view of real people in a real world'; Melvyn Bragg in *Punch* thought it a 'supremely well achieved and absorbing novel' – and Molly Keane, author of *Good Behaviour*, called it 'a wonderfully moving and important book'.

WILLIAM TREVOR

Fools of Fortune

PENGUIN BOOKS

PENGUIN BOOKS

Published by the Penguin Group
27 Wrights Lane, London W8 5TZ, England
Viking Penguin Inc., 40 West 23rd Street, New York, New York 10010, USA
Penguin Books Australia Ltd, Ringwood, Victoria, Australia
Penguin Books Canada Ltd, 2801 John Street, Markham, Ontario, Canada L3R 1B4
Penguin Books (NZ) Ltd, 182–190 Wairau Road, Auckland 10, New Zealand

Penguin Books Ltd, Registered Offices: Harmondsworth, Middlesex, England

First published by The Bodley Head 1983
Published in Penguin Books 1984
9 10 8

Copyright © William Trevor, 1983
All rights reserved

Printed in England by Clays Ltd, St Ives plc

To Jane
and in memory of
my father

CONTENTS

Willie 7

Marianne 105

Imelda 149

Willie 177

Marianne 185

Imelda 189

WILLIE

I

It is 1983. In Dorset the great house at Woodcombe Park bustles with life. In Ireland the more modest Kilneagh is as quiet as a grave.

To inspect the splendours of Woodcombe Park and to stroll about its gardens, visitors pay fifty pence at the turnstiles, children twenty-five. The descendants of the family who built the house at the end of the sixteenth century still occupy it and are determined to sustain it. They do not care for the visitors, the car parks they have had to make, the litter left behind. But naturally they do not say so.

Near by, the small town of Woodcombe – to which the family gave their name and where, traditionally, military ribbons and puttees are manufactured – is famous for the delicacy of its mullioned windows. After an inspection of the manor showpiece the visitors like to linger there, consuming in the Copper Kettle and Deborah's Pantry the butter-scones and shortbread for which the town is famous also in 1983. They do not know that nearly a hundred and sixty years ago an Anna Woodcombe, then a girl of seventeen, married an Irishman called William Quinton who took her to live in Co. Cork, in the house called Kilneagh, not far from the village of Lough, not far in turn from the town of Fermoy. They do not know that two generations later an army colonel who was a poor relation of the Woodcombes of Woodcombe Park found himself stationed with his regiment in Fermoy; his daughter, too, married a Quinton and became mistress of Kilneagh. His second daughter married an English curate, a fortunate marriage for the young man, since the Woodcombes of the manor had in their gift the living of the town. This couple's only child was brought up in Woodcombe Rectory and later caused history again to repeat itself, as in Anglo-Irish relationships it has a way of doing: she fell in love

9

with a Quinton cousin and became, in time, the third English girl to come and live at Kilneagh.

It is the voices of these cousins that are heard there now. In 1983 no one pays fifty pence to see Kilneagh or to stroll about its gardens. No one points out to tourists that it was the Anna Woodcombe of the nineteenth century who planted the Kilneagh mulberry orchard, remembering the one at Woodcombe Park; or that the name Kilneagh might possibly mean the place of the church, perhaps even a foundation of St Fiach. No one suggests that the family name of Quinton must derive from St Quentin, a name originally of Normandy.

A mile and a half away, the village of Lough is without attractions, its concrete convent dominating the single street, with agricultural machinery displayed next door to it. There are no teashops, only Sweeney's garage and public house, where a cup of tea might possibly be had, and Driscoll's all-purpose store, where it would not occur to visitors to linger. The sense of the past, so well preserved in the great house and the town in Dorset, is only to be found in echoes at Kilneagh, in the voices of the cousins.

2

I wish that somehow you might have shared my childhood, for I would love to remember you in the scarlet drawing-room, so fragrant in summer with the scent of roses, warmed in winter by the wood Tim Paddy gathered. Arithmetic and grammar books were laid out every morning on an oval table, red ink in one glass inkwell, black in the other. In that distant past I didn't even know that you existed.

'*Agricola*,' Father Kilgarriff said on the day I began to learn Latin. 'Now there's a word for you.'

On the sides of the brass log-box there were embossed scenes, and the one I liked best was of a farmhouse supper. Men sat around a table while a woman served, one of them reaching behind him to seize her hand. You could tell from the way he had twisted his arm behind him that it was a secret between them. Was the woman another farmer's wife? Was this man coveting her, or were they taken in adultery? The brass people were almost faceless because the working of the metal didn't allow for much detail of feature. It was odd that the men wore their old-fashioned caps while having supper.

'In Latin we decline the noun, Willie. Nominative, vocative, accusative, genitive, dative and ablative. *Agricola, agricola, agricolam, agricolae, agricolae, agricola.* Do you follow that, Willie?'

I shook my head.

'Farmer,' said Father Kilgarriff. 'O farmer, farmer, of the farmer, to the farmer, by with or from the farmer. Have you caught the idea of it, Willie?'

'I don't think I have, Father.'

'Oh, Willie, Willie.'

Father Kilgarriff always laughed when he said that. He was unfrocked, but in our Protestant household he continued to wear the clerical black and the collar that marked his calling. It suited him: he was as dark as a Spaniard, and said himself that he must have Spanish blood. His laugh was soft and in his sallow, handsome face his eyes were without bitterness, in no way reflecting the disgrace in his life. He lived in the orchard wing with Aunt Fitzeustace and Aunt Pansy, having been taken in by them as their lodger after his misfortune. According to Johnny Lacy, who worked at our mill, Father Kilgarriff was able to pay only very little for the food he ate, which was why he looked after the cows and taught me my lessons. He came originally from the village, but it was in a parish in Co. Limerick that he'd been unfrocked. He would have crept into a Limerick slum room, so Johnny Lacy said, if he hadn't been taken in at Kilneagh. I thought of him as old but I don't imagine he could have been more than thirty at that time. He was the gentlest man I've ever known.

'Does *agricola* mean farmer, Father?'

'You're getting it now, Willie.'

Carved into the white marble of the mantelpiece were one hundred and eight leaves, in clusters of six. Four tall brass lamps had glass globes shaped like onions; the Chinese carpet was patterned with seven shades of blue. My great-grandfather, framed in gilt above the mantelpiece, had most of his hair on the right-hand side of his head and looked like a spaniel. Born in the year of the French Revolution, he was the most extraordinary of all my Quinton ancestors. He had planted two lines of beech trees on either side of the avenue to celebrate the victory at Waterloo; and thirty years later he made himself famous through his eccentric memorial to his wife, whose portrait hung above the mantelpiece also. Anna Quinton had travelled the neighbourhood during the Famine of 1846, doing what she could for the starving and the dying, her carriage so heavy with grain and flour that once its axle broke in half. *The meat goes bad in the heat*, she wrote, *but even so they grab it from my hands*. When she died of famine fever her dog-faced husband shut himself into Kilneagh for eleven years, not seeing anyone. It was said that she haunted him: looking from his bedroom window one morning he saw her on a distant hill – an apparition like the Virgin Mary. She told him that he must give away the greater part of his estate to those who had suffered loss and deprivation in the famine, and in his continuing love of her he did so. His son, my grandfather, who was twenty-five at the time and should have inherited these acres, looked wryly on. According to Johnny Lacy, he hadn't had the heart to bother much with what was left: it was my father who had pulled everything together again.

'We decline the noun, Willie. We conjugate the verb.'

'I see, Father.'

It was the spring of 1918 and my father wanted to send me away to a boarding-school, but my mother wouldn't hear of it until I was older. That time would come soon enough, she used to say in a way I found ominous, for I had no wish ever to leave Kilneagh. I was eight in 1918, a straw-haired boy with the family's blue eyes and a face that caused strangers to enquire if I were delicate.

'Will we tackle a bit of history?' Father Kilgarriff suggested, pushing aside the green Latin grammar. History excited him, but he was suspicious of the victory that followed battles, and of war as a means to an end. His hero was Daniel O'Connell, who had brought freedom to the Catholics of both Ireland and England and had not cared for violence either. Father Kilgarriff spoke of him often, but also dwelt on the long gallery of men and women who had enlivened the story of our rebellious island: Queen Maeve and the Kings of Munster, Wolfe Tone, Lord Edward Fitzgerald, Robert Emmet who had loved Sarah Curran, Thomas Davis who had written poetry. England was always the enemy: at the great battles the blood of the contenders mingled in a torrent, and the greatest encounter of all was the Battle of the Yellow Ford.

'It should have been the end of everything,' Father Kilgarriff stated. 'The beginning of a whole new Ireland, but of course it wasn't. You can't put your trust in battles.'

I didn't quite know what he meant, but I did know that victory had somehow been turned into defeat, for even as I learnt about that new beginning in 1598 Irish soldiers were fighting for England in the German war. The village was empty of men, and so was Fermoy, where the army barracks were. 'It's a long way to Tipperary,' the soldiers sang together, whether they came from Lough or from Sheffield. Johnny Lacy used to sing that song for me, explaining that he hadn't gone to the war himself because of his short leg.

O'Neill, who was the gardener at Kilneagh, had been too old to go, his son, Tim Paddy, too young. But I could remember two or three of the men who worked in the mill showing off their uniforms and their haircut. They'd been delighted with themselves, but later had perished with other men of the Munster Fusiliers at Sedd-el-Bahr. And before that, in the first few days of the war apparently, Aunt Fitzeustace's husband, an Englishman to whom she'd been married for only a month, had been killed in France. Soon afterwards she returned to live again at Kilneagh, although all that is outside my memory.

Every day at half-past twelve Father Kilgarriff left the drawing-room and returned to the orchard wing, so called because of the mulberry orchard that stretched behind it. Kilneagh had been built in 1770, its gardens laid out at the same date, the orchard added later. Ten white-framed windows dominated a stone façade; there were pillars and steps and urns, and a white hall door; some clever piece of architecture had arranged the chimneys so that they were not visible above the slated roof. The house itself was shaped like an E with its middle prong missing, the two wings protruding at the back, with a cobbled yard between them. The kitchen wing, containing the kitchen of the main house, had a long, cool dairy that opened on to the yard, and a warren of upstairs rooms, only a few of which were used; behind it was O'Neill's vegetable garden. In the orchard wing there was a smaller kitchen, so that my aunts, with their maid Philomena and Father Kilgarriff, were independent of the workings of the main house. Aunt Fitzeustace and Aunt Pansy were my father's sisters, Aunt Fitzeustace of strong, muscular appearance and with a notable jaw, given to wearing tie-pins and tweed hats, Aunt Pansy meek, with apple-pink cheeks. They were often to be found in the garden, Aunt Pansy looking for flowers to press, Aunt Fitzeustace cutting areas of grass which crusty old O'Neill said did not require cutting, or manuring shrubs which he said would not benefit from manure. They had their own pony and basket-trap to bring them to Lough or Fermoy, and they had collected a large number of stray dogs which my father objected to but did not forbid.

'Well, how did you improve the morning?' he enquired at lunch on the day I began to learn Latin, and when I told him about *agricola* and how you had to think of it in six different ways he hastened to change the subject. He touched his forehead with the tips of his fingers, a gesture which reflected a claustrophobic affliction aggravated by too much, or too rapid, talk. My father liked a tranquil pace in all things, and time for thought. With his two black labradors nosing the backs of his legs his favourite walk was down the avenue, wrapped in the silence induced by the beech trees that celebrated Napoleon's defeat. Their branches looped and interwove overhead, their leaves held off the sky: in spring and summer the avenue of Kilneagh was as silent as a cave, which was when my father liked it best. He would listen for ages to O'Neill or Father Kilgarriff provided they didn't rush at him with speech, which both of them had learnt not to do. My mother didn't either, but sometimes it was difficult for Tim Paddy to remember because he was young, and it was difficult for me and for my sisters. At table my mother made quietening gestures with her hands, and in the kitchen Mrs Flynn, the cook, would warn a new maid that my father disliked noise or voices raised. He always smiled when touching his forehead with the tips of his fingers, as if he considered his weakness a little silly. Nor did he ever himself insist that tranquillity was his due: that wasn't, as my mother would have put it, his style. He was a bulky, lazy-looking man in tweeds, with a weathered brown face, very much the Irish seigneur. He said himself that his chief characteristic was a Cork man's failing: he could never make up his mind or come to a decision on his own. 'I don't know what I'll wear today,' he'd say at breakfast, sitting there in his pyjamas and a teddy-bear dressing-gown, waiting for my mother to advise him.

My mother was tall, with a delicate oval face and eyes that reminded me of chestnuts. She had black hair, parted in the middle, and below it her nose was delicate and straight and her lips like a dark red rosebud. She presided over the household with untroubled authority, over my father and myself and my sisters, Geraldine who was seven at that time and Deirdre who was six. My grandparents on my father's side of the family had lived with us in the main house but they had both died a year ago, in the same month. Besides Mrs Flynn in the kitchen there was a single housemaid at Kilneagh, and Hannah who came from Lough on Mondays and Thursdays to scrub the floors and do the washing. O'Neill and Tim Paddy lived in the gate-lodge, its tidy little garden colourful with hollyhocks and herbaceous borders. Because Mrs O'Neill was no longer alive they had their meals in the main kitchen and sat there for a while in the evenings. Both of them were stunted, O'Neill completely bald, Tim Paddy with a ferrety look.

'Well, what's the way of it this afternoon?' my father asked that lunchtime, and my mother said that she and the girls were going to ride. 'And Willie? Walk over to the mill?'

'Don't forget your homework, Willie.'

'Oh, after tea,' my father said.

A new maid was to arrive that afternoon and because the previous maid had already left Mrs Flynn brought in the tapioca pudding herself. Geraldine and Deirdre ate it with dollops of raspberry jam but my father and mother added cream and I followed this grown-up example, although I would much have preferred the jam. My father told us about an occurrence at the mill that morning, how an old tinker had arrived there, claiming he was dying. When everyone's back was turned he had helped himself to an ounce of Mr Derenzy's snuff and various documents that were valueless to him.

'Oh, poor old fellow!' Geraldine cried.

'Poor Mr Derenzy, you mean,' Deirdre corrected. '*Dear* Mr Derenzy.'

They giggled through their mouthfuls of tapioca and were told not to by my mother. My sisters laughed inordinately at anything that was even faintly humorous. For the rest of the day they would talk about this lone tinker, wondering if he slept with the rain beating down on his face, as the tinkers who wandered the country-side on their own were said to. On our walk to the mill I asked my father if the story was true or if he'd made it up to amuse the girls. He smiled, and I knew he'd just been having fun.

After that we proceeded in silence for a while, the labradors obediently at our heels. The path from the house began in a shrubbery of towering rhododendrons, continuing through a gate that neither my father nor I ever opened, choosing instead to climb over it. Cows grazed in the sloping pasture beyond, and at the top of this there was a spot from which the mill and the house could both be seen, and the distant Haunt Hill, so called because of its haunting by my great-grandmother. We descended steeply then, through a birch wood and by the edge of a field that was ploughed in March and thick with growth by June, a mass of corn in August. Before we reached the mill my father said:

'You'll enjoy it, you know. You know you'll enjoy it, Willie.'

He spoke of my going away to the school he'd been at himself, in the Dublin mountains. He worried sometimes in case Father Kilgarriff was not preparing me well enough, which was why he had wanted to send me to a preparatory school.

'You'll play rugby, Willie, and cricket maybe. You'd never find games like that in Lough.'

My father laughed, amused at the sophistication of cricketers in our village. I had never seen the games he spoke of played, but on our walks to and from the mill the rules of both had been explained to me and I had pretended to understand.

'The teaching's famous there, Willie. Pakenham-Moore became a circuit judge, you know.'

I nodded, endeavouring to display enthusiasm. He had also told me about a game called cock-fighting, a boy perched on another boy's shoulders and smacking with his fists at a third boy, similarly mounted. There was fagging, and the tradition of flicking pats of butter on to the wooden ceiling of the dining hall. Prefects could beat you with a cane.

We reached the mill and I accompanied my father to his office, where Mr Derenzy was copying figures into a ledger. A fire was blazing in the grate, its coal recently renewed, the hearth swept. Mr Derenzy brought sandwiches every day and ate them at his desk during the lunchtime break. Afterwards, if the weather was to his liking, he went for a walk and was often to be seen staring down into the water of the leat, a man devoted to Kilneagh Mill and to my father – and in a different kind of way to Aunt Pansy. Red hair fluffed into a halo about Mr Derenzy's skull-like head and his blue serge suit shone here and there, polished where his bones protruded. Clipped to the top pocket of this suit was a row of pens and pencils, their neat presence a reflection of his pernickety nature. He disliked rain and heatwaves and warned Aunt Pansy against drinking from a cup with a crack in it. He carried a supply of snuff with him at all times, in a tin that had originally contained catarrh pastilles: *Potter's, the Remedy* it said, red letters on a blue ground.

Unlike the other men at the mill, Mr Derenzy was a Protestant, which allowed him to have pretensions in the direction of my aunt. But considering himself socially inferior, he had never thought it proper to propose marriage. 'Oh, for heaven's sake, man,' my father used to urge him, 'say the word to her and have done with it.' But Mr Derenzy would look away in excessive embarrassment. Every Sunday afternoon he arrived at the orchard wing to take Aunt Pansy for a walk and afterwards returned to Sweeney's public house in Lough, where he lodged. According to Johnny Lacy, who appeared to know everything that went on in Sweeney's, he spent Sunday evening drinking cups of weak tea and worriedly dwelling upon his presumption.

'I'm getting the February overheads in, Mr Quinton,' he said now. 'Afternoon to you, Willie.'

'Good afternoon, Mr Derenzy.'

'Liver and tapioca pudding,' my father reported. 'Were Mrs Sweeney's sandwiches up to scratch?'

'Oh, never better, Mr Quinton.'

I knew that one day I would inherit this mill. I liked the thought of that, of going to work there, of learning what my father had had to learn about grain and the machinery that ground it. I liked the mill itself, its grey stone softened with Virginia creeper, the doors of lofts and stores a reddish brown, paint that over the years had lost its shine due to the sun; in a central gable the green-faced clock was always a minute fast. I loved the smell of the place, the warm dry smell of corn, the cleanness even though there was dust in the air. I enjoyed watching the huge wheel turning in the mill-race, one cog engaging the next. The timber of the chutes was smooth with wear, leather flaps opening and falling back, then opening again. The sacks had *Quinton* on them, the letters of our name arranged in a circle.

Memory fails me when I think about the men of the mill: names are forgotten, except for Mr Derenzy and Johnny Lacy. Faces return instead, and arguments about the revolution that had exploded in Ireland in 1916 and was not over yet. 'I wouldn't drink a bottle of stout with de Valera,' a voice protests scathingly. 'I wouldn't stand beside him at a crossroads.' And a cool reply comes, that Dev was above the drinking of stout with anyone.

One man was tall and thin, another's face was half obscured by a hedge of moustache, a third wore a black hat that never left his head. Johnny Lacy had a way with him and was always laughing, his face crinkling up with merriment when he told his stories. These had mainly to do with the people of our own household and the men of the mill, but there was also the one about the dwarf's wife, late of Fermoy, who could eat French nails, and the one about the soldier at the barracks who had ridden a horse through Phelan's shop window to win a bet. There was the deranged man from Mitchelstown who claimed to be the King of Ireland and the woman who bred fleas because she liked them. Johnny Lacy had a reputation as a rake and was a star turn on the dance-floor in spite of his short leg. He was particularly fond of the fox-trot and would often demonstrate the step for me, clasping in his arms an imaginary girl. The round shape of Haunt Hill with its little jagged tip was like a woman's breast, he told me, wagging a neat, oiled head which smelt of carnations. A suave devil, my father called him.

That spring afternoon I loitered in the part of the mill where the men were working, as I often did. Mr Derenzy hurried in twice with invoices, his clerkly Protestant voice pitched high above the rush of water and machinery. It wasn't a busy time of year. The chutes were being repaired, sacks sorted out. Johnny Lacy and the man whose moustache was like a hedge were working a scales, and for half an hour or so I moved the weights for them. Then I began to walk back to the house, not waiting for my father because he wouldn't be ready until much later. There were Mr Derenzy's figures to look through and then he would answer any letters that had come, the labradors sprawled by his feet in front of the fire. He would walk about the

18

mill, having a word with the men: all of it took time and usually I preferred to return home on my own, running down the slope of the pasture to the gate in the rhododendron shrubbery, my feet crunching a moment later on the gravel that was spread in a semicircle around the house. I still think of approaching Kilneagh like that. The beech-lined avenue with the tall white-painted iron gates at the end of it was as impressive as my father ever claimed, but in my childhood I liked best of all the walk through the birch wood and the fields.

As I entered the house I was still thinking about the school in the Dublin mountains. My father's good-natured efforts to ease me into its traditions had become a source of mild terror and I regularly lay awake at night wondering about being savaged with a bamboo cane. 'Ah, no, no,' I would make Dr Hogan from Fermoy pronounce. 'No, Mr Quinton, I'd say Willie's too delicate for a place like that.' But I also knew that my delicate appearance was misleading. 'Healthy as a nut,' Dr Hogan had stated more than once.

'We didn't see that tinker,' Deirdre remarked at teatime. 'Did you see the poor old fellow, Willie?'

I shook my head, my glumness not quite slipping away, as usually it did when I was no longer alone. My father's school trunk would be taken from the attic, where he had told me it still was. Our initials were the same: we could have the white paint that marked them freshened up, he had said, and the brass lock cleaned.

'No, I didn't see him,' I replied.

We sat, spaced far apart, around the big mahogany dining-table that was always covered at teatime with a white linen tablecloth. There were egg sandwiches, and brown bread and soda bread and bread with raisins in it. There were scones that were still hot, and coffee cake. My mother asked me if everything had been all right at the mill. I said it had, and she told me about their ride through the bluebell spinney near Haunt Hill, over country that had once been Quinton country, home by the old quarry. Sometimes I went on that ride myself, on Geraldine's pony, Boy.

'The new maid's called Josephine,' my mother said, cutting the coffee cake. 'Tim Paddy's gone to Fermoy for her.'

'Was Kitty sacked because she broke the chrysanthemum vase?' Geraldine enquired.

'Well, actually, Kitty's getting married.'

'I told you,' Deirdre cried, dramatically flashing her eyes, a habit that moments of triumph brought out in both my sisters.

'Oh, I know she's marrying that beery fellow.' Geraldine disdainfully sniffed. 'I only wish she wouldn't.'

'I don't think we should call him beery,' my mother protested. 'A red complexion doesn't always mean a person drinks too much.'

'Mrs Flynn says he drinks like a bottle. She says he'll lead Kitty a right old dance. Actually, I'm never going to marry anyone.'

'Will Kitty and the beery fellow have a honeymoon?' Deirdre asked, and Geraldine said she could just imagine them, drinking like bottles on a strand somewhere. Pretending they were unable to control their laughter, they pressed their fists against their mouths until my mother said that was enough now.

When the giggling had subsided and each of us had eaten the single slice of coffee cake we were allowed, Geraldine asked me what Mr Derenzy had said when I'd seen him, for the utterances of Mr Derenzy were of great interest to my sisters.

'Only "good afternoon".'

'Did he ask after Aunt Pansy?'

'He never does.'

'Did he offer you a pinch of snuff?'

'No, not today.'

'I wish he'd marry Aunt Pansy and come and live in the house. Wouldn't it be lovely, having Mr Derenzy walking about the garden?'

'If I had to marry anyone,' Deirdre said, 'I'd marry Mr Derenzy.'

'Oh, so would I.'

Soon after that my sisters went off to the stables and my mother said she'd help me with my homework, if I should need any help. I said I would because I enjoyed it when we sat together at the oval table in the drawing-room, working out the cost of five dozen clothes-pegs at three-farthings each, or learning about the continental shelf.

That day we investigated the conflict which Father Kilgarriff considered so important, the Irish victory which the clever English had later turned into defeat. '*August 15, 1598,*' I read aloud. '*Sir Henry Bagenal, marching out of Newry, was defeated on the River Blackwater by Hugh O'Neill and Red Hugh O'Donnell. The victory was a total one, and the disaffected throughout the land everywhere took up arms.'*

In a moment we put the history book aside and my mother spoke of the long English occupation which had succeeded that famous battle, and of how advantage was at present being taken, as it had been taken in the past, of England's foreign war, even though Irish soldiers were helping to win it. 'I wish the rising had succeeded that Easter,' she said. 'The whole thing would be over by now.'

But at some point while she was speaking my mind had drifted away, to the school in the Dublin mountains. I knew that when the moment came to mention it to her my mother would be sympathetic. It was she who really made the decisions, she who was more in touch with things. She spoke French and German, she understood the intricacies of mathematics: far more than my father, she would appreciate that Father Kilgarriff's teaching was perfectly adequate, that boarding-school was quite unnecessary.

'Well, that Josephine'll be here.' She smiled at me as she stood up, lightening the mood which the talk of war and revolution had inspired in her and which my gloomy face no doubt suggested she had inspired in me. 'One of these days it'll all be all right,' she added.

I puzzled my way through algebraic equations and pages of tedious fact about natural resources in Lancashire. I learnt part of 'The Deserted Village', and then I took my books and the two inkwells from the oval table and placed them in a drawer of the big corner cupboard with my pens and pencils and blotting paper. My father insisted that all signs of my lessons should be removed from the drawing-room by the evening of every day.

I made my way to the cobbled yard between the two wings at the back of the house, over which Tim Paddy was brushing water. He was smoking a Wild Woodbine cigarette and as a greeting he slanted his head at me in a way he had. It was pleasant in the yard or the big old dairy at that time of day, everything clean again after the milking of the cows, the buckets laid out, upside down in a row, hens and ducks waiting in the doorway for Tim Paddy to finish. Sometimes he would lean on his brush handle and his ferrety face would bristle with excitement as he told me how he intended to enlist in the Munster Fusiliers the very minute he was old enough. He had heard talk in the village of adventure and companionship in foreign parts, of cities rich with wine and scented women. 'You're the biggest eejit this side of Cork,' his old father used snappishly to grumble at him. 'Can't you stay where you are and not go looking for destruction?' But he might be washing the cobbles of our yard for ever, Tim Paddy pointed out, while the whole world passed him by.

That evening, when he saw me, he didn't remove the Wild Woodbine from his mouth in order to settle himself for leisurely conversation. 'The new maid's prettier than Kitty,' Geraldine called out, passing through the yard with Deirdre, who added that the new maid had lovely hair.

I pretended to be not much interested, although I was. I watched while Tim Paddy finished his task and threw away the butt of his cigarette. 'Wouldn't you go and take a look at her?' he eventually suggested. 'She's nice all right.'

I remembered my mother showing Kitty where O'Neill's vegetable garden was when Kitty was new, but when I went to look there O'Neill was on his own, crouched among drills he had dug, planting potatoes. He didn't reply when I spoke to him; he rarely addressed either my sisters or myself.

I left the vegetable garden by a door in its high brick wall. The door was set in a narrow arch and was painted the same colour as the woodwork of the mill. Mr Derenzy had once told me that a large supply of this brown-red paint had been on sale at the Admiralty supply stores in Cork, cheaply priced at the end of the reign of Queen Victoria. I remembered his saying it as I stood by the door hoping for a sight of the new maid. My father ambled through the high rhododendrons, returning from the mill with his labradors dawdling behind him. He would go straight to the dining-room and pour himself a glass of whiskey, as he did every evening. Then he would settle himself down in one of the leather armchairs with the *Irish Times*.

Daisies were beginning to shower the lawns, where there had been snowdrops not long ago. The sound of the Angelus bell carried through the clear evening from Lough, and I imagined O'Neill crossing himself among his potato rows, and Tim Paddy doing the same in the yard, and stout Mrs Flynn pausing for a moment in the kitchen, and my aunts' maid pausing also. From the distance came the barking of their stray dogs, out for an evening run through the fields.

'This is Josephine,' my mother said, stepping through the French windows of the morning-room, on to the grass. Already the new maid had changed into her uniform: the hair Deirdre had spoken of was fair and smooth beneath the same white cap that Kitty had worn, her lips had a pretty pout. The fragility of her face might have been reflected in her hands but, like Kitty's, they were chapped and coarse. For some reason I noticed that at once.

'How d'you do?' I said, and Josephine made some shy reply.

My mother led her away, into the morning-room again, to begin her duties. I did not know then that our household was complete, that Kilneagh was as I've always since remembered it.

3

Would we have loved one another then in whatever way it is that children love? You might have lived at Rathcormack or Castletownroche, even in Lough itself. During all the years that have passed I've often pretended that you did. I've closed my eyes and seen you in church on Sundays, your blue dress, that artificial rose in the band of your hat. I've glanced across the pews at you, unable to prevent myself, as Mr Derenzy could not prevent himself from glancing at Aunt Pansy.

'O Lord, correct me, but with judgement,' old Canon Flewett pleaded every Sunday morning; 'not in Thine anger, lest Thou bring me to nothing.' Mrs Flewett played the organ, the psalm of the day was said, the *Te Deum* and the Creed; my father read both lessons. Geraldine and Deirdre observed Mr Derenzy's admiration of our aunt, nudging one another with their elbows. When they became bored they blew through their teeth and my mother frowned at them.

Mr Derenzy collected the money, a moment of great excitement for my sisters because it was Aunt Pansy's turn to admire her admirer, which with discretion she did. She gazed straight ahead of her, permitting a glow of pride to suffuse her apple-like features when he offered the wooden plate to Canon Flewett, who placed it on a larger one, of polished brass, and offered this in turn to the Almighty.

'Well, thank you so much, Mr Quinton,' Canon Flewett invariably said in the churchyard, and then thanked Mr Derenzy for going round with the plate. The other Protestant families of the neighbourhood stood around, conversing about agriculture or the weather. Many of them were related, cousin marrying cousin, as the local habit was. In a procession we would pass through the lich-gate, its black ironwork arching above us. Mr Derenzy walked the length of the village street with Aunt Pansy, and my father and Aunt Fitzeustace were occasionally put in mind of some incident in the past. 'Who's that woman in the purple?' I remember his once enquiring, and Aunt Fitzeustace reminded him that she was a distant relative of the Quintons over whom he had upset a blackberry ice cream when he was five. One way or another, there were quite a number of distant Quinton relatives.

During church our dog-cart and Aunt Fitzeustace's basket-trap were left in Sweeney's yard, the horse and pony munching oats from their nosebags. 'Safe journey home,' Mr Derenzy wished us, helping Aunt Pansy and then Aunt Fitzeustace into the basket-trap. He would be over as usual in the afternoon, he promised Aunt Pansy, and as the trap and the dog-cart left the yard his hand reached into his pocket for the tin that contained his snuff. It was a gesture that caused Geraldine and Deirdre to giggle delightedly, Geraldine saying that Aunt Pansy was the luckiest person in the world to have Mr Derenzy after her. 'Now, don't be unkind,' my mother would chide but the girls insisted they meant every word of it, that Mr Derenzy was gallant.

There was another love story at Kilneagh, or at least talk of one: Johnny Lacy told me that Father Kilgarriff had been unfrocked in Co. Limerick because of his love of a convent girl who was now in Chicago. It didn't occur to me to question this account of the unfrocking, not even when Johnny Lacy described the convent girl's teeth glistening in the dark confessional, and the tap of her heels on the tiles when she walked, her black-stockinged ankles slim and shapely. As if he'd been there he described how Father Kilgarriff had been on his knees for an hour in the bishop's palace and how the ringed finger had been snatched away from his pleading grasp.

Greatly intrigued by all this, I walked to Lough one afternoon and went into the Catholic chapel. Mrs Flynn referred to it as the Church of Our Lady Queen of Heaven, a title I considered more pleasing than St Anthony's Church of Ireland, which was what our own place of worship was called. The pews were of varnished pine; there were holy pictures on the walls and a cross on the altar. Lighted candles surrounded a Sacred Heart effigy, and the confessional smelt of dust, as if its green curtains needed airing. In the vestry there were more candles, locked away behind the two glass doors of a dresser. A red bulb gleamed beneath an image of Christ as a child, one hand raised in blessing, a puffy crown on the figure's head. A surplice hung from a hook on the wall and in a corner there was a sweeping brush. I wondered if Father Kilgarriff and the convent girl had stood together in such a vestry. I wondered if his hand had reached out to touch her, as the man on the log-box reached out towards the woman. 'A grievous sin,' Johnny Lacy had said in a sombre voice. 'That's what the bishop would have called it, Willie, a most grievous sin.'

But Tim Paddy hinted that this story should be taken with a pinch of salt. Tim Paddy was known to be jealous of Johnny Lacy, to envy him his easy ways and his success in Fermoy's dance-hall. He gloomily described to me the girls Johnny Lacy used to buy biscuits and sweets for, the prettiest girls of the night's dancing. 'Like Josephine,' he added one day.

Tim Paddy was painting a greenhouse when he said that and he slanted his head as he spoke, drawing his white-coated brush along a line of putty. Inside the greenhouse his father was pricking out seeds and I knew that if he had not been there Tim Paddy would have lit a cigarette and settled down for a conversation.

'Your sister's right,' he said. 'She has better looks than that Kitty had.'

'I thought you liked Kitty, Tim Paddy.'

He wrinkled his ferret's nose, dipping the brush into the paint. 'I wouldn't give you twopence for her.' Again he drew his paint-brush along the edge of the putty, one eye on his father's bent head. 'Josephine's different,' he said.

O'Neill came out of the greenhouse and told Tim Paddy to be sure to remove any splashes of paint from the glass. It was his arthritis that caused the old man's cantankerousness: when his affliction was particularly bad he used to crawl about on his hands and knees among the vegetables and flowerbeds, like some creature from the woods. That and his hairless head made him seem old enough to be Tim Paddy's grandfather.

'Don't be idling with the boy,' he muttered before re-entering the greenhouse. 'Get on with your work now.'

Tim Paddy made a face, continuing to paint the narrow surfaces of wood and putty. I went away and stared at the rows of sprouting peas, and the twigs that had been stuck into the soil to attract their tendrils. Traps had been set among the beans to catch fieldmice.

Tim Paddy was in love with Josephine, I said to myself, and that was the third of the Kilneagh love stories. I went in to tea and there she was in her afternoon black. She was eighteen years old, although I did not know it at the time: ages afterwards, when I was no longer shy with her, nor she with me, she told me her eighteenth birthday had taken place the week before she arrived at Kilneagh. She told me that it was her father, a farrier in Fermoy, who had arranged for her to go into service. He had received a letter from my mother, who had heard of Josephine's existence from Mr Derenzy, he having heard of it through Mrs Sweeney of the public house. My mother had gone to Fermoy to interview the family. 'She's quick to learn,' Josephine's father assured her, and having asked a question or two my mother declared herself satisfied.

Three weeks later, on the morning of her leaving home, her father talked to her for an hour and then sent her to see their priest, who told her to take care in a Protestant household. 'If there's no fish served on a Friday,' he said, 'see if they'd supply you with an egg.' But this predicament never arose because everyone in Kilneagh had fish on Fridays, that being the simplest arrangement: Mrs Flynn and O'Neill and Tim Paddy could not eat Friday meat either.

Josephine had liked Kilneagh from the start. She hadn't minded Geraldine and Deirdre giggling at teatime and she considered my father easygoing, even though she wasn't allowed to rattle the crockery in his presence. He was nice, she thought, sitting there at the breakfast table wondering how he should dress himself for the day. But it was my mother who made her feel at home in a world she did not know and in a house that seemed enormous to her. Its landings and half-landings, front staircase and back one, the kitchen passages, the Chinese carpet in the scarlet drawing-room, the Waterford vases in the hall, endless porcelain figures in the morning-room, the silver pheasants, the rosewood trays: all this was a strangeness that whirled about her, like colours in a kaleido-scope. Soup-spoons were round, dessert-spoons oval, the larger fork must be placed on the left, the smaller accompanied the dessert-spoon at the top. Kindling was kept near the range, gravy boats and soup tureens on the first shelf of the cupboard in the wall. Meat must be covered in the larder, milk jugs placed on the cold slate slab.

Wash both night and morning, Mrs Flynn commanded, rise at six-fifteen. Do not speak in the dining-room unless invited to, carry the vegetable dishes to the left of the person being served. She warned Josephine against Johnny Lacy, who had upset Kilneagh girls before and was older than he looked, besides having a short leg. 'Yes, Mrs Flynn,' Josephine endlessly repeated during her first few days of awkwardness and bewilderment. She blacked grates and shone brass, and seemed for ever to be sweeping floors. Her own small attic room, with its white enamel bowl and pitcher, was as strange as anywhere else.

On Josephine's first Sunday afternoon Tim Paddy took her down to the mill, allocated this duty by Mrs Flynn, who presumably considered him too much of a youth to be a nuisance in the way Johnny Lacy might have been. The water tumbled in the mill-race, the Virginia creeper on the walls was dotted with specks of spring-time growth. Tim Paddy drew attention to the green-faced clock of the central gable, one minute fast, the date on it 1801. Together they peered through the bars of the office windows, and Tim Paddy pointed out Mr Derenzy's stool and my father's desk and his swivel chair. They returned to Kilneagh the long way, round by the road, through the tall white gates and up the avenue of beeches. They took a path to the right before they reached the gravel sweep, ending up at the back of the house. 'On a day off you don't walk in front of the windows,' Tim Paddy explained, 'although I go by them maybe a hundred times on an ordinary day.' Josephine understood that. It was like my mother showing her the garden on the afternoon she arrived: for a quarter of an hour she had been a visitor at Kilneagh, and she knew she would never feel so again. On that Sunday evening she and Mrs Flynn and O'Neill and Tim Paddy sat down to their six o'clock tea in the kitchen and then she went upstairs to put on her uniform.

Years afterwards, when Josephine related all that, we tried to establish between us when it was that Michael Collins had first come to Kilneagh and decided it must have been a few months after she came to the house herself, in the early summer of 1918. She remembered my father saying in the hall: 'I'm honoured to meet you, Mr Collins.' She remembered being puzzled because Michael Collins didn't seem the kind of man for someone like my father to make such a fuss of: she didn't know then that he was a revolutionary leader. He and my father remained in the study for more than two hours, and when she brought in warm water for the whiskey they ceased to speak. Two other men waited in a motor-car on the gravel in front of the house. 'Josephine,' my father said, 'bring out bottles of stout to those fellows.'

By that summer the war in Europe had been won, but this was not apparent at the time and in Ireland everything was unsettled and on edge. De Valera was in Lincoln Gaol, and Collins was increasingly in disagreement with him about Ireland's eventual status. I know that now, but even in retrospect it is impossible to guess how my father's acquaintanceship with Collins had begun, though it must in some way have been related to the Quintons' longstanding identification with Irish Home Rule. For this, we were seen by many as traitors to our class and to the Anglo-Irish tradition. The eccentricity of my great-grandfather in giving away his lands had never ceased to be remembered in the big houses of Co. Cork and beyond it. And one of Johnny Lacy's stories retailed an incident in 1797, when a Major Atkinson of the militia at Fermoy had ridden over to Rathcormack at the head of a band of soldiers and shot six men in the village street. On the way back he had called in at Kilneagh, hoping to rest his horses there, but had been angrily turned away. In the barracks at Fermoy that display of inhospitality had not been forgotten either.

'You are English, Mrs Quinton?' I heard Collins politely enquire as he left the house after that first visit.

'Yes, I am English.'

My mother's voice conveyed no note of apology. I could not see her from where I stood in the shadows of the hall, but I guessed that as she returned his stare the eyes that in calmer moments reminded me of chestnuts had gleamed fierily, as they always did when she was challenged or angry. There was injustice in Ireland was what my mother maintained: you didn't have to be Irish to wish to expunge it. She told Michael Collins that she was the daughter of an army colonel and did not add that her marriage had taken place in an atmosphere of disapproval and distrust, just before her father's regiment had been recalled to England. She had told me also, but the years that had passed must have calmed that atmosphere away for I remembered my grandfather and grandmother visiting us quite often in Kilneagh and seeming happy to be there. 'I could stay for ever,' my grandfather used to say. 'There's nowhere to touch Kilneagh.' He was tall, like my mother, and stood very straight. I liked his voice, and was sorry when he and my grandmother left England for military duty in India. They did not ever visit Ireland again.

'I'm much obliged to the both of you,' Michael Collins said in the hall. 'God bless you, sir.'

Seasons changed; time slipped by at a dawdling pace, or that at least is how it seems. Incidents remain, isolated in my memory for reasons of their own. Moments and the mood of moments make up that distant childhood. A monkey puzzle died; new dogs were added to my aunts' collection.

In his unemphatic way Father Kilgarriff pursued in our history lessons his theme of warfare's folly, still illustrating the absurdity of it with reference to the Battle of the Yellow Ford. 'That bald English queen,' he softly murmured, 'answered defeat by dispatching Robert Devereux, who paved the way for yet another fateful battle. When she decided to behead him the destiny of Ireland hung on a thread again: at Kinsale this time.'

Neither the mildness of his manner nor his even, handsome features were ever disturbed by agitation. I mentioned Michael Collins to him, but he displayed no interest or curiosity in the revolutionary leader's visits. If only people would remember Daniel O'Connell, he murmured, if only they honoured his pacific spirit. He spoke also of my great-grandmother, Anna Quinton of the Famine. In the drawing-room portrait she was shown to be plain but Father Kilgarriff, extolling her mercy, granted her beauty as well. He knew a lot about her tribulations. She had begged the officers at the nearby barracks to retail the misery and starvation they saw around them to the London government. She had begged her own family, in Woodcombe Park in England, to seek to influence that government. So passionate did she become in her condemnation of the authorities that in the end her letters were returned unopened. *You spread calumny over our name*, her irate father wrote. *Since you will not cease in your absurd charges against this country, I have no choice left but to disown you.* The returned letters were in my father's possession, kept in the safe at the mill. Because he was interested, Father Kilgarriff had read them all. I don't believe my father had ever bothered to.

Occasionally I wondered if Father Kilgarriff was content, helping Tim Paddy with the cattle and teaching me in the drawing-room. I didn't know what to think about the girl in Chicago, but he spoke so warmly of my great-grandmother's compassion and drew my attention so often to the sadness of her eyes in the portrait that I came to feel she was almost alive for him – surely as alive as the girl in his confessional now was.

'Oh, fool of fortune,' my father commented when I tried to make him talk to me about Father Kilgarriff on one of our walks to the mill. He would say no more, and I had known him to apply that assessment to almost everyone at Kilneagh. It was his favourite expression, and one which at that particular time probably better defined Tim Paddy. 'Does she ever mention me?' Tim Paddy humbly asked, and I lied and said I'd heard Josephine say he was amusing. But it was the suave Johnny Lacy, with his dance-hall fox-trotting and his stories, who amused her more.

In spite of Mrs Flynn's disapproval he often now arrived in the kitchen. He and Josephine would go for walks in the evening, while Tim Paddy went off on his own and miserably set rabbit snares. In the end he didn't speak to either Josephine or Johnny Lacy and would savagely brush water over the cobbles in the yard, not pausing once to take the Woodbine out of his mouth. 'Oh, he does love her so!' Deirdre cried after she and Geraldine had spent a whole morning following the unhappy youth about the garden. They said they'd seen him hitting his head against an apple tree, and that he'd cried, a wailing sound like a banshee's howl. One Saturday night Johnny Lacy took Josephine to a dance in Fermoy and Tim Paddy got drunk in Sweeney's and was found sprawled out in the backyard by Mr Derenzy. In spite of the anguish they claimed on his behalf my sisters delighted in enacting that moonlit scene: the prone Tim

Paddy, Mr Derenzy bending over him, enquiring if he would care for a pinch of snuff.

All around us there seemed to be this unsettling love, for even his polite courting of Aunt Pansy left Mr Derenzy occasionally looking wan. He was not made for love, I'd heard my father say, as Johnny Lacy so clearly was. Mr Derenzy had been borrowed from his ledgers and his invoices, from the solitary Protestant world of his upstairs room at Sweeney's. Yet it was said that he had loved Aunt Pansy for thirty years.

I didn't want Tim Paddy to be unhappy, any more than I wanted Father Kilgarriff or Mr Derenzy and Aunt Pansy to be: I wanted everything, somehow and in the end, to be all right. Nothing could be done about O'Neill's aching joints, or Mrs Flynn's widowed state. But in spite of the old gardener's shortness of temper and Mrs Flynn's severity over the rules she laid down in her kitchen, they neither of them appeared to be discontented. Josephine sometimes sang very softly while she worked and my sisters said it was because she was in love. She at least was happy and I was happy myself, apart from my single nagging trepidation.

'It's just that I don't see the sense of it,' I said to my mother.

'You have to go to school, Willie.'

'It's awful, that place.'

'Your father wouldn't send you to an awful place.'

'Does he think Father Kilgarriff isn't any good?'

'No, of course he doesn't think that.'

'Then why's he want to send me?'

'You have to meet other boys. Play games and take part in things. Kilneagh isn't the world, you know.'

'But I'll live in Kilneagh when I'm grown up. I'll always be here.'

'Yes, I know, Willie, but that's all the more reason to see what other places are like.'

I did not reply. I had realized as soon as I'd spoken that my efforts would be useless. All I could do now was confess my feelings to my father, which I'd been nervous of doing in case they belittled me in his eyes. My mother pointed out that several years had yet to pass before the grim establishment could claim me. She offered that as the only consolation there was.

*

The men of the village came back from the war. Only one of them returned to the mill, a man called Doyle with a grey, slightly crooked face, who for some reason was unpopular with the others. Johnny Lacy told me my father had taken him back reluctantly, feeling obliged to since the mill was a man short. A suspicion of some sort hung about him; I never came to know him. I continued instead to listen to the other men's conversation about the confusion in the country and whether or not de Valera was right, although what about I was not precisely certain. I knew that an alternative government had been set up in Dublin and that fighting continued between the imperial and the revolutionary regimes. I heard names that had a ring to them: Cathal Brugha, the Countess Markievicz, Terence MacSwiney, but I didn't know who these people were. The escape of de Valera from Lincoln Gaol had been arranged by Michael Collins, and at least I knew about him.

I remember being surprised to hear my mother saying she had liked Collins the first time she met him: there had been, after all, that moment of awkwardness in the hall. But my mother was strange in this respect, given to blaming herself for taking offence when offence was not intended, and that may have been so on this occasion. Collins had an honest laugh, she insisted, his blue eyes had tenderness in them. If he ordered assassinations there was justice in what he ordered, for such death was an element in a war that was little different from the war her own countrymen had been waging against the might of the Kaiser. More energetically than my father, she supported the revolutionary cause and it was she who made him contact Collins again after his initial visit to Kilneagh. *Dear Mr Collins*, my father wrote, in a letter that exists today. *Since you called in on us some time ago I have been thinking about many of the matters we discussed. As arranged, I have forwarded what we agreed to the address you left with me, but I am wondering now if more might not be done on my side. It could be to the advantage of the common ground we share if we met again. Except for Fridays, when I go into Fermoy, I am always at home here, if not in the house never less than twenty minutes from it, in the office of my mill. Should you again be passing near I would be delighted to offer you a drink, or lunch or supper. Yours sincerely, W. J. Quinton.*

A force of British soldiers known as the Black and Tans because of the colour of their uniform had been sent to Ireland to quell the spreading disobedience. By reputation they were ruthless men, brutalized during the German war, many of them said to have been released from gaols in order to perform this task. The Irish gunmen who rampaged through the countryside had become, in turn, ruthless themselves. They gave no quarter and, knowing the lie of the land, were often more successful in the skirmishes that took place. There was a Black and Tan force at Fermoy, which brought this spasmodic but intense warfare close to us.

It was perhaps brought closer still by the visits of Michael Collins. When he came the second time he was on his own, but on all future occasions there were the men who waited in the motor-car while he and my father talked. And the second occasion was the only one on which he arrived on his motor-cycle.

'I'm delighted you could find the time for us,' my mother said, bringing me with her into the drawing-room, where Collins and my father were standing by the French windows on an excessively hot day in June. I remember Collins as being a little ill at ease, tall and heavy in his brown motor-cycling leather, the cast of his features suggesting a simplicity which was contradicted by a snappish gleam that came and went in his eyes. I didn't know at the time that without a revolution to make him famous he would have been working as a clerk in a post office.

'I'm pleased to be here again, Mrs Quinton.'

'And this is Willie,' my father said.

'How are you, Willie?'

They talked about the weather, hoping the heatwave we were having would last. 'Let me fill that up for you,' my father said, reaching out for the visitor's glass. 'No,' Collins said.

There was tomato soup for lunch, and chops and summer pudding, and wine. The conversation was desultory. My father talked about the mill, Collins listened. When he might have spoken himself, he appeared to prefer silence.

'I believe you know Glandore, Mr Collins,' my mother said in one of these lulls.

'I know it well, Mrs Quinton. I come from round about.'

'A charming place.'

'Ah, it is of course.'

My sisters did not have lunch with us that day, and it must have been a Saturday because Father Kilgarriff hadn't been to the drawing-room that morning. I remember the windows being open and the scent of flowers wafting in. I felt it was an honour to be sitting there with a famous revolutionary in motor-cycling clothes, even though I did not once speak.

'You'll remember today,' my mother said afterwards as we walked together through the garden in search of my sisters. My father and Collins were in the study, drinking coffee. I did not see him again, but heard the roar of his motor-cycle on the avenue. And a fragment from a conversation my parents had that evening remains vividly with me. They talked together in the gathering gloom of the drawing-room, not arguing yet faintly disagreeing.

'It's money he came for, Evie.'

'Maybe, but even so.'

My father sighed, and for a moment nothing was said. Then my father spoke again.

'Doyle has been threatened. I shouldn't have taken that man back.'

'Is Doyle spying for them?'

'God knows, God knows. Look, I promise you, Evie, the best we can do is to give Collins money. There is no question whatsoever of drilling fellows at Kilneagh. Absolutely not.'

I crept up the dark stairs and afterwards lay awake, astonished at the sternness there had been in my father's voice. I wondered what Father Kilgarriff would have thought if he'd heard this talk of drilling men at Kilneagh, and I was sorry that my mother's wish had not prevailed: nothing could surely have been more exciting than revolutionaries on the lawns and in the shrubbery. I dreamed about them, with Michael Collins in his motor-cycling clothes, but when I woke up in the morning the first thing I remembered was the authority of my father's insistence that Collins should only be given money. Could it be possible that his apparent indecisiveness, his self-claimed lack of resolution, were no more than superficial traits, contrived to make a talking point? I thought about it for a while, but came to no conclusion.

'No, I didn't lay eyes on the man,' Father Kilgarriff replied when I asked him if he'd seen Mr Collins. 'Wasn't there hay to be made?'

'You heard his motor-bike, though, Father?'

'I don't think I did. Now, tell me this. New Zealand has a temperate climate. Why would that be?'

*

One Saturday evening during that same heatwave our parents and Aunt Fitzeustace and Aunt Pansy went to dine with people called D'arcy who lived in a house not unlike our own on the other side of Lough. I couldn't sleep because of the heat and went along to my sisters' room to pass the time. We played cards on Geraldine's bed and then, to our very great surprise, were aware of the sound of music. Since it appeared to come from the kitchen, we crept down the back stairs in our nightdresses. Unfortunately we ran into Mrs Flynn, who happened to be crossing the kitchen passage just as we entered it. We were noisily reprimanded, but after much pleading on the part of my sisters were eventually led into the kitchen itself. A bizarre sight at once silenced the giggling that had begun to twitch Geraldine and Deirdre's lips; it stunned me also. Seated at the big oak table and looking no less grumpy than usual, O'Neill was playing an accordion. Johnny Lacy was teaching Josephine a dance step, Tim Paddy and a red-cheeked girl we'd never seen before were smoking Woodbines at the table. Mrs Flynn was flushed; the others were laughing. In a high-backed chair, close to the range, my aunts' maid, Philomena, was drinking a cup of tea. It was extraordinary beyond belief that old O'Neill should be performing on an accordion, the kind of instrument that beggarmen played on the streets of Fermoy. No one had ever told us that he possessed such a thing, we had never heard a note of it coming from the gate-lodge. And who on earth was the girl with the red cheeks?

'That's Bridie Sweeney,' Mrs Flynn whispered. As she spoke Tim Paddy saw us and waved across the kitchen, not in the least woebegone or sorry for himself any more.

The tune came to an end, and another began. This one had a different rhythm, and the two couples spun about the kitchen, Tim Paddy and the girl still smoking their Woodbines, Johnny Lacy whisking Josephine as if she were a feather. When he danced you'd never guess he had a short leg.

'Well, how's the three of you?' he said to us, coming over when the music ceased. 'Will you take a turn with me, Deirdre?'

O'Neill, as usual, did not acknowledge our presence: intent on his accordion, I don't believe he looked up once while we were in the kitchen. Johnny Lacy danced with Deirdre and then with Geraldine, and Josephine tried to show me how to waltz. Tim Paddy introduced Bridie Sweeney to us, saying she was one of the

35

Sweeneys from the public house. The way he spoke it seemed as if he had never been in love with Josephine. He stuck his chin out and smiled as proudly as a sultan. All of it puzzled me very much.

'You'll break chaps' hearts,' Johnny Lacy told my sisters, the smell of carnations potent in his hair. He laughed and gave each of us a halfpenny. *'What's the news, what's the news?'* he suddenly began to sing, and O'Neill picked up the tune of *Kelly the Boy from Kilanne*.

'Ah, they're lovely children,' Bridie Sweeney said. Tim Paddy was holding her hand and she was pressed up close to him, with an arm around his waist. 'I s'pose it's lessons for yez the entire time,' she said. 'God, I couldn't abide lessons.' She asked us a riddle, something about skinning a rabbit, and then Johnny Lacy broke off in his singing and took a mouth-organ from his pocket. He played it skilfully, making it screech above the lilt of the accordion, and I could see the Sweeney girl eyeing him, even though she still had her arm around Tim Paddy's waist. He winked at her, and I looked quickly over to where Josephine was sitting by the range, but she hadn't noticed. *'Enniscorthy's in flames and old Wexford is won,'* sang Johnny Lacy, and I noticed then that Father Kilgarriff had entered the kitchen.

He stood by the door, not saying anything, slightly smiling. The festivities were taking place because advantage had been taken of my parents' and my aunts' absence; Father Kilgarriff didn't matter because he had no position in the household. Had he been a real priest the music and the dancing would have ceased on his entrance and only commenced again when it was clear that his approval had been gained. Had he been a Quinton relative or a friend of my parents there would have been embarrassment in the kitchen. Tim Paddy slanted his head at him in his particular way; Johnny Lacy saluted him familiarly. I realized it was the first time I had been in the main kitchen when he had been there also, if indeed he had ever been there before. He stood for a moment longer by the door, still smiling, seeming pleased because of the music and the dancing. Then he went away.

'Up you go now,' Mrs Flynn said, and all the way up the back stairs we could hear Johnny Lacy singing another song. I wondered if Father Kilgarriff could hear it too, in his bedroom in the orchard wing. My aunts' stray dogs had begun to bark, and it was perhaps more likely that he had shut the windows in order to protect them from the unexpected disturbance. I didn't know why I went on thinking about him, his Spanish looks vivid in my mind, his voice insisting softly that argument and persuasion were the only way. I had never been in his room, but I supposed it would have the red glow of a holy light and a statue of the Virgin, and a crucifix on the wall. It was odd to think of him there, dwelling upon Daniel O'Connell and the compassion of my great-grandmother, when but for a convent girl he might be esteemed and respected in Co. Limerick. And then, quite strongly, I sensed that Tim Paddy was right when he'd hinted that Johnny Lacy's love of a story had resulted in a confusion of the truth: knowing Father Kilgarriff, there was something about his romance with a convent girl that did not quite make sense. I saw the girl's teeth glistening in the confessional and heard the tap of her feet on the tiled floor: I wondered if she'd ever even existed.

I couldn't sleep that night. I went on thinking about Father Kilgarriff, and then I thought about Josephine and Johnny Lacy and Tim Paddy and Bridie Sweeney. I kept seeing the wink that had caused that look to come into Bridie Sweeney's eyes, and remembering how Josephine hadn't noticed any of it. If Johnny Lacy began to go for walks with the Sweeney girl instead of Josephine Tim Paddy would be miserable all over again, and so of course would Josephine. Eventually I got out of bed and gazed from my window out over the garden. Even though it was after ten o'clock it was still light. I pretended that a Black and Tan was lurking among the mass of rhododendrons and that I crept downstairs and crossed the lawn with my father's shotgun. I led him into the kitchen, with his hands above his head, and everyone was astonished.

The music of the accordion floated up to my window, and then abruptly ceased. It did not begin again. Tim Paddy and the Sweeney girl crept into the garden and while I still watched they kissed one another, thinking they were hidden by the rhododendrons. Through the gloom that was gathering I saw a flash of something white and realized that it was the Sweeney girl's petticoat. Her flowered skirt was on the grass, and as I watched she lay down beside it and Tim Paddy lay down also. They had not ceased to kiss and their arms were still around one another; I could see her bare flesh where the petticoat had been bundled up to her waist and Tim Paddy's hands pulling at her underclothes, and her own hands

37

pulling at them also. Then, from the far distance, came the rattle of the dog-cart on the avenue and the lovers vanished.

The next day, after mass, Josephine told my mother she wanted to marry Johnny Lacy. 'He's been home with me last week to Fermoy, ma'am,' she said. 'They know he's all right.' My mother gave us this news on the way to church, and my father shook his head in mock disapproval, saying that Josephine was the quietest maid we'd had in the house for many a year. 'Fools of fortune,' he murmured. 'We'll be having to say our Protestant prayers for them.' And after church, as Mr Derenzy fell into step beside Aunt Pansy for the walk to Sweeney's, my father called out loudly: 'Did you hear that news, Derenzy? There's talk of a wedding.'

Aunt Pansy went the colour of a sunset and Mr Derenzy agitat-edly pinched snuff from his tin box. Aunt Fitzeustace, who always remained silent when the union of Mr Derenzy and Aunt Pansy was raised by my father, groped in her large handbag for her cigarettes and matches. Aunt Fitzeustace smoked constantly but never on the village street. With a huge, grateful sigh she would light her first cigarette when the basket-trap left Sweeney's yard.

'Everything's parched with the heat,' Mr Derenzy said, as if he hadn't heard my father. 'I was noticing that.'

He and Aunt Pansy walked ahead, and my mother told Aunt Fitzeustace that she was concerned about the match because Josephine was a singular girl.

'Will he lead her a dance?' Geraldine asked. 'Like the beery fellow and Kitty?'

But nobody answered that. Aunt Fitzeustace, who could look most severe at times, played with her packet of cigarettes.

'Yes,' she said at length. 'A singular girl.'

'And he, of course, is flirtatious.'

'You'll have them in the divorce courts before they've started.' My father laughed rumbustiously. He walked with Geraldine and Deirdre on either side of him, holding their hands. I brought up the rear, behind my mother and Aunt Fitzeustace.

'I wish you'd take it seriously,' my mother upbraided crossly.

'Sure, they can only try it and see.'

'Yes, they can only try it,' Aunt Fitzeustace said.

*

38

Father Kilgarriff was saying something uninteresting about the Gulf Stream when through the drawing-room window I saw my father hurrying beneath the rhododendrons in a way that was unusual for him. 'Evie!' he called loudly, somewhere in the house. 'Evie! Evie!' And that was unusual too.

'Something's happened,' I said, and we both listened. There were hasty footsteps on the stairs, and ten minutes later Tim Paddy led the dog-cart past the window and my parents drove off in it. Father Kilgarriff attempted to continue with the geography lesson, but neither of us had any concentration left. It was Josephine, coming in with the mid-morning tea, who told us that the grey-faced Doyle had been murdered.

Father Kilgarriff crossed himself; Josephine had been weeping.

'He was hanged from a tree,' she said. 'His tongue was cut out.'

There was a long silence after she left the drawing-room. The tray of tea and biscuits remained untouched on the oval table. I remembered my father saying he shouldn't have taken Doyle back. I began to say something about that but Father Kilgarriff spoke at the same time.

'How can people be at peace with themselves after doing a thing like that?'

'Who would have done it, Father?'

'I don't know, Willie.'

He read to me for the rest of the morning from *The Old Curiosity Shop*, but instead of the adventures of Nell and her grandfather I saw Doyle's crooked grey face and the blood rushing from his mouth. When Father Kilgarriff began his journey back to the orchard wing my sisters pulled at me in the hall. 'What did they do with Doyle's tongue?' Geraldine kept asking. 'Did they take it away?'

All three of us went to the kitchen, but Mrs Flynn knew as little as Josephine, so went to look for Tim Paddy. 'The poor bloody bugger,' he said, but didn't say much else. We even dared to ask O'Neill, tracking him down to his onion beds. He actually spoke to us. He told us to go away.

My father and mother didn't return at lunchtime. Geraldine, Deirdre and I sat around the dining-room table in a way that seemed very strange to us. Geraldine had been in the room with my mother when my father began to call her name in the hall below. 'They've hanged Doyle,' was what he had said when they stood together on the landing. 'He was missing all night.' I explained to my sisters about death by hanging because I'd asked Father Kilgarriff and he'd told me that the weight of the body snapped something in the neck. Deirdre began to cry. Tears dripped into her cold rice pudding; Geraldine scolded her.

'Doyle was involved with the Black and Tans,' my father told me later that afternoon, and did not say more except that the murdered man had sold information in the neighbourhood, to a Sergeant Rudkin. He had had no political leanings himself, neither Republican nor imperialist. 'They'd have regarded his tongue as the instrument of his treachery,' my father explained.

Deirdre had a dream about the body hanging from the branch of a tree, the bloody tongue picked up by a magpie. Geraldine drew a picture that included this magpie, in which Doyle was represented as a devilish-looking creature with staring black eyes. But when my mother found the drawing she furiously burned it, saying that a dead person must be respected no matter how despicable he had been in life.

'Ah now, it's best forgotten,' Mr Derenzy replied when I asked him about the murder. He shook his head, causing the red fluff of his hair to spring up and down. He began to talk about something else, and it wasn't until our conversation had come to an end that I realized he was afraid. When I asked Johnny Lacy he told me that the Black and Tans were loyal to their spies and rarely failed to avenge a death, justly or unjustly finding another victim. 'I wouldn't cross the yard in the dark,' Mrs Flynn announced.

Yet life settled down again and when I think of that hot summer at Kilneagh I still hear the whisper of Josephine's singing as she dusts and polishes. Aunt Fitzeustace cuts the grass, old Hannah arrives from the village to scrub the floors and do the washing, Tim Paddy leaves spinach for Mrs Flynn at the back door, O'Neill is hunched among his high delphiniums. The mill-yard bakes in the afternoon sun, my father walks the length of the avenue, his labradors slouching with him. '*I am old, but let me drink*,' my mother prompts in the scarlet drawing-room and adds in the silence that follows: '*Bring me spices, bring me wine.*' Even while she speaks the shadow of Doyle hovers in the drawing-room, as it hovers everywhere else. The magpie from Deirdre's dream swoops for the tongue, flies settle on the blood as I had seen them settle on the carcass of a sheep. One of these days it will all be all right, my mother says again; and my father assures me that it can't be long now before the Black and Tans are recalled to England.

In early September Aunt Fitzeustace and Aunt Pansy went to the sea for their summer fortnight. Their many suitcases were loaded into the basket-trap one Friday morning and Tim Paddy stood ready to accompany them to the railway station at Fermoy. They stayed in Miss Meade's boarding house in Youghal, and my father used to urge Mr Derenzy to take his holidays at the same time in order to accompany them. He swore that Aunt Pansy would come back engaged, but Mr Derenzy could never be persuaded, no doubt considering the suggestion improper.

'Good-bye, good-bye,' we shouted after the basket-trap, and Aunt Fitzeustace and Aunt Pansy waved. Their dogs barked in the orchard wing and Father Kilgarriff hurried to calm them, an extra duty in the absence of my aunts. Philomena went to stay with her twin sister in Rathcormack.

Later that same day, when my father and I were in Fermoy ourselves, we saw a soldier whom my father identified as Doyle's friend Sergeant Rudkin. The man was lighting a cigarette at a street corner, one hand cupped against the wind. Noticing my father, he raised that same hand in greeting.

'He's just inherited a greengrocer's shop,' my father said quietly. 'In Liverpool.'

He watched Rudkin turning a corner and then said he'd once met him, here in Fermoy one night. 'Oh, very agreeable, he was. He had a drop too much taken when he told me that about his shop.'

I enjoyed these Friday outings to Fermoy, collecting groceries that had been ordered the week before, buying household items for my mother and Mrs Flynn, and sometimes for my aunts. We always went for tea and sandwiches to the Grand Hotel, where my father talked to people I did not know. 'Well, fellow-me-lad,' a man would say and, finding it difficult to continue, would laugh and tap me on the head. Others would remark on my growth, or notice that I had the Quinton eyes. I liked it best when we went early to the hotel so that I could have my tea and then do what shopping remained, rather than wait in the hallway while my father conversed with his friends in the bar. The shop people always asked after my mother and my aunts, and occasionally after Mrs Flynn.

On the Friday when we saw Sergeant Rudkin there was green knitting wool to be matched and an order placed for oilcloth. There was a set of bolts to be collected from Dwyer's hardware, and a cough remedy from the Medical Hall. I did all that while my father was in the hotel and at six o'clock we set out for Kilneagh. The Black and Tan sergeant was on my mind because it seemed strange to me that a member of a force which my father spoke of with revulsion should greet him on the street.

'He was with poor Doyle the night I met him,' he explained when I asked. 'It would never have done to walk past your own employee, Willie.'

I accepted that, and understood it. My father said:

'Doyle, you see, was in a difficult position. He'd fought beside that man in Belgium.'

I asked if Doyle had been married. He shook his head. A moment later he added:

'It should never have happened, Willie. That hanging was a terrible thing.'

He spoke deliberately, with an unusual firmness that reminded me of his saying that Collins's men would not be invited to drill at Kilneagh. We sat together in the dog-cart, stopping in Lough so that he could call in at Sweeney's for a drink and further conversation. I waited in the yard and Mrs Sweeney brought me out a plate of biscuits. We made our way then, slowly, through the village, between the two rows of colour-washed cottages, past Driscoll's shop and the Church of Our Lady Queen of Heaven. We turned eventually into the avenue of Kilneagh, my father humming beneath his breath as he often did on our Friday journey home.

'I hate having to go away to the school,' I said without looking at him, dropping the confidence into the euphoria which appeared to be there between us. He continued to hum during the lengthy pause which occurred before he replied.

'Oh, we can't have you uneducated, Willie. We couldn't have that, you know.'

The words were precise, with a ring of finality about them, yet my father's tone was as lazy as ever. It matched our unhurried progress as we passed through the white gates of Kilneagh and proceeded up the avenue between the two lines of beech trees. The labradors made a fuss on the gravel in front of the house, jumping up at both of us, and the stray dogs rushed round the side of the house. My father had presents for Geraldine and Deirdre and as I watched him giving them their parcels I knew I was going to have to go to the school he thought so much of. Perhaps it was the inevitability of it that caused me, for the first time, to feel that further dwelling on the matter would be something to be ashamed of, that further reference to it would belittle myself in my own eyes as much as in his. I was my father's favourite, though he tried to hide the fact by paying extra attention to my sisters. For my part, I was fonder of him than of anyone else.

I awoke with a tickling in my nostrils. I lay there, knowing that something was different, not sure what it was. There was a noise, like the distant rushing of wind in trees.

Too drowsy to wonder properly, I slept again. There were voices calling out, and the screaming of my sisters, and the barking of the dogs. The rushing noise was closer. 'Willie! Willie!' Tim Paddy shouted.

I was in Tim Paddy's arms, and then there was the dampness of the grass before the pain began, all over my legs and back. The ponies and my mother's horse snorted and neighed. I could hear their hooves banging at the stable doors.

There were stars in the sky. An orange glow crept over the edges of my vision. The noise there'd been had changed, becoming a kind of crackling, with crashes that sounded like thunder. I couldn't move. I thought: We are all like this, Geraldine and Deirdre, my mother and father, Josephine and Mrs Flynn; we are all lying on the wet grass, in pain. Aunt Fitzeustace and Aunt Pansy would be asleep in Miss Meade's boarding house in Youghal; Philomena would be asleep in Rathcormack; for all I knew Father Kilgarriff was dead.

Through the fever of this nightmare floated the two portraits in the drawing-room, my dog-faced great-grandfather and plain, merciful Anna Quinton. I seemed to be in the drawing-room myself, gathering up my school books and placing them in the corner cupboard. After that I was in the dog-cart, asking my father why Father Kilgarriff had been unfrocked. I saw that the teeth glistening

43

in the confessional were Anna Quinton's, which was why Father Kilgarriff read her letters. I would understand such things, my father said, when I went away to school: that was why I had to. I would understand the love of Mr Derenzy and Aunt Pansy, and the different love of Tim Paddy and the Sweeney girl.

'Don't move, Willie. Don't move. Just lie there.' It was Josephine who whispered to me, and then there were other voices. There were men shouting, asking questions. 'Who are you?' one question was, and someone else said: 'He's O'Neill. He's a gardener in this place. That fellow's his son.' There was a gunshot and then another. They seemed like part of the crackling noise, but I knew they weren't because they were closer to where I lay. 'Oh, Mother of God,' Josephine whispered.

Men walked by me. 'Is there a bottle in the car?' a voice asked. 'Christ, I need a drop.' Another voice said: 'Hold on to your nerves, hero.'

There were further gunshots and one by one the dogs stopped barking. The horse and the ponies must have been released because I heard them galloping somewhere. Something touched my leg, the edge of a boot, I thought. It grazed the pain, but I knew that I must not call out. I knew what Josephine had implied when she'd whispered to be still. The men who were walking away must not be seen; they had been seen by O'Neill and Tim Paddy, who must have come up from the gate-lodge. My eyes were closed, and what I saw in the darkness was Geraldine's drawing of Doyle hanging from the tree, the flames of the drawing-room fire making a harmless black crinkle of it.

4

Kisses it says, scratched on the varnish of a table. *Big Lily with her tits bare* it says on the whitewash of the lavatory, the third cubicle of the row. Initials and dates decorate a doorway, and once used to fascinate me. The doorway is in the mill, the table in a schoolroom in the city of Cork, the whitewashed lavatories in the school my father had gone to also. Kisses was a girl's nickname. Big Lily was the wife of the nightwatchman. The initials belonged to the men who, down the generations, had worked the mill.

The schoolroom was in Mercier Street, across the city from Windsor Terrace at the top of St Patrick's Hill, where my mother and I lived with Josephine. I didn't know why this school had been chosen for me, only that I was still too young to go to the one in the Dublin mountains. Mercier Street Model School had twenty-three pupils, boys and girls, all of them Protestants. It was run by Miss Halliwell.

'Willie Quinton,' she said the morning I arrived. 'Children, this is Willie Quinton.'

Josephine had walked across the city with me, and I thought of her making the journey back, shopping as she had said she would. I wished I was with her. I wished I was sitting in my mother's bedroom, on the chair she said was specially mine, beside her bed. The children in the schoolroom had the sharp features and the unfriendly eye of town children. A girl had giggled when Miss Halliwell repeated my name.

'Well, dear,' Miss Halliwell said now, 'and which class shall receive you, I wonder? Children, I believe Willie has a scholarly look about him.'

Miss Halliwell was lean, with the look of a wilted cowslip. I had heard my mother describe her as a girl, but she did not seem like a girl to me.

'Geometry?' she enquired. 'Algebra? You've made a start with both? And French likewise? So, too, with history and geography? Arithmetic, with Latin, we take for granted.'

She smiled at me, the tired petals of her face reviving for a moment. She was being sympathetic, but in the schoolroom you could tell that this was not her usual mood, that strictly speaking she was cross.

'I haven't learned any French,' I said.

'Ah.'

She sat at a large table, around which were spread the members of her most senior class. At the smaller tables sat the junior classes, in twos and threes. The walls of the schoolroom were green, covered with shiny maps and charts. I was soon to learn that while the senior class grappled with parsing and analysis or the elaborations of a

45

French verb, Miss Halliwell's voice would follow the movements of her cane over a reading chart with pictured objects on it: *A for Apple, B for Boot, C for Cat.*

'That's a pity about French, dear.'

'Father Kilgarriff didn't know French. My mother was going to teach me.'

'Ah.'

She smiled again. She said:

'Kilgarriff? That's a funny name. A priest, Willie?'

Father Kilgarriff had been shot when he'd appeared in the yard, but unlike O'Neill and Tim Paddy he had survived his wounds. Aunt Fitzeustace and Aunt Pansy, returning from Youghal as soon as they heard the news, had nursed him in the orchard wing, which was the only part of Kilneagh that had not been destroyed. The gate-lodge had been burnt to the ground, a final gesture as the Black and Tans hastened away in their motor-car.

I didn't say anything when Miss Halliwell remarked that Kilgarriff was a funny name. Amusement passed from face to face in the schoolroom. There was more giggling.

'Stop that unpleasant noise,' she snapped, anger flaming her cheeks. 'If there is something to snigger at, one of you can put a hand up and say so. A priest, dear?'

'Father Kilgarriff is a priest.'

'It's perhaps not surprising then that he didn't know French.'

Laughter followed this remark, obedient and noisy, not like the sniggering. Miss Halliwell paused, waiting for silence before she said:

'The priests of Ireland are not well-travelled. Not renowned for travel, Willie.'

I moved my head, half nodding it. I felt disloyal to Father Kilgarriff. 'I thought the monks,' I began, about to repeat what he had told me: that the Irish monks of many centuries ago had travelled endlessly, bringing to a heathen Europe the Christian faith.

Miss Halliwell interrupted by shaking her head. Her eyes glistened, and to my horror I realized that the tears which were gathering had to do with her concern for me. 'Sit there, my dear,' she softly commanded, gesturing towards a table at which the children were younger than I was. 'Poor Willie,' she whispered later that morning when she inspected a piece of work she had set me. She did not blame me for being backward because a priest had taught me. She did not blame me for anything. Her fingers touched my head in passing, her eyes were lurid with compassion. 'We'll do our best,' she whispered at the end of that day. 'Together we'll do our best, dear.'

More than anything I didn't want sympathy. The scarlet drawing-room no longer existed. Never again would Tim Paddy lean on his brush handle, nor Mrs Flynn set off to mass in her Sunday clothes. Never again would I walk to the mill with my father, up the sloping pasture, down through the birch wood. Yet at night in bed I no longer sobbed before I went to sleep. I could think about my father and my sisters without involuntarily tearing at the palm of one hand with the fingernails of the other. I could even imagine Geraldine and Deirdre in the heaven I had heard so much about, a territory that remained vague even though I now had greater reason to wonder about it. I imagined Mrs Flynn and Tim Paddy and O'Neill there also, and of course my father.

'Together we'll do our best, dear,' Miss Halliwell whispered. 'I am here to be your friend, Willie.'

My mother and I might have lived in the orchard wing with my aunts and Father Kilgarriff, but my mother had said she could not. Father Kilgarriff looked after the cows on his own now. My mother's horse and the ponies had been given away. My father's labradors had been shot that night with the other dogs.

'I'm really quite all right, Miss Halliwell.'

'Dear Willie, of course you are.'

After that first day I made the journey on my own from the house in Windsor Terrace to Mercier Street Model, and back again each afternoon. The city had been badly damaged in the fighting; half of Patrick Street was gone, shops and buildings blown apart by the Black and Tans. I hurried by them, always preferring the quays and docks. Often I stopped to watch the cargo ships unloading, wondering what it would be like to be a seaman. I wandered slowly home by roundabout routes, past the warehouses of Tedcastle, McCormick and Company, past Sutton's Mills. I learnt the names of the streets: Anglesea Street, where the drunk woman stormed abuse at her reflection in a shop window, Cove Street, where the burnt-down laundry was, Lavitt's Quay and Fapp's Quay and Kyrl's Quay.

Often I found myself miles out of my way, lost in the slums. Other children shouted at me, ragged creatures, dirty and barefooted. Shawled women begged, but I had nothing to give them. I watched pitch and toss being played, and once a man who trailed a greyhound on a string told me this animal could race faster than any dog in Ireland. 'Blarney Boy's the name we've given him. You'll tell people yet, son, you saw Blarney Boy on the streets of Cork.' But I never did.

During that time peace came hesitantly to Ireland. The fighting which had succeeded the revolution eventually ceased; Michael Collins was dead, killed in an ambush during that civil war. Josephine had read me a piece from the *Cork Examiner* which stated that a treaty with England recognized the sovereign state of twenty-six Irish counties. The red letter-boxes were painted green; statues of imperial figures were removed; the Irish language was to be revived. My mother mentioned none of it, having lost all interest in matters of that kind.

'A grand time to be growing up,' an old man assured me as I lingered one afternoon in Merchant's Quay. 'I'd rather have your time than mine.' But the strangeness of the city streets and shops impinged more upon me than the national freedom or the future that was there for growing up in. The city's weather mattered also, as weather had not before: there was wind and cold to journey back and forth through, or dozy, pleasant heat. On wet days the rain-water gushed like a torrent down St Patrick's Hill, tumbling over the steps in the pavement, overflowing from the gutters. Lilac fluttered in spring, tumbling over the red stone walls. 'Then what's your name?' wizened Mrs Hayes asked me the first time I entered her shop at the corner of Rathbone Place, sent by Josephine for rashers and a Bermaline loaf. This shop was the nearest one to us, cramped and busy, the goods it sold piled up in a jumble, sawdust on the floor. Flies settled on the wire-mesh covers that protected butter and cheese, wasps buzzed near the sticky strips of paper that hung from the ceiling. A brown cat slept on the counter, curled in close to itself, never moving. 'Young Hayes is wanted,' Josephine had enigmatically remarked, and in time he returned from wherever he had been, a bespectacled young man in a brown shop-coat like his mother's, with a cap pulled low on his forehead. 'The Amnesty,' Josephine said, but I wasn't curious about what that meant.

My sisters would have delighted in Mrs Hayes's shop, in Mrs Hayes herself and in her son. They would have sucked their cheeks in and imitated the particular way the old woman picked at the cheese when she was cutting it, and the way her son looked at you intently through his cracked, wire-rimmed glasses. I could never prevent myself from thinking about my sisters when I entered the shop, and I continued to miss them because I made no friends in Mercier Street. I was not disliked, but Miss Halliwell's excessive pitying of me, and the allowances she subsequently made for my shortcomings, generated in my classmates a degree of suspicion and unease. 'Adamant?' she said in a spelling lesson and the smile I dreaded crept into her faded countenance. The word she uttered dangled in front of me, yet in my confusion I could not distinguish the letters that formed its composition.

'I didn't know we had to learn that one,' I stammered back, knowing that already I had been forgiven.

'It's one of the ten, dear.'

'I'm sorry, Miss Halliwell.'

'Spell *oyster*, Willie. Was *oyster* one of the words you learnt?'

I spelt the word incorrectly, and Miss Halliwell came to the table where I sat and put her hand on my head. I could feel her fingers caressing my hair. They touched my ear and then the nape of my neck. 'O-y-s-t-e-r.' Slowly, drawing her lips back and rounding them about each letter, she spelt the word and I repeated what she had said. I was aware of an intimacy in all this and did not care for it, the twin formation of our lips, the twin sounds following one another.

She returned to her table. A boy called Elmer Dunne had a habit of dropping his pencil and then poking about on the floor looking for it. In the playground he would report that he had managed to catch a glimpse of Miss Halliwell's underclothes and the flesh at the top of her stockings. 'Oh Jesus Christ!' he would moan, and then describe how, given a chance, he would unbutton her long brown cardigan and slowly remove her long brown skirt.

'Now try again, dear,' she said.

'O-y-s-t-e-r.'

'Very good, Willie.'

I spelt other words too, my face like red-hot coal, and then laughter gurgled in the schoolroom because Elmer Dunne had appeared from beneath the table, rolling his eyes to indicate his indelicate desires. Savagely Miss Halliwell scolded the miscreants, among whom I longed to be. I longed to shout out what Elmer Dunne wanted to do to her lean body, to linger over each obscenity.

'You are slow and ignorant,' she furiously upbraided the others. 'Poor Willie has been taught by an uncouth country priest and already he is passing you by. You will end up behind the counters of low-class Catholic shops, while Willie makes good his progress.'

Every day her sympathy lingered with me, long after I'd left the schoolroom. It accompanied me on my travels about the city and was still there when I examined the goods in the window of the pawnbroker's shop at the bottom of St Patrick's Hill: old racing binoculars and umbrellas, knives and forks and crockery, occasionally a pair of boots. While it hovered around me I would begin the steep ascent to Windsor Terrace, to our narrow house painted a shade of grey, tightly pressed between two others.

I couldn't tell my mother about the awfulness of the schoolroom because it would be upsetting, and the doctor who sometimes came to see her said that upsets should be avoided. When I sat with her in her bedroom I told her instead about the ships that were docked at the quays or how I'd seen a milk-cart toppling over on its side when its horse slipped on an icy street. I described the people I'd noticed, the tramps and drunks and foreign seamen, anyone who had appeared to be exotic. I brought her reports of actors and singers I had imagined in the Opera House, culling their names from the play-bills that decorated the city's hoardings: I made up quite a lot in order to keep our conversations going.

She listened vaguely, occasionally making the effort to smile. The letters which came from India, from my English grandparents, remained unopened in her bedroom, as did the letters from Aunt Fitzeustace and Aunt Pansy. 'Write to your aunts,' she commanded in the same vague way. 'Tell them you are well. But add please that I am not quite up to visitors yet.' She did not venture out of the house for many weeks on end and then would very slowly make her way down the hill to the city, sitting for an hour or so in the Victoria Hotel. 'I thought it cold today,' she'd say. 'The first day it's warm again I'll have another walk.'

On several occasions I tried to explain to Josephine about Miss

50

Halliwell's disturbing sentiments. But it wasn't easy to conjure up the atmosphere of the schoolroom and I felt shy of revealing that Miss Halliwell stroked the nape of my neck or that Elmer Dunne said Miss Halliwell had a passion for me. He was not teasing or mocking me in any way, but simply stating what he believed to be the truth. 'It's not that at all,' I protested, walking one day along the quayside with him. 'It's just that she's sorry for me. I wish she wasn't.' But Elmer Dunne laughed, and spoke again of unbuttoning our teacher's clothes.

'Oh, Willie, she's only being kind,' Josephine said in the kitchen when finally I presented her with an approximation of my worry. I pretended to accept that opinion, for as soon as I'd brought the subject up I didn't wish to pursue it. The kitchen was small, but I liked its cosy warmth and the smell of Brasso when Josephine laid out for cleaning the brass pieces that had come from Kilneagh. When I finished my homework she would talk about her childhood in Fermoy, and it was then that she told me about her first days at Kilneagh and how strange its world had seemed to her – as strange as the world of the city now was to me. Sometimes the bell in the passage would jangle and she would remain with my mother for an hour or so while I sat alone, close to the heat of the range. Now and again I wandered into the dank sitting-room or dining-room, both of them noticeably narrow, as everything about the house was. There was room for only one person at a time on the stairs, and you had to wait on a half-landing in order to permit someone else to pass. Each of these half-landings had a long rectangular window, the bottom half of which comprised a pattern of green and red panes in a variety of shapes. The two main landings had similar windows, though rather larger, and the patterned motif was repeated on either side of the hall door and in the hall door itself, through which sunlight cast coloured beams, red tinged with green and green with red. Incongruous on the stairway walls were the gilt-framed canvases that had been saved from the fire. In the narrow sitting-room and dining-room familiar furniture loomed awkwardly now, and on the landing outside my mother's room the tall oak cupboard that had held my sisters' dolls in the nursery took up almost all the space there was. I opened it once and saw what appeared to be a hundred maps of Ireland: the trade-mark of Paddy Whiskey on a mass of labels, the bottles arrayed like an army on the shelves.

'No, Josephine,' my mother said as I entered her bedroom one evening to say good-night. 'You have a life of your own to live.'

'I want to stay with you, ma'am.'

'I'll soon be myself again.'

'I couldn't marry him now, ma'am. I couldn't settle in that neighbourhood.'

'A little drink?' my mother suggested.

'No thank you, Mrs Quinton.'

I said good-night but my mother did not hear me. She spoke of parties at Kilneagh before her marriage, of decorating the church for the Harvest Festival, and how my father used to pick his Christmas presents for her from Cash's Christmas catalogue: bottles of scent and lavender water, talcum powder and bath oil. 'There now,' Josephine murmured because my mother had become agitated, speaking now of the damp lawn and its coolness soothing the pain. 'I didn't want to live,' she sometimes said.

I remembered her when Josephine and I had returned from the hospital in Fermoy. She had been wearing a green overcoat, standing with Aunt Fitzeustace in the garden. The overcoat had been my father's and had hung, hardly ever worn by him, in one of the kitchen passages. 'No, it cannot be believed,' Aunt Fitzeustace had been saying, tears dripping on to her blouse and her tweed tie.

'Good-night,' I said again.

'Ah, Willie, I did not see you there. Yes, of course it's time for your bed.'

She did not kiss me, as she had at Kilneagh. I closed her bedroom door and climbed up another half flight of stairs. Often I dreamed of that moment in the garden, of Aunt Fitzeustace's weeping, and my mother in the green overcoat.

'Mr Derenzy is coming today,' Josephine reminded me one morning, and when I returned from school there was a fire in the dining-room and my mother had dressed and come downstairs. The dining-room door was ajar, and with some excitement Josephine said: 'You are to go in at once, Willie. Just comb your hair.'

She combed it herself with a comb that had been ready on the kitchen draining-board. She made me wash my hands, and damped the comb beneath the tap. 'Look up at me,' she said, and then hurried me to the dining-room, where a mass of papers and ledgers was spread out on the table. My mother, in a black and red striped dress, had a tray of tea things in front of her. The room smelt of her scent, the first time I'd noticed it since we'd come to the house in Windsor Terrace. She had touched her cheeks with rouge and had piled her hair up, the way she used to for a party at Kilneagh. 'Willie'll be better at understanding,' she said, smiling and pouring tea.

I shook hands with Mr Derenzy, who hadn't changed in any way whatsoever. He wore the same blue serge suit, the same pens and pencils clipped to its top pocket. His red hair still gave the impression of sustaining a life of its own, the hand that gripped mine felt more like bones than flesh.

'Ah, Willie, it's good to see you.'

'The poor man's having a terrible time explaining to me, Willie.'

'Ah no, no,' Mr Derenzy protested, sitting down again.

My mother offered me a piece of Swiss roll, and when Mr Derenzy began to talk about sales and purchases at the mill I realized that my task was simply to listen. The sums and subtractions were a formality, but once Mr Derenzy paused and, addressing me rather than my mother, explained that a legal agreement necessitated this long report of the continued management of the mill. I had not even thought about any of it before, or wondered what was happening there. That afternoon I realized Mr Derenzy was now in charge of everything, no longer a clerk but the mill's manager.

'Coal, £12,' he said. 'Carpenter's repairs to the chute supports, £3. 4s., Midleton Sacks and Company Limited, £14. 12s.' He took from his pocket the tin that once had contained catarrh pastilles and now held snuff. As I listened to his fluty voice I reflected that the container couldn't always have been that same one: the words *Potter's, the Remedy* would not still have been as easy to read across the table if he had carried the tin about with him for years. It was odd that Geraldine and Deirdre, so interested in everything about Mr Derenzy, had never wondered if he suffered from catarrh and bought these pastilles regularly.

'Wicks,' he said, 'half a crown. I'm thinking,' he added apologetically, 'would the mat inside the office door have had its time? Mr Quinton didn't say order a new one, but it's gone threadbare and only a while ago the traveller from Midleton Sacks got his foot caught in it. I had Johnny Lacy take a look at it, only he said there's nothing can be done with the fibre the way it's manufactured. And if we don't replace it at all –'

'Oh, replace it, Mr Derenzy,' interrupted my mother, as if waking from sleep. 'Simply replace it.'

'That's nice of you, Mrs Quinton. Only I don't think that mat could be repaired. But then again I wouldn't want you to think there's an extravagance in buying a new one.'

'An office has to have a mat.' My mother smiled, but the strain of the afternoon was showing beneath the powder and the rouge. 'Mr Derenzy,' she suggested, 'I think we might have a little drink.'

She rose as she spoke and approached a decanter on the sideboard. Glasses had been arranged in a row in front of it, as if other guests were expected. Neither the glasses nor the liquid in the decanter had been there when I'd last entered the dining-room.

'Ah no, not whiskey for me, Mrs Quinton. No, thanks all the same.'

'There's gin somewhere. There's sherry.'

'I never touch a drop, Mrs Quinton.'

'You don't drink? I never knew that.'

'It's not on temperance grounds, Mrs Quinton. It's only I have no head at all for it.'

'Oh, but surely a little thimbleful?'

'I'd be on my bed for three days, Mrs Quinton.'

Not properly listening even though she managed to conduct the conversation, my mother had poured herself a measure of whiskey and now added water to it from a cut-glass jug. With this she returned to where she'd been sitting.

'Is there anything, Mr Derenzy? Soda water? There might be lemonade. Willie, go and ask Josephine if she has lemonade for Mr Derenzy. Or maybe that ginger stuff.'

'Ah no, don't bother.' Wrenching his face apart, a skeleton's smile was full of apology for the trouble this disinclination to drink whiskey was causing.

But my mother nodded at me in a way I remembered from Kilneagh, indicating that I should do as she had bidden me. 'And ask Josephine to make up the fire.'

There was no lemonade, nor any ginger stuff, so Josephine sent me out to Hayes's while she went herself to the dining-room to put coals on the fire and to say I wouldn't be long. When I returned with two bottles of soda water Josephine put them on a tray, with glasses that were larger than the ones on the sideboard, and in the dining-room I poured some for myself and some for Mr Derenzy. The conversation, clearly no longer about accounts and office replacements, had ceased when I entered. As he received his glass from me, Mr Derenzy attempted to guide my mother's attention back to the business of the mill but she at once interrupted him.

'You know the facts,' she said sharply. 'You are a person, Mr Derenzy, who knows everything. About Kilneagh and Lough, indeed about Fermoy. You have told Willie and myself that an office mat is threadbare and we have been attentive; Willie has gone out for soda water. The mill is running profitably, that is clear to see. But there is something more important.'

'I wonder in front of Willie, Mrs Quinton? If you recall, you said you would prefer to have this private between us.'

'I have changed my mind.'

In my absence the decanter had been removed from the sideboard and was now beside my mother's glass. So was the jug of water.

Mr Derenzy shifted his feet about and repeatedly swallowed. He was here at the request of Lanigan and O'Brien, he said; it was a legal requirement that he should regularly make the report he was endeavouring to make.

'Was it Sergeant Rudkin?' enquired my mother, and in my mind's eye I instantly saw the man in soldier's uniform lighting a cigarette at the street corner in Fermoy. 'Rudkin?' my mother repeated.

The fluffy halo nodded, and for a moment there was agitation in the mill manager's eyes. His lips had begun to quiver, anger grated in his voice.

'Rudkin walked about Fermoy,' he said, 'as if nothing had occurred. The only thing that happened was the woman he was after closed her door to him.'

'What woman, Mr Derenzy?' My mother sprawled over the papers on the table, her glass held in the air.

'He was attempting to associate with a Fermoy woman. The widow of McBirney, the bicycle-shop man.'

'I didn't ever know that.'

'McBirney was killed in the Munster Fusiliers.'

55

'I don't think that matters, you know.'

'No, no, it doesn't at all. It was only that you enquired about the woman –'

'Are people in Fermoy certain about the other thing? How do people know?'

'Oh, they know all right, Mrs Quinton. One of the young fellows with Rudkin that night ended up in a terrible state. He deserted from the barracks and was gone for two days until they found him near the Mitchelstown Caves. He couldn't stop talking about Rudkin and the petrol tins. He was unhinged by the whole affair: a finger wasn't laid on him because everyone knew the Tans would do it for them when they heard he'd talked.'

'In the circumstances isn't it surprising that no one had the courage to shoot Sergeant Rudkin? Wouldn't you say that, Mr Derenzy?'

'Rudkin slipped the net. As soon as he saw the lie of the land with McBirney's widow he got himself shifted up to a barracks in Dundalk.'

It was difficult to believe now that the Sergeant Rudkin they spoke of had waved genially at my father and on some previous occasion had told him he owned a vegetable shop in Liverpool. He might even have shaken my father's hand, the way a bleary farmer had often done in the Grand Hotel.

'It's still surprising,' my mother insisted, 'that nobody shot Rudkin.'

She leaned back in her chair again, her glazed manner returning, not listening when Mr Derenzy said that he had heard of stories in which revenge had been planned. Sergeant Rudkin would have suffered, he said, if he hadn't slipped the net.

'He did what he did,' my mother whispered, speaking more to herself than to either of us, 'because Doyle was hanged on our land. That's all the reason there was. It had nothing to do with Collins.'

'There's a portion of slating to be seen to,' Mr Derenzy said after a moment of silence. 'The roof of the right-hand loft. A matter of say two dozen new slates, Mrs Quinton.'

'I cannot understand why nobody shot him. I cannot understand that. He'd be back in Liverpool now, selling people vegetables. If I've followed you, that would be right, would it, Mr Derenzy?'

'Mrs Quinton –'

'Does nobody think we're worth it? Well, perhaps we're not.'

'Oh now, that's not the way of it at all.'

'Do you still go over to Kilneagh on Sundays, Mr Derenzy?'

'Well, yes, I do.'

'I would be grateful if you would explain to my sisters-in-law that we are not ready for visitors yet.'

'They're only concerned at not having had a line from you, Mrs Quinton.'

'That has to be, Mr Derenzy. I would ask you to say also that I would prefer not to receive letters.'

My mother rose. She shook hands with Mr Derenzy and abruptly left the room. Her scent was more noticeable when she moved, and her red and black dress made a pleasant swishing sound.

'Ah now, I hope I haven't tired her,' Mr Derenzy worriedly remarked. He reached under the table for a brown leather suitcase and carefully placed in it his ledgers and bundles of papers. He had not drunk any of his soda water.

'And have you settled in, Willie?' he enquired, ending the silence he had evoked in order to mark his concern for my mother.

'At school d'you mean, Mr Derenzy?'

'Well, at school certainly. But in general terms, Willie. Isn't Cork a great place now?'

'Cork's all right.'

'More to do, Willie. More than in Lough, you could say. And d'you like the school you're talking about?'

I shook my head, but Mr Derenzy didn't notice.

'Do your lessons well, Willie, and pay good attention to what the teacher says. I'm keeping the mill going for you, until the moment's right for you to take over.'

'Thank you, Mr Derenzy.'

'Your mother'll be getting better, Willie. All the time she'll be getting better.'

A few weeks after Mr Derenzy's visit my mother requested that she and I should meet in the Victoria Hotel on my way home from school one afternoon. We were then to proceed to the offices of Lanigan and O'Brien, who had been the Quinton family's solicitors for many generations. In the hotel she ordered tea but didn't have any herself, none of the triangular ham sandwiches nor the little iced sponge-cakes. She whispered to the waiter and received instead what might have been a glass of water.

'Would this place remind you of the Grand in Fermoy, Willie?'

She was doing her best, endeavouring to make conversation. She was thinner than she'd been at Kilneagh, but in the hotel her undiminished beauty caused people to glance at her a second time.

'A bit it reminds me,' I said. 'Only a bit.'

'Maybe we'll go to the Opera House one night, Willie.'

'That would be nice.'

'Did Josephine take you? My memory's gone to pieces, you know.'

'Yes, she did.'

'Of course she did. I remember now. And what was it you saw, Willie?'

'Paddy the Next Best Thing.'

Catching the waiter's eye, she waved her hand at him and a moment later he arrived with another glass for her.

'The first time I came to Kilneagh, Willie, I knew I'd end up living there. "You can't go marrying a Quinton," my father said to me. Wasn't that ridiculous? D'you remember your grandfather, Willie? Very tall and thin.'

'Yes, I remember him.'

'He's keeping the flag flying in India now, since it's not permitted to fly here any more. He and your grandmother.'

'Yes, I know they're in India.'

'You'll write to them for me, Willie? Just say we're all right.'

I nodded, finishing a raspberry-flavoured cake.

'Tell them not to worry, Willie.'

'Yes.'

'I'll pay the next time,' my mother said suddenly, rising before I had finished and waving the waiter away. The man didn't demur. No hurry whatsoever about paying, he said.

'What I'm anxious about,' my mother said without preamble in the offices of Lanigan and O'Brien, 'is all this business with Mr Derenzy and the mill. I've brought Willie with me because my memory's poor these days. We'll make a new arrangement about the mill, Willie, which you'll have to remember because I'm certain I shan't.'

The solicitors' offices were in the South Mall, heralded by a shiny brass plate among many similar ones, all of them drawing attention to the services of legal or medical practitioners. Mr O'Brien was long since dead, but Mr Lanigan's presence made up for the loss. He was a person of pyramidal shape, a small head sloping into the slope of his shoulders, arms sloping again as he spread them over his desk. A chalk-striped brown suit imposed a secondary shape of its own, with a heavy watch-chain slung across a waistcoat so tightly fastened over the slope of Mr Lanigan's stomach that it appeared to be perpetually on the point of bouncing a dozen tiny buttons all over his office. Two beady eyes, not dissimilar to these buttons, were almost lost in the smooth inclines of his face, and artificial chins, created by a stern celluloid collar, all but obscured the flamboyance of a polka-dotted brown bow-tie Mr Lanigan's smile perpetually twinkled.

'I would have come to the house, Mrs Quinton, for it's more than a shame to have you walking to the South Mall. The next time there's anything, Willie, let you leave a message in here with Declan O'Dwyer and I'll travel at once to your mother's bidding.'

With a hint of impatience my mother said it did her good to get out. She was always being told that, she pointed out to Mr Lanigan: by the doctor and by Josephine, even by Mr Derenzy. 'Now, concerning Mr Derenzy,' she said.

'And how is our dear friend? Would that name derive from the French, d'you think? I often say, do you know, the French have left their mark on Ireland. And if they have, Mrs Quinton, we mustn't complain about it. Willie, do you speak French well?'

I shook my head. I said I was only beginning to learn French with Miss Halliwell.

'Ah, good Miss Halliwell! A born teacher, a privilege to have her in Cork.' While speaking, Mr Lanigan reached behind him and struck the wall with an ebony ruler. Almost at once a small man in a frock coat entered the office. He had a nervous, quizzical expression, eyes busily darting behind pince-nez.

'Declan O'Dwyer,' said Mr Lanigan, 'I believe refreshment would be in order. Mrs Quinton, there is wine or there is tea. Willie, there is a good fruit cordial.'

My mother asked for wine; I agreed to sample a glass of fruit cordial. Declan O'Dwyer's hands, held chest-high like the paws of an expectant dog, were abruptly pressed together as if in prayer. His grey head shot rapidly up and down. He hurried from the room.

'Our clerk these forty years,' Mr Lanigan said. 'Now tell me this, Willie: would you guess our good friend was without the blessing of speech?'

I shook my head. My mother shuffled in her chair.

'It has never made the smallest difference, Willie, and I would say there is a moral in that. Declan O'Dwyer is the sharpest solicitor's clerk in these two islands. If the good Lord taketh away, Willie, He also giveth. If it is a privilege for this city to have Miss Halliwell in charge of Protestant children in Mercier Street, it is a privilege also for Lanigan and O'Brien to retain the services of Declan O'Dwyer.'

At that appropriate moment a tray containing two glasses of red wine and one of pinkish cordial was carried into the office by the mute solicitor's clerk.

'Good man, good man,' said Mr Lanigan, his entire being seeming now to be consumed by the radiance of his smile. 'Mrs Quinton, your health. As Voltaire has so eloquently put it –'

'I have come to ask if it is necessary for Mr Derenzy to bring all those papers and accounts to the house every six months. Mr Derenzy is the most trustworthy of men, and as regards the management of the mill Willie and I are perfectly happy to leave matters to him.'

Mr Lanigan, before replying, commented upon the wine. It was a fine burgundy, he said, a delicate French burgundy and a privilege to drink. Cork was a fortunate city, he said, to have received a shipment of such wine. 'And the cordial, Willie? Is the cordial to your liking? Declan O'Dwyer purchases it for me in the London and Newcastle Tea Company. As to the matter you raise, Mrs Quinton, the difficulty would be the circumvention of the wishes expressed in the late Mr Quinton's will. It is a fact of life, borne out by so many of the intricacies of my profession, that the wishes of the departed take precedence over those of the quick. As Voltaire might indeed have put it –'

'I do not wish to hear about Voltaire. Mr Derenzy's visits are a nuisance to me. If my husband had been aware of that he would most certainly have ordered matters differently.'

My mother had stood up, having first drunk her wine in one or two gulps. A little had spilt and now stained the frill of her bodice; small beads of perspiration had broken out on her forehead; she swayed in front of Mr Lanigan's desk.

'I am excessively sorry, Mrs Quinton. We are unfortunately up against the letter of the law. But after all, Mr Derenzy comes only twice a year –'

'I wish him not to come at all. I wish to be left in peace, and not reminded.'

'I understand, I understand. But the law –'

'I am simply requesting that Mr Derenzy's visits might be made to yourself or not made at all. There is no need for them, no need whatsoever.'

Mr Lanigan ponderously shook his head and heaved the slopes of his shoulders. He regretted, he stated, more than he could say; it grieved him to be unable to accede to the most reasonable request that had been put to him. My mother brushed these sentiments aside.

'You are not being helpful to me, Mr Lanigan. You are not being kind. It is not easy for me, you know.'

'I assure you I do know that, Mrs Quinton.'

'I receive letters from my sisters-in-law which I do not open. I have requested Mr Derenzy to inform them that I do not wish to receive them. Another arrived this morning.'

'I could send a message –'

'And to India. I would like a message sent to India.'

'India, Mrs Quinton?'

'Letters come from my father and mother in a place called Masulipatam. I cannot be doing with them.'

'People are perhaps concerned for you and Willie. It is only that.'

'Willie is kindness itself. He has agreed to inform his grand-parents that we are well, but please understand that it is difficult for poor Willie to say more.'

'What message would you wish passed on, Mrs Quinton?'

'That I do not care for being bombarded with communications from this Masulipatam. That I wish the letters would cease.'

'Oh, I do not believe I could put it quite like that –'

'Why not? Why are you being obstructive, Mr Lanigan? You are a gross and unfeeling man.'

'Mrs Quinton, I do assure you –'

'Please request your clerk to show us out.'

Panting a little and deprived at last of his smile, Mr Lanigan struck weakly at the wall with his ruler and Declan O'Dwyer arrived in the office. I knew my mother was drunk; and I wished I might have told Mr Lanigan that. It was clear to me that my father's wishes were the law.

'What did I say to that man?' she asked when we reached Windsor Terrace. As we entered the house I told her that she had called him gross and unfeeling. She shook her head, saying she had not meant it. She stared at me in a puzzled way. 'Why did we go there, Willie? Did that man send for us?'

I didn't reply. She frowned in even greater bewilderment, swaying on the stairway. I walked away to write the letter she had asked me to write.

'Oh, don't be cross with me, Willie,' my mother cried after me, but I didn't reply to that either.

I wrote to Father Kilgarriff as well, who in his reply quoted from a letter of Anna Quinton's which he had not before known of. *November 15th, 1846. Corpses in the ditches lie as they have fallen. The people of the cottages eat grass and bramble leaves, and the roots of ferns. At the barracks they were offended when I would not stay to lunch. For God's sake, bring your persuasion to bear on this most monstrous of governments.* Her black horse had been called Folly, Father Kilgarriff recalled, and after that she came into the dreams I had about Kilneagh, seeming to be there with my sisters and my father. 'That's Anna,' my great-grandfather said, pointing across the landscape at Haunt Hill, and clearly I saw the troubled, unpretty Englishwoman on her horse. The family was titled in Dorset, Father Kilgarriff had told me: she might have been Lady Anna, but never chose to call herself so.

'Eschew the company of Elmer Dunne,' Miss Halliwell warned me, but in the playground I continued to laugh with the others when he talked to us about her undergarments. 'Would you never think of slipping a hand up under her skirt?' he said on the day he left the school for ever. I knew Miss Halliwell was watching from the schoolroom window and had seen him drawing me aside. 'I swear to Jesus she's on for it, Quinton. She'd love a touch, that one.'

I felt proud that Elmer Dunne, who was big and heavy and stupid, several years older than I was and a real chancer, should seek my company, calling me Quinton in that manly way. Slowly he gestured with his head and I followed him behind the lavatories, out of Miss Halliwell's line of vision. He took a packet of cigarettes from his trouser pocket and casually offered me one. He was going to become a clerk's assistant in the new woollen goods factory, and as he held a match to my cigarette he said that some of the girls who worked there would knock spots off the ones at school.

'D'you know what it is, Quinton? Catholic girls are the best for a ride.' He laughed noisily. Drawing unwelcome smoke into my lungs, I replied that I'd always heard that to be true.

'If ever you get a feel of her, Quinton, will you tell me what it was like?'

He was the nearest thing to a friend I had made in Mercier Street and I was sorry he was leaving, although I knew I would never be able to oblige him in the way he wished me to. 'OK so, Quinton,' he said, and crossed the playground with the cigarette in his mouth. He waved at Miss Halliwell, who was still watching from her window.

'Good riddance,' she snapped after she had rung the handbell and the clamour had quietened in the schoolroom. 'A boy nine years in this school and nothing to show for it. With uncouthness like that he'll not last an hour in the post he's got.'

That day, when all the others had gone, Miss Halliwell did not even open the French grammar book she was to teach me from. She sat at her table gazing in front of her at nothing at all. 'A boy like that,' she whispered again. 'Nine years in my school, Willie.' Once when she had asked Elmer Dunne to recite the second verse of 'The Brook' he had stood up and recited instead:

> 'Paddy from Ireland, Paddy from Cork,
> With a hole in his britches as big as New York.'

He had remained standing, taller than Miss Halliwell herself. Defiantly he had waited for her to approach him with her ruler, holding out the palm of his hand for the punishment that must inevitably follow. 'Thanks, Miss Halliwell,' he had said when she'd finished.

'I am sorry you associated with him,' she upbraided me now, 'when I asked you not to. You especially, Willie.'

I felt the familiar burning in my face, spreading from my cheeks into my forehead and my neck, an embarrassed flushing which I associated entirely with Miss Halliwell, for it was in this schoolroom that it had begun.

63

'I'm all right, you know, Miss Halliwell.' My mouth was parched, my lips suddenly so dry they were almost sore. 'Really, Miss Halliwell.'

'No child should be harmed as you have been.'

'I don't feel harmed.'

'I will always have a place in my heart for you, Willie.'

I looked down at the ink-stained surface of the table, at the blue cover of my French text-book. Miss Halliwell repeated what she had just said, and a lean hand reached out for one of mine. Then, for the first time, she kissed me. Her lips left a moist coolness on the side of my face, her fingers stroked my wrist.

'He gave you a cigarette, didn't he? He made you smell of smoke just to offend me. Ever since I began to teach in this city there have been boys like that, Willie.'

'It's embarrassing when you favour me, Miss Halliwell.'

'We will always be friends, Willie, you and I. Together we have found comfort in our tribulations.'

Again she kissed me, and a feeling of desperation rushed somewhere inside me, making me dizzy. I wanted to say anything that would make her stop, to protest that I didn't like it when she came so close, to say I knew she was wearing violet-coloured underclothes. But in the midst of my panic what I heard myself saying was:

'Should we get on with our French now, Miss Halliwell?'

'I will always be here. When you leave this school please don't forget that. Will you write me letters? Promise me, Willie. Promise you'll write me letters.'

'Yes, Miss Halliwell.'

A hair curled from a mole on her chin, and I thought if I asked her why she didn't cut it off she would weep. Her tears would fall like rain on to my blue French book. The faded flowers of her face would become as ugly as Aunt Fitzeustace's when she had wept in the garden.

'When they told me about you, when they told me what had happened, I knew there would never be another child in this schoolroom who could mean as much to me as you have.'

'I've learnt the *Passé Composé. J'ai commencé.*'

'Do you like me, Willie?'

I said I did, but it was not the truth. I hated her mole and her moist lips and her talk of comfort in our tribulations. I was glad she'd smelt the tobacco on my lips, I was glad Elmer Dunne had coarsely said she was on for it. I couldn't imagine myself ever writing to her and certainly didn't intend to. In my dislike of her I felt calm again, and without emotion I said:

'Please don't favour me, Miss Halliwell. Please don't touch the back of my neck in class.'

'Willie, dear —'

'Elmer Dunne used to drop his pencil on the floor so that he could look up your skirts.'

She did not say anything. Her face was slightly turned away from me. Beneath the blush that now suffused it there was a sudden prettiness. I said:

'*Tu as commencé, il a commencé, nous avons commencé, vous avez commencé, ils ont commencé.*'

When I had finished Miss Halliwell still didn't speak. I stood up and gathered my books together, buckling them into my satchel. I left the schoolroom, not looking again in her direction, not saying good-bye as I usually did.

After that I was never again kept back when school was over, and on my last day in the schoolroom I imitated Elmer Dunne: knowing that Miss Halliwell was watching me from her window, I walked across the playground with a cigarette in my mouth. Someone cheered and then the bell rang out, but I continued on my way. I left my satchel and my books and my pencil-case in the schoolroom, and went on walking, through the city and up the hill to our house.

That day was a Wednesday and Mr Derenzy had come to make the half-yearly report my mother had attempted to dispense with. From the hall I could hear his voice in the dining-room, with a few monosyllables from my mother. I opened the dining-room door and took my place at the table. Miss Halliwell would be weeping in the schoolroom by now, alone after her pupils had gone.

'There's a bill I have to question from Midleton Sacks,' Mr Derenzy said. 'There's a charge for a gross we didn't receive, so I'll be writing a complaint concerning that.'

The afternoon dragged. Josephine brought in tea. My mother drank whiskey, saying it was good for a toothache she had developed. I was glad I had been cruel to Miss Halliwell.

'Johnny Lacy's getting married,' Mr Derenzy said. 'One of the Sweeney girls.'

'Johnny Lacy?' My mother's lips remained parted after she spoke. She stared, frowning, at Mr Derenzy. 'Johnny Lacy?' she said again, with greater emphasis. *'Johnny Lacy?'*

'He's been courting Bridie Sweeney for a long while now.'

'But Josephine –'

'Oh, I'd say all that was over, Mrs Quinton.'

My mother slowly shook her head. In her bewildered way she said she had kept urging Josephine to return to Lough.

'Well, there you are,' said Mr Derenzy.

'Now, someone's on my mind,' my mother said from her bed later that same evening. She had poured herself a little whiskey, she explained, because she was still suffering from toothache. Her face puckered in irritation while she endeavoured to establish who it was that hovered mysteriously behind her thoughts. I thought it might be Miss Halliwell, that somehow or other Miss Halliwell had been in touch with her, to complain of my behaviour. But after a moment's consideration I knew that of course it wasn't. More likely to be Josephine, I thought, but did not say so.

My mother frowned and shook her head, appearing to dismiss the subject. She said that when she was first married she used to wait at the mill every afternoon so that she and my father could walk back together to the house. 'I remember the day you were born, Willie. I remember the broken veins in Dr Hogan's face and how his shiny boots reminded me of a huntsman. "Now, now, Mrs Quinton," he said, "make your effort when I tell you."'

She poured herself more whiskey. She told me I had been creased and red, my eyes squeezed tight. And then, abruptly, she exclaimed, interrupting what she was saying:

'It's that man who's on my mind. You know how that kind of thing is, Willie? Suddenly, when you're not thinking at all it comes to you. That horrible Sergeant Rudkin, Willie.'

She went on talking about him, asking me if I could visualize him in his vegetable shop in Liverpool, selling produce to people who didn't know he had been responsible for a massacre. Would they have eaten the parsnips and cabbages if they knew? Would they have laughed and joked with him if they knew he had ordered the shooting of the dogs? She described his vegetable shop to me so minutely that she might have visited it herself,

66

potatoes in sacks, tinned fruit on a shelf, bananas hanging from hooks.

'The Devil incarnate,' my mother said.

5

Woodcombe Rectory it says on the writing-paper and I see that rectory clearly, although I've never visited Dorset. *Do please come to Woodcombe*: regularly the invitation was repeated, but like the pleas from my aunts and from India the letters from the rectory lay about my mother's bedroom unacknowledged, sometimes unread except in idle moments by myself. One mentioned you: in the September when first I went to the school I had so dreaded in the Dublin mountains you were to leave the rectory for a boarding-school in Hampshire. You were aware of my existence then; and I, without interest, of yours.

My father's name is on a board here, I wrote to Father Kilgarriff, *because he was in the rugby team, although I don't think he ever told me that. I have made friends with two boys in particular, Ring who comes from Dublin and de Courcy from Westmeath. The day is like this:*

At a quarter past seven the rising bell is rung, and then the ten-minute bell. After the second one if you're caught in bed you are punished. Breakfast is at five to eight, and Chapel afterwards. Chapel is the centre of school life, so the headmaster says. He's an English clergyman, as round as a ball, with a crimson complexion. His wife wears blue stockings and has grey hair that bushes out from the sides of her head. Their butler is called Fukes. He looks like an assistant at a funeral, de Courcy says, with his black clothes and deathly face.

Classes go on all morning, with a break at eleven o'clock for milk. Buckets of it are placed on a table outside Dining Hall and you dip your mug in. That's a tradition here. So is flicking butter on to the wooden ceiling of Dining Hall, which is something my father told me about. Classes continue after lunch and then there are games, tea and Preparation. Cloister cricket is a tradition too, but that's only played in the summer term. In class and Chapel and Dining Hall we have to wear gowns. On Sundays we wear surplices in Chapel, and the masters have academic hoods, all different colours.

The chaplain was a good-hearted man with a stutter, keen on rugby. Old Dove-White, who was my housemaster, sought a quiet life, never minding when we read books during his Latin lessons, or played cards or dice. Mad Mack, the mathematics master, had a ginger moustache and ginger hair and twisted the lobes of your ears. There was a man in a white coat who dealt in scientific subjects, and bald Monsieur Bertain who liked to talk about the part he'd played in the German war. Hopeless Gibbon, younger than one of the prefects, couldn't keep order. Dove-White's pipe tobacco had burnt holes all over his clothes.

Exposed to the winds that swept across the gorse-laden hillsides, the school that contained these people was a cloistered world of its own, different in every way from Mercier Street Model. None of my new mentors resembled the two teachers I had previously experienced, and the sexual obsessions of Elmer Dunne paled to ordinariness when related to the exploration of that same subject by my classroom companions. The headmaster was known as the Scrotum and his wife as Mrs Scrotum.

In my letters to my mother I did not repeat that nickname, nor say that Mr Mack was violent or that Hopeless Gibbon had difficulties in the classroom. *The Chaplain has a tin of biscuits*, I wrote, *like the tins there used to be along the counter of Driscoll's in Lough, with glass over them. A boy whose name I don't know has got into trouble because of the mice he keeps, and his jackdaw pecked poor Fukes and had to be given its freedom, even though the boy had taught it to say 'Amen'.* In reply there was a letter that was difficult to read. Some of the ink had been smudged, and the sentences rambled on, often remaining unconcluded. My mother's handwriting was jagged and unfeminine, sprawling as if a spider had trailed its way from the inkwell across the page. She described a walk she had taken, and how she'd sat on a low wall and a cat had crept into her lap. Vaguely she said she missed me.

Ring and de Courcy and I used to smuggle bread out of Dining Hall beneath our gowns and toast it in the furnace-room on the end of a length of wire. On Sundays we had tea with Dove-White, who invited a few other boys as well. He always had Fuller's cakes, which he had sent up specially from Dublin, and he let us make toast at his fire, a less difficult operation than poking slices of bread into the coke furnace. We sat for hours in his cluttered room, full of the belongings of boys who had long since left the school. Stacked away in corners, filthy with dust by now, were cricket bats and tennis racquets, books, overnight cases, deflated rugby balls, rugs, canes, caps, scarves, hats, hockey sticks, and a useful supply of gowns, surplices, blazers and House ties. 'Oh, now, now,' Dove-White would protest with a half-hearted sigh when the conversation touched upon Big Lily the nightwatchman's wife, who was the source of the graffiti in the school's whitewashed lavatory cubicles. Big Lily worked in the kitchens, returning in the late evening to a cottage halfway down the back drive. Her husband, O'Toole, would then get up and prepare himself for his night's duty in the furnace-room. It wasn't until he was safely ensconced in a chair among the piles of coke that surreptitious journeys were made to the windows of his cottage, where the culminating excitement was the sight of Big Lily washing herself at the kitchen sink. I made the journey myself, since to do so had long since become a ritual experience for all new boys.

'Blood Major knocked on the door,' de Courcy said in Dove-White's room, and Dove-White gave his sigh. Blood Major was no longer at the school, but the night he had knocked on the door while Big Lily was washing herself was one of the most repeated of all Sunday-afternoon stories. No one tired of retelling it, with variations from week to week.

'"Is that you, Blood?" she says. "Come in, Blood, I can't see you in the dark."' De Courcy paused, allowing expectation to rise: de Courcy's versions were always good. '"Evening, Mrs O'Toole," Blood says, "I was passing and I saw the light. Is this penknife Mr O'Toole's?" He holds out his own penknife and Big Lily shakes her head. She had covered herself up with a sheet she'd pulled off the line above the range. "Someone said it was Mr O'Toole's," Blood says. "I'm sorry to trouble you, Mrs O'Toole." The next thing is he's sitting down having a cup of tea and Big Lily is putting safety-pins in the sheet to keep it around her. "You're a fine big boy, Blood," she says. "You have lovely strong arms. Will I sit on your knee, Blood?" The next thing is she's up on his knee and he has two of the safety-pins taken out of the sheet. "God, you're a terrible boy,

69

Blood," she says, and in steps O'Toole, back for his tobacco. "Poor Blood got a fly in his eye," she says, "I'm trying to lift it out with a corner of this sheet." O'Toole gives a jerk of his head and says you have to be careful with anything in the eye. "Ah, there's me tobacco," he says, and as soon as he's gone Big Lily has Blood down on the table.'

'She's a most respectable woman,' Dove-White protested, as he always did, when de Courcy had finished. 'It's sheer nonsense, de Courcy.'

'She spends four hours in Confession every Tuesday, sir. The priests go mad with excitement.'

'I doubt that very much.'

There were other accounts drawn from the private life of the nightwatchman's wife, and many adventures concerning the legendary Blood Major. One in particular told how he had cycled down to Dublin one night and had been approached by a heavily made-up woman in Bachelor's Walk. 'Are you game for a drink?' she suggested to him. 'Will we go to Mooney's?' With alacrity Blood Major agreed and in the brighter light of the public house he noticed that the woman was a good deal older than his mother. Her coat was of worn fur, her hair a shade of brass. Each time she laughed the sound ended in a bout of coughing which caused her several chins to wobble. 'They have good-class mahogany in here,' she said after Blood Major had bought her a glass of Smithwick's. 'Spanish mahogany, the best you can get.' She was particularly fond of mahogany, she revealed, and a desultory conversation about the timber then commenced, during which Blood Major edged a knee closer to one of his companion's. On her recommendation, he examined the mahogany counter and the drinking cubicles, and the frames of the mirrors which advertised different brands of spirits. You'd never find better mahogany than that, the woman assured him. 'Will we try another glass, dear? Isn't it lovely and warming?' As she spoke, she returned the pressure on her knee and placed a hand on Blood Major's thigh, saying he was a fine big boy. 'Take care with that one,' a man in a bowler hat warned him at the bar. 'She's up to her neck in the pox.'

It was stories such as these, and the use of improper language and obscene references, that inspired the crusade of Mad Mack, whose avowed intention was to cleanse the school of verbal grime. He had a band of minions, stern-faced youths whom he'd imbued with his puritan zeal and invested with the authority of prefects.

'Abominable man,' was Dove-White's unvarying opinion of the mathematics master. They had not addressed one another for fourteen years, Mad Mack in turn considering Dove-White ludicrous and ineffectual.

'Take yourself to the back,' Mad Mack had ordered during my first mathematics lesson, and I joined the row of farmers' sons, whom daily he referred to as peasants. In Chapel he occupied one of the throne-like seats behind the choir, strands of his ginger hair plastered across his head, lips hidden by his ginger moustache. Gowns draped the differently disposed figures of his colleagues among the carved oak gargoyles that lent distinction to this special area, an arm raised here and there, fingers gripping a chin or touching a cheek-bone. But Mad Mack always sat bolt upright, as if in pain.

'Trench reported Mrs Scrotum to him,' de Courcy remarked to Dove-White, 'for eyeing Hopeless Gibbon. She likes being friends with the young ones, doesn't she, sir?'

'Abominable woman.'

Unfailingly Dove-White emerged from his sleepiness to condemn these people. The headmaster himself was his most particular *bête noire* and if we could get him going on a Sunday afternoon he would hold forth for hours about the red-fleshed clergyman's under-graduate days at Keble College, Oxford. These mysteriously acquired recollections – for Dove-White himself had not been to that university – appeared to belong in the same category as the sagas of Blood Major, and reminded me also of the stories Johnny Lacy had told me about the circus dwarf's wife who ate nails and the soldier who'd ridden a horse through Phelan's shop window in Fermoy. We Irish were intrigued, my father used to say, by stories with a degree of unreality in them.

'D'you think Mad Mack should be given the sack, sir?' de Courcy would regularly enquire. 'I mean, since he's depraved?'

'A man like Mack shouldn't be allowed in any school. Heaven knows why they can't see that.'

'The headmaster's not intelligent, sir.'

De Courcy was thin and jumpy, always moving about. He had hair that was paler than my own, white almost, and smooth as a pebble. Beneath the neat curve of his fringe a sallow face perpetually changed expression, eyes flickering nervously, lips chattering or laughing. Ring was the opposite, a massive boy with a sledge-hammer head, slow of thought and speech. They'd been at the same preparatory school in Co. Wicklow but some element was missing in their friendship which I, to my surprise, apparently supplied. We sat next to one another in Dining Hall and in Chapel and in class. We roamed together over the hills at the back of the school, we smoked cigarettes together, and on exeat Sundays we all three walked down to Ring's house in Rathfarnham and spent the day there. Ring's father was a manufacturer of lemonade who'd been at the school at the same time as my own, a big man with a chunky bald head. Ring was proposing to manufacture lemonade as well; de Courcy wanted to become an actor.

'No, that ridiculous man's not intelligent,' Dove-White would thoughtfully agree, the conversation following a pattern. Burning tobacco would fall from his pipe on to his waistcoat, to be followed by a smell of singeing, which he ignored. At Keble, he would invariably add, the headmaster had been considered mentally deficient.

'Let's go over to Bolger's,' de Courcy suggested one Saturday afternoon in the furnace-room, and after some calculations we agreed that between the three of us we had enough money for the outing. Bolger's was a house about a mile across the hills, where tea – with fried eggs and bacon – might be purchased at a modest cost. Afterwards, funds permitting, a call might be made to Lamb Doyle's public house.

We thrashed our way through the gorse, Ring singing a lugubri-ously indecent ballad, de Courcy enthusing about his future in the theatre. They both knew a little of my history, but I did not often talk about the past and they did not ask. I never mentioned my mother.

'Have you sausages today?' Ring asked the waitress at Bolger's in his drawling, lazy voice. 'Six sausages each, and fried bread, black puddings and potato cakes.'

'Isn't she a lovely creature?' de Courcy whispered while the girl laid out knives and forks for us. Freckled and stout, she blushed in confusion.

'What's your name?' Ring demanded.

'Noreen.'

'And where are you from, Noreen?'

'Mullingar.'

'Noreen of the wild ways,' de Courcy murmured when she'd gone, a remark which Ring repeated to her as soon as she returned.

'Errah, get on with you,' said the girl.

We drank cups of tea with the fried food, and ate slices of soda bread smeared with blackberry jelly. 'I wonder have we enough for a jar in Lamb's?' Ring suggested when we'd finished, and de Courcy and I placed what remained of our money on the table.

'Are you doing anything this minute, Noreen?' Ring enquired of the waitress. 'Would you wet your whistle with us in the Lamb's?'

'Sure, amn't I up to my neck?'

'Slip out the back, Noreen. Your man here has an eye for you.'

De Courcy kept his head bent during this exchange. Although he talked a great deal about girls, he was excessively shy in their presence and found it difficult to converse normally with the maids at school, several of whom he had declared he would lay down his life for.

'D'you get any time off, Noreen?' Ring persisted. 'Would you be free in the evenings ever?'

As he spoke, he placed one of his huge arms round the girl's waist, causing her to jump backwards as if stung by a wasp. 'Lay off that stuff,' she cried, glaring at all three of us from a distance. 'Keep your hands to yourself now.' Cautiously she approached the table again in order to stack the plates on to a tray.

'It's your man here who's keen for you, Noreen. It's not me at all.'

'I haven't a fancy for schoolboys.'

'As a matter of fact, Noreen, we're sailors off a ship.'

The girl did not reply. She carried the tray away, and since she did not return we set out for Lamb Doyle's. We occupied a table near a window which afforded a wide view of the approach to the public house, for it was not unknown for Mad Mack or his proselytes to come snooping.

'Did you ever in all your days see a more graceful creature?' de Courcy demanded as we lit our cigarettes. 'Wouldn't you lay down your life for her, Quinton?'

I replied that I didn't think I would, but de Courcy continued to speak with some extravagance of the waitress's beauty, lending emphasis to his romantic mood by declaiming the poetry of W. B. Yeats. Ring laughed coarsely.

'You'd do better than that skivvy in the first kip-shop you'd come to,' he said. 'An uglier lump I never laid eyes on.'

'You are without a soul, Ring.'

'You'd need a soul and a half to see anything in that one.'

As he spoke, the only other drinker in the bar approached us. He was a man in a stained Donegal suit and a stained hat. He had broken front teeth.

'Excuse me.' Blear-eyed, he looked down at the three of us. 'Are you from the college?'

'We're sailors off a ship,' Ring said.

'I was at the college myself one time.'

He paused while politely we acknowledged this fact. We'd never seen the man before.

'Thirteen years ago. I used to teach geography.'

He turned and walked away. We drank what remained in our glasses and mechanically hid our cigarettes in the cups of our hands. It was never a good idea to drop into conversations with strangers in a public house. Even the most genial of them had been known to contact the headmaster a day or two later, sobered by conscience and anxious for our welfare. We were actually on our feet, about to go, when the tweeded man addressed us from the bar.

'I've got you one for the road.' He pulled a chair in to the table so that we might drink together. 'You're right enough for an hour,' he said. 'If you're back there for Chapel they'll not notice anything else.'

He gave us fresh cigarettes and made us clink our glasses against his. He asked us who we were and we gave him the names of three other boys. He didn't reveal his own.

'Is Mack still in action?' he enquired. 'Is he back on speaking terms with Dove-White?'

The amount he knew about the school convinced us that he was speaking the truth when he claimed a connection with it in the past. Nor did his grubbiness seem entirely out of place, or preclude him from the schoolmastering profession: there was nothing particularly prepossessing about the gingery appearance of Mad Mack or Dove-White's burnt clothes.

We sipped the porter we'd been bought and smoked the

cigarettes. De Courcy inaccurately described the waitress in Bolger's, informing the man that if he could see her he'd wish to lay down his life for her. 'In that case we'll take another glassful,' said the man and again approached the bar.

With his eyes closed, de Courcy continued his eulogy of the waitress, referring to her as an exquisite sea-bird. 'Frail blessed bird,' he murmured, but Ring told him to give over immediately or he'd frighten our benefactor off.

The man returned, laden with drink and further cigarettes. He handed us a packet each and made us again raise our glasses.

'We could get into terrible trouble, sir,' Ring said, 'if any of this leaked out.'

'How could it leak out?'

'As long as you realize we'd be in trouble, sir.'

'I was sacked for sodomy,' the man said.

Slowly, admiringly, Ring moved his head from side to side. It could happen to a bishop, he said in his slow voice.

'After that I went to England. I was in a school near Nottingham only I had a bad bit of luck there too.'

'That girl has started a storm in me,' de Courcy suddenly exclaimed, standing up and swaying.

The man laughed pleasantly. 'I have a small proposition,' he went on, 'which could earn you a pound, boys.'

Recalling the reference to sodomy, I hastily rose to my feet also. We would have to go now, I explained, otherwise we'd be late for Chapel. We'd see him some other time, Ring promised, we'd definitely be back.

De Courcy said nothing, intent on making an unsteady course across the bar. We followed him, and when the tweeded man called after us Ring assured him we'd listen to any proposition he had to make the next time we had a drink with him. De Courcy staggered in the yard, before covering its grey cement with sausage and fried bread.

'Hills of the North, rejoice,' we sang in Chapel. 'Valley and lowland, sing.' The boys around us glanced in our direction, attracted by the loudness of our voices and the stench of porter. The good-natured chaplain stuttered his way through a sermon about St Simon, and all during it I thought to myself that the tragedy at Kilneagh was over and done with. There was no Miss Halliwell daily to remind me of it, nor was there my mother every evening to say good-night to. According to Father Kilgarriff, my aunts had taken in another collection of dogs; the rhododendrons still flowered; Mr Derenzy had assured us that little had changed at the mill. One day I would be back there. It was not impossible that one day Kilneagh would be as it had been.

'A most dangerous person,' Dove-White said in the course of a Latin lesson. 'Incredible impertinence that he should be anywhere near this place.'

'He's a homosexual, is he, sir?' de Courcy politely suggested. 'That's what he said anyway.'

'Keep well away from him, de Courcy.'

'He offered us money, sir. He mentioned a proposition.'

'Where've we got to, Tuthill?'

'. . . *omnem Galliam ab injuria Ariovisti*, sir.'

Ring was playing patience. With a piece of broken mirror propped up on his desk, a boy known as Lout MacCarthy was squeezing his blackheads. A. McC. P. Jackson was reading an Arsène Lupin book. Thynne Minor was asleep.

'Continue on then,' Dove-White commanded Tuthill. '*Hac oratione habita ab Divitiaco.*'

'The thing is, sir,' de Courcy interrupted again, 'it's interesting your friend coming back like this. As you say, sir, you'd think he'd keep away.'

'He was no friend of mine, de Courcy. *Hac oratione –*'

'I think the boys should know what he got up to, sir. If he's a danger, sir, shouldn't the boys know what to beware of? Did he have a name, sir?'

'Of course he had a name, de Courcy. Don't be silly now. *Hac oratione*, Tuthill?'

'*When this speech –*'

'I think you should tell us, sir. I mean, if he's going round offering money –'

'Oh, for heaven's sake, de Courcy! The wretched man was sacked because he took boys out on a picnic. He gave them cider laced with gin.'

'Is that all, sir?'

'There are parents who scrimp and save, de Courcy, so that they can send their sons to this school. They hardly do so in order to place them at the disposal of the sexually perverted.' Dove-White's voice was tired. He closed Caesar's *Commentaries on the Gallic War* and pulled his burnt, chalky gown more cosily about him. He asked for silence and then, like Thynne Minor, he drifted into sleep.

That afternoon we crossed the hillside to Lamb Doyle's, hoping to find the sacked geography master there, and in this we were not disappointed. He approached us as we entered and at once bought us drink and cigarettes, which we accepted without demur. Now that we knew the extent of his crime we felt we could cope with whatever attentions he plied us with, although we resolved to keep a watchful eye on him when he was having our glasses refilled at the bar.

'It was Mad Mack who did for me,' he confided. 'It was Mad Mack reported the thing.'

'The picnic, sir?'

'Ah, they told you, did they?'

'Dove-White told us.'

'Sure, where was the harm in having a picnic with a few lads?'

'No harm at all, sir,' de Courcy agreed smoothly. Ring guffawed, striking his knee with his fist, as his habit was when amused.

'Tell me this, lads, does Mad Mack still occupy the same old bedroom?'

None of us was able to answer this question, since none of us knew which bedroom Mad Mack had slept in thirteen years ago, but it was soon established that his sleeping arrangements had in fact changed. The mathematics master now slept in a downstairs room in the masters' house, the room next to his study: he had been elsewhere before.

'I was afraid of that,' the man said. He remained lost for a moment in thought, his eyes screwed up against the smoke from his cigarette. Ring clattered his empty glass suggestively on the table, and our companion obediently crossed to the bar for more porter. When he had delivered it to us he spoke again of the mathematics master. He then astonished us by weeping. He turned his face away so that we should not see how it had contorted; his hands shook so much that for a moment he was unable to light his cigarette. 'Christ,' Ring muttered.

Eventually recovering himself, the man said:

'I have begged for threepenny pieces on O'Connell's Bridge. I have cleaned out the latrines of the gaol where I was in England. Mack brought all that on me. If Mack was humane I would still be your geography master and no harm done.'

Alarmed by this display of emotion, Ring said we should be getting back now. But de Courcy shook his head. He displayed concern for our companion by deploring the misplaced zeal of the mathematics master. 'The trouble is, sir,' he said, 'Mack's insane.'

The man placed a pound note on the table. It was ours, he said, if we would agree to lead him, in the middle of the night, to the window of Mad Mack's bedroom.

'We'd be delighted, sir,' de Courcy responded immediately. It was the least we could do, he pointed out, after all the drink and cigarettes we'd been bought.

'We could get into terrible trouble,' Ring began. 'Appalling trouble –'

'There'll be no trouble whatsoever, boy, if you keep your mouth shut. We might need the loan of a ladder, though.'

'There's a fire escape running up by those windows,' de Courcy said. 'But we'll get hold of a ladder if it's better.'

'The fire escape might do the job for us. I think I remember it now.'

'It's great to have met you, sir,' enthused de Courcy.

Shortly after that we left the public house, Ring and myself considerably apprehensive, de Courcy jubilant. The arrangement was that we were to meet behind the chapel at two o'clock on a Sunday morning a week later. 'We'll never stay awake,' Ring objected, and on the night in question he fell heavily asleep soon after lights-out. De Courcy and I, however, managed not to. We roused Ring when a distant church clock chimed half-past one.

The man arrived promptly at our rendezvous. He didn't speak, and in the continuing silence we led the way to the masters' house and pointed to the black fire escape that ended its descent beside Mad Mack's bedroom window. As always, the top half of the window was open, an element in Mad Mack's puritan zeal being his devotion to fresh air. The sacked geography master climbed to a height of six feet or so. He paused before pressing the lower half of his body against the opening, above the sleeping mathematics master. A faint sound disturbed the still night.

'My God,' whispered Ring, 'he's having a slash on him.'

Sunday-morning breakfast was a leisurely, if somewhat formal, occasion. Standing in our gowns in the darkly panelled dining hall, we waited in silence while the Scrotum and Mrs Scrotum led the small procession of masters to the high table, where the funereal Fukes awaited them with a silver-plated coffee-pot. '*Benedictus benedicat*,' intoned a prefect known as Bamboo Jones because of his upright stance, '*per Christum Dominum nostrum*.' Mad Mack sat down next to Mrs Scrotum, with Monsieur Bertain on the other side of him and the chaplain next to Dove-White. Hopeless Gibbon hurried in late, red-faced and whispering an apology. The science man lived out, as did the other masters who were now absent.

Mad Mack appeared not to have suffered from the attention paid to him while he slept. Certainly he had not woken up at the time: we knew that because we had remained where we stood until the geography master had adjusted his clothes and descended to the ground. Without addressing a word to us, he had marched off into the darkness.

While the butler now hovered behind him with the coffee-pot, Mad Mack's harsh voice rang out, deploring the fact that his shaving water had been tepid. And from boy to boy, from table to table, word went round the dining hall that he had been urinated upon during the night. Sniggering swelled into laughter. Heads turned towards the high table, eyes searching the gingery countenance of the mathematics master. Mrs Scrotum chattered across him to Hopeless Gibbon. Sleepily, Dove-White reached for the toast.

'Why is there this laughter?' The Scrotum was on his feet, the crimson orb of his face pushed out at us, his little knuckles resting on the table-cloth. He turned to Bamboo Jones, who was seated at the head of the table nearest to him, as by dining-hall tradition the duty prefect should be.

'Why are we being treated to laughter, Jones?'

'I don't know, sir.'

'Cease this unpleasantness at once,' commanded the Scrotum noisily, and then sat down.

Mad Mack would have thought it was raining, Ring said, poking at the lumps in his porridge. He would have woken up and shut the window, wiping a few drops off his moustache. The laughter had dribbled away, but eyes still glanced in the direction of the high table and again the word went round: that it was the sacked geography master, already known by repute because of what we had reported, who had done the deed.

Again the Scrotum rose. 'Why are you boys looking at Mr Mack? Why are they, Jones?'

'I'm afraid I don't know, sir.'

A boy called FitzPayne, at a table not far from where the Scrotum stood, was selected as a source of possible elucidation.

'FitzPayne, why is Mr Mack the object of your interest?'

'I don't know, sir.'

'What do you mean, you don't know?'

'I'm not looking at Mr Mack, sir.'

'Are you telling me lies by default, sir? Remember what we agreed between us about lies, FitzPayne. Less than half a minute ago you were staring at Mr Mack with an impertinent grin on your face. We are waiting to hear why that was so, FitzPayne.'

'I don't know, sir.'

'Step up to High Table, sir. Mr Dove-White, move your chair to one side so that FitzPayne may the better stare at Mr Mack.'

The maids, still handing round plates of porridge, had stopped in their tracks. Fukes, in the shadows of a recess behind the head-master, was investigating the condition of his teeth with a fore-finger. The matron's ladle was poised dramatically above the enormous white enamel porridge container. Her assistant, placing thick slices of bread on plates, paused also. 'Well now, FitzPayne,' the headmaster urged, and FitzPayne, a youth ravaged by acne, said he begged the headmaster's pardon.

'You will please tell us why your attention was drawn towards Mr Mack.'

The silence was so complete and so intense that it felt like a sudden presence – as if God, de Courcy afterwards suggested, had chosen to pass through the dining hall on some minor mission. Mad Mack registered bewilderment, the chaplain looked concerned. Mrs Scrotum, the growth of her grey hair more horizontal than usual on a Sunday morning due to her Saturday-night washing of it, was impatient to return to her conversation with Hopeless Gibbon.

'Did you once,' pursued the Scrotum, 'have a nursemaid, FitzPayne?'

'No, sir.'

'Had you once had a nursemaid, she might have informed you that it is distasteful to stare.'

'Yes, I know, sir.'

'It is gratifying that you know something.'

'Yes, sir.'

'We are still waiting to hear from you, FitzPayne. Mr Mack, can you throw any light on FitzPayne's conceit of staring at you?'

'I most certainly can not, Headmaster.'

'In that case it must be left to you, FitzPayne. We have heard the view of Mr Mack, we have heard the view of the duty prefect. If you and I have to stand here all day, FitzPayne, we shall do so. The inconvenience to staff and boys is of course to be regretted. Fukes, I would have another cup of coffee.'

The probing of the butler's cavities ceased, the forefinger wiped on the napkin he carried. Coffee was poured, the silence continued. Eventually FitzPayne broke it.

'It had to do with a story that's going round, sir.'

'What story is this, FitzPayne?'

'That something happened to Mr Mack in the night, sir.'

'Did something happen to you in the night, Mr Mack?'

The mathematics master, who smiled rarely, permitted himself that relaxation now. A row of even false teeth appeared beneath the ginger moustache and then was gone again.

'As a matter of fact, I dreamed I was teaching Shell B, Headmaster.'

Laughter, too long held in check, was gratefully released.

'Well, FitzPayne? Mr Mack states he adventured no further than the land of dreams. Are you implying it was in a dream that something untoward occurred?'

There was further laughter. The porridge plates nursed by the maids were eased on to the serving table. FitzPayne said:

'In the night, sir, a man passed water on Mr Mack.'

The Scrotum's eyes bulged, and even over the distance that separated us I believed I could see the flushed flesh whiten. The lower half of his face twitched; Dove-White told us afterwards that he moaned. FitzPayne spoke again.

'Through the window, sir, that Mr Mack keeps open.'

Mad Mack was standing up. Dove-White told us that the vein in the centre of his forehead had begun to throb, always a danger signal.

'Headmaster,' he began, and was ignored.

'You will come at once to my study, FitzPayne.'

'Headmaster –'

'I'd be obliged if you would kindly accompany us, Mr Mack. FitzPayne, you will apologize to my wife. You will apologize to Matron and to her lady assistant. You will apologize to the maids.'

'I'm sorry, sir.'

'Mr Dove-White, no one is to leave this room until we have returned. Breakfast will naturally not be taken today.' He turned to his wife and his voice lost the quiver it had developed when he lowered it to address her. 'My dear, I think it better that you accompany us also.'

He led the way. Mrs Scrotum, who had a way of holding her arms stiffly elongated, with her hands clasped in front of her, marched next in line. Then came Mad Mack, fury enlivening every aspect of him. FitzPayne was grinning through his acne.

Bamboo Jones crossed to the high table and spoke to Dove-White, who nodded. Bamboo Jones said we might sit down but must not converse. The head prefect, Wiltshire Major, bustled up to him and then bustled up to Dove-White. Whispering broke out among the masters, Wiltshire Major spoke to the matron and the undermatron, both of whom immediately rose and left the dining hall, taking the maids with them. Bamboo Jones stationed himself by the door, alert for the headmaster's return. From time to time he ordered us to be quiet and when eventually he heard the head-master's footfall he hurried to the serving table and struck it repeatedly with a soup-spoon, another dining-hall tradition.

Obediently, we stood up. Mrs Scrotum did not return, nor did Mad Mack. FitzPayne went straight to his place. The Scrotum said:

'We are going to pray. You will please kneel.'

Deliverance was asked for. 'O Lord, to cleanse us,' is a phrase that was quoted, and afterwards de Courcy remarked that though boys and masters might be cleansed of the distastefulness FitzPayne had exposed us to, the same might possibly not be true of the women who had left the dining hall, nor indeed of Mad Mack himself.

'To Thy honour and Thy glory again we dedicate our miserable lives.'

'Amen,' said Dove-White.

'Amen,' said we, and rose from our knees.

'We have heard a lie this morning.' The Scrotum paused, the scarlet flesh of his neck bulging above his clerical collar. 'A lie,' he repeated, 'which this unfortunate boy saw fit to perpetuate. Stand out, FitzPayne. Approach High Table, please.'

For the second time FitzPayne left his place and did as he was bidden.

'Turn around. Face your peers, FitzPayne.'

Obeying this instruction placed FitzPayne at an advantage. With his back to the Scrotum, he at once allowed his mouth to drop open, drawing back his lips in a squinting grimace. Heads were bent, laughter stifled. Bamboo Jones started forward, then changed his mind. Wiltshire Major glared threateningly at FitzPayne.

'This boy,' pronounced the Scrotum, 'has been misled by evil gossip. This boy has apologized to Mr Mack for the distasteful nature of the lie he saw fit to repeat, knowing it must needs be a lie. Mr Mack and I have accepted that this boy did not himself invent the lie, which indicates that its source is among you still. Whomsoever is responsible I would wish to converse with before an hour has passed.'

His gown flapped as he strode from the dais which raised the high table above the other tables. He clutched a mortar-board to his chest and looked neither to the right nor the left. Hopeless Gibbon brought up the rear of the procession that passed from the dining hall.

'Stay!' shouted Wiltshire Major. He closed the door and stood with his back to it. He told us to sit down.

'I want to see you, FitzPayne,' he said, 'immediately after this. As to what the headmaster has just requested, will whoever started the ridiculous tale about Mr Mack report to him *without delay*. I have to warn you that if there is no owning up the entire school will be punished.'

During this speech Fukes clattered the high-table breakfast dishes, gathering them on to a tray. Wiltshire Major, who liked making speeches, continued:

'If ever again there is anything like a repetition of such a stupid and pointless rumour it will be a most serious matter, I can assure you.'

It was difficult to know what to do. Wiltshire Major meant what he said, and already there were those who must have guessed where the story had begun. 'I'd say we're stumped,' Ring suggested. 'I'd say it's a cop all right.'

But de Courcy was more sanguine. 'We didn't do much when it comes down to it.'

'We took money from the man,' I reminded him, 'and we got up in the middle of the night.'

'We could say we saw a stranger prowling.'

We hurriedly discussed the matter with Dove-White, who advised confession. He approved of de Courcy's suggestion that, on the way to or from the lavatory, he had glanced from a window and seen a suspicious figure in the moonlight. Out of a sense of responsibility, he had woken Ring and myself and a decision had been reached: concerned about the school's valuables, we had decided to investigate.

'I see,' said the Scrotum.

'After which, sir, we hastily dressed. We followed the man to the masters' house, sir, thinking he might be going to break in.'

'I had one of MacCarthy's golf sticks, sir,' Ring put in. 'I picked it up when we passed through the locker-room. In the circumstances, I didn't think he'd mind, sir.'

The headmaster's study was large and gracious, as impressive as the drawing-room next door, which featured two water-colours by Turner. Both rooms, richly carpeted, were full of knick-knacks and occasional tables. I stood beside the chair over which one bent when receiving punishment. It was tapestry-covered, yellow and blue, the same chair that had been there in my father's day. 'You'll get to know it,' my father had said.

'The man climbed four steps up the fire escape, sir, and then he unbuttoned his trousers –'

'That'll do, de Courcy.' The Scrotum spoke snappishly, as he often did. His English voice had a nasal quality, sharply accented. His origins were low, Dove-White had told us, pointing out that though the headmaster's 'h's' were all carefully in place, words like 'house' and 'noun' acquired an extra dimension beneath his tongue and that, apparently, was not quite the thing.

'What I mean is, sir,' de Courcy went on, 'we were in a quandary because it wasn't clear immediately what was happening. There was this sound, sir, and the window being open at the top and the man being on a level with it –'

'Will you kindly cease, de Courcy?' Tetchy impatience snapped at us again. Some internal struggle took place because the Scrotum's small white knuckles, clenched to rap the surface of the desk, did not do so. His temper was as unreliable as Mad Mack's, but his position in the school forbade resource to casual physical attack. For him the only reward for anger was the calm formality involving the tapestry-covered chair, and as if in recognition of this fact his nasal voice now acquired the churchman's cadences so familiar to us in Chapel.

'Mr Mack reports that he shut his window during the night because of a shower of rain.'

'Yes, sir.'

'So what you are saying is invented.'

'We didn't like to go too close, sir. All we were concerned for was Mr Mack's safety.'

'I see.' The anger cooled a little more, the voice dropped further. 'I accept what you say concerning a trespasser on School property, and I would suggest to you that this man was unsober. I would suggest to you that he climbed up the fire escape when he wasn't in command of himself. Drink is the curse of this country.'

'We said afterwards he mightn't have been sober. Didn't I say that, Quinton?'

'We all said it.'

'I would suggest to you that in the poor light of the night you could have been mistaken in what you imagined occurred.'

'It's possible we were, sir,' Ring agreed. 'It was just that it looked like that. The sound we heard could have been anything. Maybe a bird.'

'A bird?'

'I think there's a bird makes a sound like that, sir. When it's flying by, sir.'

'It was a terrible thing, sir,' de Courcy said, 'for boys of our age to see a man drunk. He was definitely unsteady on the fire escape, sir.'

'There is still no excuse for irresponsibly repeating all this. Why did you not wake a prefect? Or come straight to me?'

85

Ring proceeded to offer an explanation, but de Courcy interrupted him.

'We were intending to, sir. Quinton was all for waking you up, sir, only Ring said you mightn't like it. We were discussing at breakfast about coming in here straight afterwards, only the unfortunate thing was that someone must have heard what we were saying.'

'Even though we were keeping our voices down, sir.'

'And you, Quinton? You haven't said much to me about this unhappy incident.'

'I'm very sorry about it, sir.'

'How do you imagine poor Mr Mack feels?'

'It was Mr Mack's safety, sir –'

'I know, I know, boy.' The knuckles again became impatient. Another struggle waged in the crimson face; again the Christian spirit prevailed. 'When I came to this school, Quinton, the chapel was not the centre of school life, as it has since become. The kind of unpleasantness you have had the misfortune to witness was not uncommon. Bullying, for instance, was rampant.'

'Yes, sir.'

'The bullies would take the new boys up the hillside and beat their legs with bramble sticks. A boy was branded once with the point of a white-hot poker.'

'We've heard of that, sir. We're grateful to you, sir, for all you've done.'

'I shall be asking Wiltshire Major to make an announcement before lunch in the presence of Matron and the maids, to the effect that the man in his confusion simply climbed up the fire-escape steps and immediately came down again. Drink is a great scourge. It is fortunate that we weren't burnt in our beds.'

'Burnt, sir?' Ring repeated in a startled voice. '*Burnt?*' he said again, but de Courcy swiftly intervened.

'It's that we were concerned about, sir. Ring was all for hitting at the man with MacCarthy's golf stick to see if he maybe had a box of matches on him.'

Ring essayed a slow smile as the value of this variation dawned on him. 'And maybe,' he chattily added, 'if he was intoxicated, sir, he could have imagined he'd started up a fire already. Maybe what he got up to, sir, was an effort to quench it.'

'That's a disgusting suggestion, Ring. We have agreed between us that nothing of that nature took place. And why are you laughing in that distasteful manner? Is there some joke I have missed? Do you share Ring's joke, Quinton?'

'No, sir.'

'You are the stupidest boy, Ring, I have ever encountered. You are dense to a degree I would not have believed humanly possible.'

'All I meant, sir –'

'What vocation have you, Ring?'

'Vocation, sir?'

'The future, boy, the future. How do you see yourself?'

'My father makes lemonade down in Dublin, sir.'

'I am aware that your father makes lemonade. I asked you about yourself.'

'I'll be doing the same, sir.'

'All I can say, Ring, is that I wouldn't care to drink it.'

'It's not bad stuff at all, sir.'

'Do not be impertinent to me, Ring. You shall be punished for that.' The crimson face was turned towards mine and the conversation more lightly continued. 'Quinton, what vocation have you? You are becoming a veterinary surgeon?'

'I think that's Dunraven, sir.'

'Ah yes, yes. A flour mill, is it? Near Fermoy?'

'Yes, sir.'

'Be careful how you choose your friends, Quinton. Do not bend as the wind takes you. De Courcy?'

'Sir?'

'What vocation have you, de Courcy?'

'The stage, sir. The theatre.'

The Scrotum briefly shook his head. 'Has it ever occurred to you, de Courcy, to enter schoolmastering?'

'I don't think I would be good at it, sir.'

'That may not be for you to say, sir. Duty is not silent, remember. Duty speaks. I am glad we have had this conversation.'

'So are we, sir.'

'Wiltshire Major will give out his notice, the contents of which we have agreed between the four of us in this room. You will apply to Mr Dove-White for a suitable punishment for leaving your dormitory in the night. You will apologize to Mr Mack and offer to make amends in any way he suggests. You will apologize to my wife. You will stand beside Wiltshire Major when he makes the explanation and when he has finished you will apologize to him for the inconvenience you have caused. You will apologize to Matron and her lady assistant, a very young girl who may well be upset by the distasteful nature of what was said. You will apologize to the maids, some of whom are young also, and you will apologize to the duty prefect. You, Quinton, will be the spokesman. You, Ring, will request further punishment from Mr Dove-White for being impertinent. This matter is now closed. I am glad we have disposed of it in a sensible manner.'

A small blue bulb on the wall above the Scrotum's door, controlled by a switch near his desk, was extinguished as we passed beneath it. When glowing, it indicated that serious matters were on hand in the study, and that no disturbance would be tolerated. Beatings called for the ignition of the bulb, as did confirmation classes, which the Scrotum liked to conduct at the deskside. We hurried through the great flagged hall that lay between the headmaster's house and the rest of the school, feeling lucky that the bulb had been extinguished after so brief an incarceration in the study. We had assumed our concocted story would be brushed aside and, Sunday notwithstanding, had anticipated severe chastisement.

'He said you were to punish us, sir,' Ring reported in Dove-White's room.

'What on earth for?'

'Witnessing the distasteful occurrence, sir. Drink's a scourge, sir.'

Tea was brewed from a kettle of water on a gas-ring. Dove-White said the treatment meted out to Mad Mack was probably the best thing that had happened since the school was founded in 1843, even though the act had been performed by a man he had sternly warned us against. While he was speaking, a boy came in and announced that Mr Mack wanted to see us. 'Oh holy Jesus,' said Ring, and we made our way without enthusiasm to the mathematics master's study.

'The headmaster has spoken to me of your revelations.' Furious already, Mad Mack shouted at us as soon as we appeared. 'Not a word of that is the truth, de Courcy.'

'The headmaster –'

'There was no man on that fire escape. Isn't that so, Quinton? Answer me, Quinton.'

'There was a man in a Donegal suit, sir.'

'That's a filthy lie, Quinton.'

'De Courcy looked out the window, sir, on his way back from the lavatory –'

'The three of you climbed on to that fire escape and committed an act of filthy indecency.'

'We'd never do that, sir,' de Courcy protested.

'We told the truth, Mr Mack,' Ring said, 'and we've received our punishment from Mr Dove-White for leaving our dormitory under shadow of darkness.'

'You'll end up in the Dublin sewers, Ring.'

'Actually, sir,' de Courcy corrected, 'Ring's going to make lemonade. The headmaster is taking an interest in Ring's future, sir.'

A scrawny hand darted through the air. Its fingers lashed twice at de Courcy's cheeks, a swift, expert action that immediately drew blood. Mad Mack looked away and when he spoke again there was a croaking in his voice.

'Who was it,' he asked, 'if it wasn't you?'

'A geography master who was sacked,' de Courcy said.

The truth hung there, unchallenged and at last accepted, as it never could have been in the Scrotum's study.

'That man was horrible,' Mad Mack said at last, his voice still croaking.

'He was in gaol for a while,' de Courcy said.

'I'm glad he was in gaol.'

With his back to us he told us to go away and in the course of that day, humiliated by what had occurred, he left the school. He went without saying good-bye to anyone, and his defection shocked us. For three weeks we were without a mathematics master, before the arrival of a brisk man with a bow-tie whom the Scrotum had found somewhere in Lincolnshire.

Terms went by. My correspondence with Father Kilgarriff continued; at school there were letters from Aunt Fitzeustace and Aunt Pansy, and one from my grandparents in India, which requested information about my mother. *We have suggested that you and she might like to live with us, here in Masulipatam*, the letter ended, *far away from what has happened*. But in my reply I did not refer to that, knowing that neither my mother nor I would ever wish to live in India. Josephine wrote regularly, my mother not again. In the dormitory after lights-out one night I found myself retailing the story of the tragedy.

Every Christmas and again at Easter I returned for three weeks to Cork; and for two months every summer. I read Dickens and George Eliot and Emily Brontë; I continued to shop for Josephine in Mrs Hayes's grocery, reflecting less poignantly now on how my sisters would have appreciated her and her son. I walked about the streets and docks, as I had always done.

'You have never written,' Miss Halliwell said. 'You promised to write.' She had emerged from the Munster Arcade as I passed it and we stood together on the crowded street, the first time we had met since the days of Mercier Street Model.

'I'm sorry, Miss Halliwell.'

'Years have passed and you have not written. Your mother, Willie –'

'My mother's all right.'

'You still live in Windsor Terrace, Willie? You haven't returned to the place near Fermoy?'

'We still live in Cork.'

'Don't go back there, Willie. Don't hurt yourself by going back.'

'I'm quite all right, Miss Halliwell.'

'Don't ever visit it. Have you visited it since that night, Willie?'

'No.'

'Stay here in Cork. I often think of you, you know.'

'Miss Halliwell –'

'Willie, I would like to give you tea. In Thompson's perhaps?'

'I have to get back home.'

I left her standing there, dressed in her familiar brown, the hair still curling from the mole on her chin. In my letters I had continued to apologize to Aunt Pansy and Aunt Fitzeustace for my mother's refusal to receive them. Two nights ago I had dreamed of the rhododendrons and the walk to the mill, and had woken up longing to be back at Kilneagh. 'Willie,' Miss Halliwell called after me, her voice shrill, strangely floating above the bustle of the street. But I did not turn my head.

On the day after that meeting I tidied the garden because I hoped to persuade my mother to sit outside. I bought a hoe and cleared the flowerbeds of weeds. I borrowed a lawnmower from the house next door, but the grass was too long and coarse for it. 'You need a hook,' the man who'd lent me the lawnmower said, and he came into the garden himself and cut the grass with a scythe. He knew about my mother. By now everyone did.

'Because it's sunny,' I said to her. 'The sun's good for you.' She smiled from her bed at me. It was early in the day, but I knew that already she had been drinking whiskey. 'Let's go for a walk,' she said, as if I hadn't mentioned the garden. 'Let's go and have lunch in the Victoria Hotel.'

She put on her red and black dress, with a hat that perfectly matched it. She wore a cameo brooch at her throat. She carried a parasol, and all the time she smiled.

'You're quite good-looking, Willie,' she said, taking my arm on the street.

We walked in the sunshine down St Patrick's Hill and over St Patrick's Bridge. I hadn't been in the Victoria Hotel since the day we'd had tea there together, but nothing had changed. My mother ordered drinks for us, and after that we had lunch. She touched her sole with a fork, eating very little. She ordered hock and burgundy.

'I love this dining-room,' she said.

Increasingly I found it difficult to know what to say to her. On this occasion I repeated a version of some incident or other at school. I spoke of Ring and de Courcy, but she didn't appear to know who they were.

'That school was what your father wanted,' she said.

'I know.' And to prevent her continuing about my father I said: 'I met Miss Halliwell the other day.'

'Who's that, dear?'

'Miss Halliwell from the Model School.'

'You will not have to be a teacher, Willie.'

'No, I wasn't thinking that.'

I ate. My mother played again with her fish. The silence went on. Then she said:

'I often think about Sergeant Rudkin. Well, I suppose you do too.'

I shook my head. By now the image of the man, lighting his

cigarette at the corner of a street, had faded away almost to nothing.

'He comes into my thoughts,' my mother said.

She reached for her glass and drank the white wine that remained in it. A waiter poured her some burgundy. I said:

'I quite liked doing the garden.'

'O'Neill did the garden surely? And Tim Paddy. Poor little Tim Paddy.'

'No, no. The garden here I mean. I've cleared it all up.'

'That's lovely, my dear.'

'Will we have tea in the garden? Josephine has found the deck-chairs.'

'Don't you think it odd, Willie, that that man perpetually comes into my thoughts? I try to forgive him, Willie. I try to say it was an act of war.'

'It's best to forget.'

'I try to say he is an ignorant vegetable merchant. I try to say he belongs in the back streets of Liverpool.' She paused for a moment, sighing a little but smiling also. 'Your father ordered those deck-chairs from Dublin.'

'We could sit and read. There's shade from the bay tree if the sun's too strong.'

'That would be lovely, darling.'

But when we returned home she went upstairs and took her dress off and got into bed. It was Josephine and I who occupied the deck-chairs.

'D'you think she'll ever be herself again, Josephine?'

'Ah, of course she will.'

'It's taking years.'

'Poor soul, Willie.'

'I know.'

Every day Josephine carried the empty bottles from the bedside table, neither she nor my mother referring to this chore any more than they referred to the weekly arrival of the wine-merchant's delivery man.

'Don't you ever get lonesome, Josephine?'

'No, of course I don't.'

She had a friend whom she had met one evening years ago at Women's Confraternity, who came now and again to the kitchen. There was also the woman next door, the wife of the man who'd helped me with the grass, and Mrs Hayes of the shop. Josephine conversed with these women and presumably discussed with them my mother's state. 'And how's your mother, Willie?' Mrs Hayes used always to enquire while she made up the grocery order, and I imagined Josephine's priest enquiring in the same way. Prayers might even have been said for my mother, a plea made for some quality to return to her which would rescue from their continuing decay her beauty and her elegance.

'Don't you ever go back to see your parents, Josephine?'

'Oh, it's a long way to Fermoy.'

Her fingers smoothed the frill of her apron, a curl of her fair hair crept from beneath her cap. We didn't mention Johnny Lacy or the girl from Sweeney's public house whom he'd married. We didn't mention what might have been or what would be. After I'd left school I presumed I would live with my aunts and Father Kilgarriff in the orchard wing, but my mother would never be able to do that. My mother was not going to recover, and somehow I guessed that Josephine would never leave her now.

We sat for a while longer in the sunshine, and when we returned to the house we found that the afternoon post had come. There was a letter with the blue head of the English King on it, which I brought up to my mother, wondering if she would open it.

'They wish to come here,' she said the next morning. 'Your aunt and your cousin Marianne.'

'To visit us?'

'Now, why ever do they wish to come to Godforsaken Ireland? Write to my sister, Willie, and say we are not ready for visitors yet.'

But I wrote instead that the visit which had been proposed might do my mother good. Well, you know, of course, about that letter.

6

Two rooms, never before used, were prepared for your arrival. A man came to freshen them up with paint and to replace some wallpaper. Both chimneys were swept in case the August weather turned chilly, and in the kitchen I helped Josephine to air the mattresses by placing them near the range.

'So you are Willie!' your mother cried, stepping down the gangway from the steamer. 'Oh, Willie, it's so very nice for us to meet you!'

Her cream-coloured blouse was buttoned all the way up to where her chins began, each button a tiny pearl. '*Such* a treat for us to visit you in Ireland!' she exclaimed in that same excited manner, and you reddened when she went on about Woodcombe Rectory and the tastes and aspirations of your father, and how she had been urged to visit my mother by my grandparents in India, who were, of course, your grandparents also. 'Oh, most awfully anxious they are,' your mother said. 'Poor dears.' You wore a straw hat with a pink rose in its band. Your dress was blue, the rose was artificial. Tiny you seemed, dwarfed by your mother's plumpness.

That summer, that last week of July and all of August, three days of September: I have loved that summer all my life. Your dark brown eyes, darker than my mother's, your oval face, your smile that brought a dimple to one cheek, your long brown hair, soft as a mist it seemed. I stole glances at you while we stood near Mrs Hayes's shop and looked down at the city, at spires and roofs and water, at the distant green hills that had always reminded me of Kilneagh. 'The bells of Shandon,' I explained when those bells rang out. I showed you the Opera House and Mercier Street Model School, the Turkish delight shop and the woollen goods factory where Elmer Dunne was now a clerk's assistant. We strolled by the river and the railway track, we watched the cargo boats from St

Patrick's Bridge. Further and further from the city we walked, and all the time I wanted to take your hand. Across the estuary, among the leafy trees, the windows of Montenotte stared inquisitively down at us. 'How nice your Ireland is!' you said.

At school you were my secret when that summer was over, during the tedium of lessons and sermons, in private moments after lights-out. When I spoke of you to Ring and de Courcy I simply said you were a cousin I had forgotten I possessed, and as the days of that autumn shortened into an icy November I continued to keep you jealously to myself. You did not belong in conversations that touched upon Big Lily at her kitchen sink or the woman Blood Major had met in Bachelor's Walk, and school itself was different because of you. 'Marianne,' I whispered, 'dear little Marianne.' I told no one else your name.

'There's a fellow from Tipperary in his grave after that stuff,' Ring would loudly state in the public houses we frequented: an attempt to improve the sales of his father's lemonade by slandering all other brands. But often I hardly heard him. Greedily I saw you in the grey and blue uniform of your boarding-school. You had described your dormitory to me, all the beds with blue covers on them, and Agnes Brontenby, the head girl, striding through it.

'God, there's a real beauty here,' de Courcy whispered in Byrne's Provisions and Bar, screwing his neck around the partition that separated the bar from the grocery. Obediently Ring and I stood up to examine the girl over the frosted glass, but her back was turned to us. A threadbare red coat hung from narrow shoulders; hair was obscured by a tattered headshawl. She was asking Mr Byrne for a Chivers' jelly and a quarter-pound of rashers.

It would be safer to put acid down your throat, Ring warned the publican, than some of the proprietary brands of lemonade currently on the market. And when Mr Byrne had finished serving us de Courcy developed his familiar fantasy about the girl in the red coat, his voice raving in the theatre of his invention. But I kept thinking of our sitting together in the August sunshine, occupying the deck-chairs I had resurrected in order to entice my mother to the garden. On our walks you had told me about the rectory and the town of Woodcombe, and the undulating Dorset countryside. The grey and blue school uniform was hideous, you said, and Agnes Brontenby tiresome.

95

'Listen,' Ring said when he and I were alone after Chapel one evening. 'I saw the mott in the red coat again.'

In his slow way he outlined a joke he had already instigated. All three of us were to walk into Byrne's Provisions and Bar and a moment later the girl in the red coat would be there also. 'I told her de Courcy was desperate for her and she was interested all right. She saw him in the John Jameson mirror when he looked round the casement at her.'

Had you been too polite to say you were bored as we trailed about on our walks? I wondered that. 'We might go to Kilneagh,' I had suggested. 'It would be nice to show you Kilneagh.' You smiled and said you'd like that, but wouldn't it be sad for me? Nothing could be sad with you, I thought, but did not say it.

'The hard man,' Ring greeted Mr Byrne on the day we were to meet the girl. 'Are you stocking Ring's yet, Mr Byrne? Did you ever note the legal statement they have on the label? "No Better Drink", Mr Byrne.'

Mr Byrne, a dour man, once a champion wrestler, did not reply. His premises were decorated with photographs of greyhounds, which matched his cheerless presence. Lugubriously surveying the racing information of a morning newspaper, he reached for his glass of porter before raising a single bloodshot eye and surveying us. A second eye, injured in the wrestling ring fifteen years ago, was permanently cloaked behind a drooping lid.

'We'll take three bottles of stout, Mr Byrne,' Ring ordered, unperturbed by the lack of welcome. 'I hear there's a woman in Enniscorthy with her kidneys gone after a glass of Mansor's.'

Heifers had crowded the single street of Lough because it was a Monday. Pigs arrived in carts; dung and muck were everywhere. I wished it hadn't been like that, that the great white gates of Kilneagh's avenue hadn't been rusty, or the roof of the burnt-out gate-lodge all tumbled in. The cool avenue of beeches had not changed, but the windowless house rose blackly from weeds and undergrowth, corrugated iron nailed over the pillared doorway. 'This is Marianne,' I said in the orchard wing, and at least Aunt Pansy and Aunt Fitzeustace were exactly as they had been, even if Father Kilgarriff was thinner than I remembered him. The dogs did not seem different from the dogs of the past.

I pointed out Haunt Hill on the way to the mill and you described the grandeur of Woodcombe Park. We imagined Anna Quinton in its palatial rooms, lingering in its yew walks by the mock-Roman summer-house. You'd seen the mulberry orchard at Woodcombe Park, the one ours had been planted in memory of.

'The trouble is,' Ring said, 'they don't wash the empties. The empties come back and they fill them up again.'

Withdrawing a cork, Mr Byrne made a slight sound. His large, shaven head moved in a kind of circle as the stout was poured. Disdain entered his one good eye, reflecting a poor opinion of his three customers.

'God, will you look who's here?' Ring suddenly shouted, thumping the counter with the palm of his hand.

Quick to assess the situation, de Courcy stared blankly at the girl in the red coat. 'Is she your sister?' he asked Ring, dropping his voice to a whisper and appearing to be considerably discomfited.

The girl's face had a woebegone look that was not much lightened by a display of darkened teeth when she smiled. She wore a white cloche hat instead of her headscarf.

'It's Mary Fahy,' Ring said. 'The girl you're mad for, de Courcy. Wouldn't she knock spots off Noreen of Mullingar?'

The girl blushed, bending her head away from us, hiding beneath her hat. De Courcy looked away also. 'There's an error here,' he said.

'Mary came in that day for rashers and a jelly. Your man said he'd lay down his life for you, Mary.'

'Ah, no, no. It was a different girl that came in for the jelly. A big girl she was. Big heavy legs on her.'

'It was me all right,' Mary Fahy said. 'I seen you in the whiskey mirror when you peeped round the casement at me.'

'Oh, mistaken identity,' muttered de Courcy, still addressing Ring, not looking at any of us. 'When she walked in that door I thought she was your sister. Haven't you a sister that's similar to this one, Ring, with the bones sticking out of her?'

The girl went, scuttling out of the public house like a scrawny, frightened sparrow.

'Cripes, I don't know where you scraped that from,' de Courcy said, his manner changing dramatically. 'A right doxy you picked up there.'

I left also, the first time I had ever walked away from my friends. I felt annoyed with both of them and wanted to let my thoughts return to you. I had not shivered as we stood on the lawn at Kilneagh or as we passed through the vegetable garden that had become a wilderness. It seemed like a dream when Johnny Lacy and the other men came out to the mill-yard and when Mr Derenzy shook hands with you.

'What's eating you?' Ring demanded when he and de Courcy arrived back from Byrne's. 'Did you have a fancy for the mott yourself?'

I shook my head and then made some excuse, not wanting to admit that my feeling for you had caused me to consider the episode with the girl cruel. While we waited at Fermoy railway station and on the train back to Cork I had longed to say I'd fallen in love with you. The tips of my fingers had brushed your arm as we climbed up St Patrick's Hill in the dark, and for a moment I had had to close my eyes. I wanted to put my arms around you, as Tim Paddy had put his around the girl who had afterwards married Johnny Lacy. But still I had not the courage even to take your hand.

At school I wished there was someone I could talk to, who would understand my feelings and my diffidence. I thought of bringing up the subject of love when the chaplain next invited me to have coffee and biscuits with him, but his stutter always made it difficult to get a word in. Hopeless Gibbon did not inspire such confidences, Dove-White would not have stayed awake. Surprisingly it was the head-master's butler who became my confessor.

I had been summoned one morning to the study, but had discovered the blue light burning above the door. In his funereal attire Fukes was polishing the various brass knobs and handles in the stone-flagged hall, where I now loitered. He jerked his head towards the study and told me that one of the barbers who regularly came up from Dublin for a day's professional services throughout the school was cutting the headmaster's hair. Fukes had an unnaturally hoarse voice, a sound that travelled laboriously from his chest and was often difficult to understand. Calling upon this phlegmy rattle, he remarked to me now:

'I knew your father in the old days.'

Although his considerable length of service had established him as a school institution, it had never occurred to me that he must have been at the school when my father was a boy. When he made his revelation I expressed considerable surprise, of which Fukes took no notice. His haggard face was just a little below the level of my own, for he was not a tall man. It displayed no emotion as he said:

'I was sorry to hear about what happened.'

'Thank you, Fukes.'

'Of course a number of old boys were killed in the war. But this was different.'

'Yes.'

'A terrible thing.'

'Yes.'

That was the first of many conversations. On subsequent occasions Fukes revealed his memories of my father as a prefect, for he had mainly come across him when in their different capacities both of them were on duty in Dining Hall. These later conversations took place in Fukes's pantry, where he performed a variety of tasks while occupying a sagging armchair drawn close to a radiator. I would sit on the edge of a stained marble dressing-table which, like the armchair, some previous headmaster had abandoned.

'And yourself?' he asked one afternoon. 'Will you be taking up where your father left off down in Fermoy?'

I was reminded of the Scrotum enquiring about my vocation on the occasion when I had been confused with Dunraven. Fukes would have made a better headmaster. He did not address himself to many boys, but he had acquired information about everyone who passed through the school. He explained that he never ceased to eavesdrop while he served dinner in the masters' common room and in the private dining-room of the headmaster and his wife; and during Chapel services he read whatever letters and documents there were on the Scrotum's desk. He possessed a remarkable memory: the boys of the past remained as vividly with him as the faces of those he daily observed from behind the dining hall's high table. Loving the school as nobody else did, he never left it and was inordinately proud both of his servant status and his loyalty.

'Yes,' I said in answer to his question. 'That's what I hope to do.'
In the evenings you would wait for me at the mill and in the different seasons we would walk together back to the house, up through the birch wood and down the sloping pasture. Fukes was polishing the

glass globe of a lamp, so intent on his work that I didn't have to avoid his eye when I said:

'I have an English cousin I've fallen in love with.'

His head, spiky with short grey hairs, slightly nodded. The polishing of the glass continued.

'I don't know what to do,' I said, 'about all that.'

Fukes smiled, and no longer looked like a funeral mute. He mentioned other boys who had sat in his pantry with him, unburdening themselves of this and that. He told me not to be dismal.

'Write that girl a letter,' he suggested. 'Enquire how she's keeping for herself.'

'D'you think so, Fukes?'

'Why wouldn't you write her a letter? What harm would it do?'

No harm at all, I thought as I lay awake that night, remembering your blue dress and your straw hat with a rose on it. *Dear Marianne*, I composed, *I hope you had a safe journey back to England. Nothing has changed much here. Ring has developed a business sense where the selling of lemonade is concerned.* I wondered if it would interest you to learn about the public thrashing of Lout MacCarthy or the theft of the communion wine. *Is Agnes Brontenby still tiresome?* I planned to ask, but when the next day came I did not write the letter.

'Oh now, that's foolish.' Fukes shook his spiky head in disappointment. No girl could be put out by a simple letter, he said.

'Yes, I know.'

Patiently he listened while I told him how we had walked about Cork and of our visit to Kilneagh. I described you in greater detail than I had to Ring and de Courcy, I explained that you lived near the house my great-grandmother had come from. I mentioned the rose and your straw hat. I told him your name.

Fukes punctuated each statement I made with a nod, devouring everything. It sometimes seemed as if he derived what nourishment he needed from such confidences, and from his eavesdroppings. Gossip hung like dust in his pantry.

'Your father would be delighted,' he said at length, and I thought that somehow that might be so.

A Christmas card came from your mother. There was a stagecoach and snow on it, with sprigs of holly around the edge. I thought of you being in the room when your mother wrote her greeting in it and wondered if for a moment you'd thought of me. I lay down on the bed you'd slept in, pressing my face into the pillow even though the pillowslip had ages ago been washed and ironed.

For my last two terms at school you continued to possess me. Fukes asked me again if I'd written to you and I lied and said I had, ashamed of my timidity. 'Good man yourself,' he said approvingly and added that one day he'd open the *Irish Times* and read of our engagement.

'I am always here,' promised the Scrotum, a slippery smile emerging from the red bag of his face. 'I always like to see an old boy.' I had never, during all my time at the school, been addressed by his blue-stockinged wife, but she spoke to me now, vaguely wishing me well. 'In life,' she added, and turned to the next boy in the line which had formed to shake hands and say good-bye. The hand of the good-hearted chaplain was shaken also, and Hopeless Gibbon's and old Dove-White's.

'I'm in love with my cousin,' I said, at last confessing to Ring and de Courcy the truth that had come to matter more than anything else to me. They knew, they said.

'Yes, I realize you have to return there,' my mother said the night before I set out to begin my career at the mill. 'Of course I understand that, Willie.'

A long time had passed since the sunny day of our lunch in the Victoria Hotel, and we had never done anything like that since. We had not once sat in the garden as I had planned. We had never gone for a walk together, as you and I so often had.

'I'll be back here at the weekends,' I said. 'I'll come back on the train every Friday.'

'You are good to me, Willie.'

Another Paddy bottle stood uncorked on her bedside table, her glass was half full. Her white nightdress was unbuttoned, the smell of whiskey was pungent in the room.

'What was that man's name? Rudkin, was it?'

She made a noise, a laugh perhaps, or a whimper. Her eyes did not appear to focus and when she spoke she did not directly address me. Nobody had trusted Doyle, she said.

'Mr Lanigan says no provision has been made for the rebuilding of the house. Until I am twenty-one I cannot authorize it.'

'The house, Willie?'

'Kilneagh. I want to rebuild it.'

'Ah, dear Kilneagh . . .' She reached for her glass and drank a little. 'Tins of peaches on the shelves, and newspaper in sheaves for wrapping. Cabbages and cauliflowers, probably even flowers – sweet-peas and bunches of asters. Children come into his shop and he may even give them toffee-apples for nothing.'

I could not help myself. My cheeks and forehead burned with the crossness I felt. I raised my voice.

'Do you have to drink like this? For God's sake, why can you not forget? Why can't you even try?'

The moment after I had spoken it was hard to believe I had addressed her so, and yet I was glad I had. But she, as if I had spoken mildly, replied:

'I sometimes have a toothache, Willie. I do really dislike the taste of this horrid whiskey, dear.'

I left her there, her voice still feebly rambling. I thought I maybe hated her. Why could I not tell her about my love for you? Why could I tell a butler and not her? Why had she never been a help to me? 'Marianne?' she would have said. 'Now, who is Marianne?'

The following morning I caught the train to Fermoy. A room had been prepared for me in the orchard wing and as the first few days went by I gradually became used to the strangeness and familiarity of Kilneagh. At the same slow pace I began to learn a miller's trade, every detail meticulously explained by Mr Derenzy. I found the work agreeable enough, but no day ever passed during which I did not long that you might be here with me, and one evening I confided my passion to Father Kilgarriff. It was then, as if he had waited for this suitable moment, that he told me about his unfrocking.

He had not loved the convent girl who had been sent to Chicago: it was she who had loved him. Unaware of that, he'd made a friend of her since she, more than anyone else in his Co. Limerick parish, shared his pacifist opinions. God's greatest gift, he preached, was the life He entrusted to us: neither war nor revolution could be just since both permitted violence and casual death. The girl's father, who vehemently detested the imperialism that had ruled in our island for so long, was a man of some note in the locality and retorted harshly to the discovery of his daughter's love of a priest whom he regarded as heretical. Charges were trumped up, the girl dispatched, the priest brought low. 'Ah well, it's over now,' was Father Kilgarriff's single wry comment.

But I wondered if it was. I wondered if the girl was still infatuated in Chicago and I wondered if I myself would end up lonely and infatuated also. I climbed to the top of Haunt Hill, from where there was a view for many miles around, the curling river, the cottages of Lough spread out below, in the greater distance the town of Fermoy. Father Kilgarriff's peace reigned at last in Ireland; I was back at Kilneagh; *Wm Quinton* it said on the sacks and the lorries, my name and my father's and my grandfather's. Yet none of it was any good unless I could share it with you.

'I'd like to see Kilneagh again,' Josephine had said, and came one Friday so that we might travel back together on the evening train. We walked together in the garden and the ruins, and in the kitchen of the orchard wing she was shy. She sat on the edge of a chair sipping at a cup of tea while Aunt Fitzeustace worriedly questioned her about my mother, and Aunt Pansy offered currant scones around. Father Kilgarriff said it was great to see her again. That day, for the first time, I noticed a tired look about him, as well as the thinness that hadn't been there in the past. Mr Derenzy had told me he suffered sometimes from the bullet wounds in his chest.

Afterwards, making our way to the mill, Josephine said:

'It's all right here now, Willie.'

'Yes, I know.'

'Thanks be to God.'

She blessed herself. One hand slipped into a pocket of her coat and I knew she was fingering the beads of her rosary. 'God's good, Willie,' she said.

In the mill-yard Johnny Lacy greeted her, smiling, saying she was looking tip-top. I went to the office for a moment and after that we returned to the orchard wing and were driven back to Lough in my aunts' trap. Josephine didn't say much and I could tell that her meeting with Johnny Lacy had been as ordinary as she had anticipated. We sat for a while in the kitchen of Sweeney's public house and Mrs Sweeney gave us tea. There was a warm smell of bacon fat and chicken meal, and before we left to catch the train in Fermoy Johnny Lacy's wife brought in her children for Josephine to see.

'It's great,' Mrs Sweeney said. 'It's great you're back with us, Willie.'

It was nice that Josephine could be there like that, in the kitchen with those children and their mother, and that she could smile and laugh with them. I felt she had come back in order to forgive Johnny Lacy, or at least to reassure him that she was content. On the train I told her how I felt about you. She listened and then she said:

'Don't lose it, Willie.'

'Lose it?'

'The love you have. It's like a gift, loving someone.'

'But I don't know if Marianne even likes me. It's no good if she doesn't.'

'Oh, of course she does. Write to her, Willie. Please now.'

She spoke urgently and for a moment placed her hand on my arm. For all her contentment in the presence of Johnny Lacy and her smiles for his wife and children, there had been some sadness that had not reached the surface, a private, lonely sadness that made me think again of the girl banished to Chicago.

'Promise me, Willie.'

And so I promised. I would write that very night; I would write simply and plainly, telling you I loved you. If you did not care for me I would understand, and bear as best I could the disappointment.

'But she *is* fond of you, Willie. I could have told you that ages ago.'

We left the subject then, and Josephine spoke of my mother. Her voice was quiet and concerned, so sympathetic that I felt ashamed of my resentment: it was my mother who had been the victim among the three survivors of Kilneagh, and if whiskey helped to blunt the hurt it would seem to have a purpose. My mother had made an effort that Josephine had appreciated and I had not: it couldn't have been easy to put on her red and black dress and walk with me down to the city, a smile clenched into place.

We entered the house and before the lamps were lit I had resolved that I would tell her about you, and how I had at last plucked up the courage to write to you. I would not mind when she could not remember who you were; I would tell her again in the morning before she'd had too much to drink. I called to her on the stairs, but in the moment before I entered her bedroom I knew that everything was different. I knew that my mother was dead.

MARIANNE

1

In Dorset in 1983, in Woodcombe Rectory, a bright young clergy-man goes about his duties. For him the times are alien, as they are for the family at Woodcombe Park, obliged to lay down car parks and pick up litter. But busying himself with a roneoed letter, the clergyman comes to terms with the present, as the family does. He does not even know about the telegram that arrived, two generations ago, in his pretty rectory on a Saturday afternoon, or how it lay on the hall-stand all afternoon, only a maid being at home until nearly five o'clock. *Mrs Quinton died*. When the shock of the message was arrested a second telegram had to be sent, from Dorset to the town of Masulipatam in India: *Evie has sadly died*. Mourning clothes were aired, remorse and guilt lay heavily on the rectory's mood.

In Co. Cork in 1983 all that is vividly remembered.

2

We both wore black, a fact that had been noted by our fellow-travellers. The consideration for our mourning implied that it rendered us delicate: people had stood aside from our path, a woman had crossed herself, men touched their caps or hats. 'The Irish are like that,' my mother had explained.

At the harbour she embraced you. She dabbed at her eyes with a black-trimmed handkerchief. 'Poor boy,' she whispered. 'Poor boy, poor boy.'

'I'm sorry,' I said. 'I'm very sorry, Willie.'

You did not reply.

A car drove us to the house and you said we must be hungry, that there was ham and salad. You led us to the dining-room where there was the same closed-in smell I remembered, not exactly fusty but suggesting a lack of use. A fire blazed in the small grate; silence hung awkwardly. The last thing in the world I wanted to do was to eat and to listen to my mother talking.

'All that terrible drinking. Well, of course, Willie, we did what we could. I mean, I said it, over and over again, Willie. When we were here last summer I pleaded with her every day.'

I asked if my room was the one it had been before. You answered brusquely, not looking at me. My mother had begun to talk again.

I left the dining-room and went upstairs. The house had remained fondly in my memory during the time that had passed, the stained glass in the hall door and the landing windows, the clutter of furniture that had escaped the fire at the other house. My bedroom was narrow, with dark walls and a single paraffin lamp: nothing had altered in it. I poured water into a flowered basin and washed myself, delaying over the task.

The funeral, you were saying when I returned to the dining-room, was to be at half-past eleven the next morning; your mother would be buried in Lough. Josephine came in, with teacups and a teapot on a tray. She arranged them on the white tablecloth and then left the room again, softly closing the door.

'It's only a pity,' my mother said, 'that they cannot come from India. They'd want to, of course. You understand, Willie? Your grandparents would wish to.'

You said you understood. My mother ate the ham and the salad, seeming to be hungry. You cut slices of fruit cake, slowly sinking the knife into the mass of raisins and sultanas, slowly withdrawing it. You poured tea and offered the cake. You didn't look at me once.

'I'll rest for an hour or two,' my mother announced when she had drunk two cups of tea. 'Why don't you two go for one of your walks? The fresh air'll do you good.'

But you quickly replied that you imagined I'd want to lie down also. You were upset, I told myself, you couldn't help sounding brusque.

'I blame myself,' my mother said. 'In a way I blame myself for not being firm about the drinking. Yet what could anyone do? My own dear sister, and what could anyone do?'

She dabbed at her eyes with her black-trimmed handkerchief and then she went away. 'I don't think I'll lie down,' I said.

Without speaking, we walked down the hill and still in silence we crossed the bridge and made our way into the city.

'My mother killed herself,' you said at last. 'She cut her wrists with a razor blade.'

You didn't pause in your walk. You led me by shop windows full of clothes and china, past Woolworth's and a chemist's shop. Wind swirled the litter about on the pavement, seagulls screamed above our heads. A storm was getting up, you muttered in that same empty voice.

'I didn't know that about your mother, Willie.'

Two women with filthy children begged and clung on to me, saying they'd offer up Hail Marys for me, pulling at my sleeve. 'Get off to hell,' you shouted at them, hitting away their grasping hands. And later you said:

'It's not permitted for a suicide to receive a normal burial. I had to beg for that.'

We passed by the school you had gone to. *Miss A. M. Halliwell, Principal*, it said on a black plaque beside a closed blue door. '*Fight the good fight with all thy might.*' You had described Miss Halliwell to me. You had hoped we might meet her on the street.

'We should not have left my mother alone that day. We should have known.'

'I'm very sorry, Willie.'

'We could have a drink in the Victoria Hotel. My mother's only rendezvous.'

You spoke bitterly, and it seemed callous to visit a hotel which she had chosen to visit also. You were different in every way from the person you had been. Even the way you moved and walked seemed different.

'Well, a glass of lemonade,' I requested in a corner of the hotel lounge. My head had begun to ache. I wished I'd agreed when you'd suggested I might want to lie down. I watched you making your way across the empty lounge, my lemonade in a tall glass, your own amber-coloured drink in a smaller one. You sat down and there was a silence that felt as if you wished to punish me. I didn't know what to say, but anything was better than the silence.

'I'm going to be in Switzerland for the next few months.'

'Switzerland?'

'An English professor and his wife take in a few girls every year. In Montreux.'

'Oh.'

'I don't know what it'll be like.'

'No.'

'Unfortunately, the girl I told you about, the head girl at school, is going also.'

You didn't reply.

'Agnes Brontenby,' I added miserably.

You gazed into your drink, still not replying.

'I know it's awful for you, Willie.'

You turned your head away. I felt a blush of shame creeping into my cheeks. Were you thinking that I was a mingy little creature, ugly in my black clothes, silly to go on so about Switzerland? Had it sounded frivolous even to mention a professor and his wife at a time like this? It was selfish to want to share with you the mood we'd shared before, selfish when your mother was lying dead, when you'd had to persuade some clergyman to give her a decent burial. Miserably I lifted the glass of lemonade. It tasted sweet and horrible. I wondered if it had been manufactured by the father of the friend you'd told me about, and felt immediately that I should not have wondered so, since that was frivolous also. You despised me for being English. Over and over again the thought hammered at me, refusing to go away. Englishmen had burnt down your house and destroyed your family, and your mother's self-inflicted death was part of the same thing.

'Oh, don't drink it,' you muttered impatiently. 'Don't have it if you don't like it.'

'I wish I could be a help to you, Willie.'

'She was tedious and embarrassing. She was unhappy: I should be glad she's dead.'

It rained. A pebble rattled on the polished wood of the coffin. I watched while you remained with your head bowed, your chin pressed hard upon your chest. Once or twice you raised a hand to your face. I knew you wept; and anguish, like pain, possessed me too. I could not offer the comfort that passionately I longed to, I could not take your hand or honestly shed tears, except on your behalf. We turned, all of us, and walked from the grave, umbrellas held against the rain.

I shall for ever remember this day, I said to myself in the porch of the church, where pale distemper flaked from the walls and rust-marked notices were attached to the baize stretched over a board. The clergyman who had permitted your mother's burial wiped raindrops from his spectacles. You held yourself apart, rain dripping from your black coat and your fair hair. There was stoicism in your Aunt Fitzeustace's face, tears on your Aunt Pansy's. 'Poor boy,' my mother whispered, 'do please remember there'll always be a welcome for you in Dorset.'

You were not present at the lunch provided by your aunts in the undamaged part of the house, and no one remarked upon your absence. Mr Derenzy and Father Kilgarriff were there; my mother kept the conversation going. I guessed you were somewhere in the garden or walking in the fields, not caring about the rain.

'She never did recover,' your Aunt Fitzeustace said. 'Poor beautiful Evie.'

My mother repeated what she'd said to you: that our grandparents would have attended the funeral had the distance not been so great. 'I blame myself,' she repeated also, 'for not being firmer about the drinking.'

Firmness might have had little effect, Father Kilgarriff softly pointed out; there was often nothing that could be done, no consolation for so grievous a loss. They spoke of you. At least you had the mill to occupy your thoughts, Mr Derenzy said. At least, your Aunt Fitzeustace said, you were no longer a child.

Still seated around the lunch table, we were given cups of tea and when eventually you appeared you drank some. Two dogs jumped up on you, others barked ferociously, as if alarmed because you were so drenched. You took no notice, and still you hardly spoke.

'If there's a shortage, Willie,' my mother said on the journey back to Cork, 'or if money's tied up –'

'There's ample money, thank you.'

'We're there at the rectory, Willie. We're always there, dear.'

I wished she would not go on so. I wished she could see that you did not want to have a conversation.

'Take it step by step, Willie.'

'Yes.'

'And what step shall you take first? What next, I mean?'

'Next?'

Perspiration broke on the palms of my hands. I drew attention to some aspects of the landscape, feeling a warmth that spread from my face into my neck and shoulders.

'Don't let yourself brood, Willie.'

'I'll just go on at the mill.'

'That's very sensible, Willie.'

When we reached the house I sat alone for a while in the narrow bedroom I had so happily slept in during the weeks of our holiday a year ago. Vividly I recalled the details of the funeral service, hearing again the words that had been spoken, wondering what their meaning had been like for you. I longed to comfort you. I longed to be alone with you again, even though it had been so awkward on our walk and in the lounge of that hotel.

'It was terrible for him, miss,' Josephine said when I went to talk to her in the kitchen. 'To find her like that was terrible.'

'Yes, I know it must have been.'

'He was going to write to you that evening.'

'Write to me? To *me*?'

'To say he was fond of you, miss. He was intending to send a letter.'

'Fond of me?'

'He has been fond of you ever since the summer you were here. He told me the afternoon of Mrs Quinton's death.'

I went away to lay the table in the cheerless dining-room, but at suppertime you did not appear: you had gone out somewhere on your own. My mother and I ate more of the ham, and put some aside for you. 'He had no lunch either,' she sighed. 'Marianne dear, you should have stayed with him.'

'I think he prefers to be alone.'

All I could think of was what Josephine had told me in the kitchen. It seemed fateful that on that night of all nights you had intended to write to me. Many times I had wanted to write to you also, to attempt to continue the conversations we had had. But when I tried to a clumsiness overtook me and I found I could not properly express what I wanted to say in letters.

In the early morning we would begin our journey back to England. We could stay no longer because of my going to Switzerland, and as it was I would be late arriving there. I waited downstairs for an hour or so, but it was much later, when I was undressing in my bedroom, that I heard your footfall on the stairs, which seemed like fate also. I pulled my nightdress over my head and slipped into the cold bed. I wept immediately. Had we been together now, would I have put my arms about you, and drawn your head on to my breast to kiss away your suffering? And would you have forgiven me for the accident of my English birth? For an hour or more I lay there wretchedly, and then I rose and lifted the paraffin lamp from its shelf.

I did not knock, even lightly, on the panels of your door but opened it instead. All judgement had gone from me, all fear and rectitude. I cared about nothing except that you should know I loved you, that you might find at least some comfort in knowing it. I placed the lamp on your dressing-table and spoke your name.

3

'Ah, Marianne, my dear.'

He always liked to meet new arrivals at the railway station, Professor Gibb-Bachelor explained. He was a man in his sixties, tall and exceedingly thin. His beard was grey and sparse, his wig jet-black, with a light wave in it.

'You are a little late,' he remarked, unchidingly, 'arriving today, my dear.'

'There was a funeral. My father sent a telegram.'

'Ah yes, of course. "I am going to meet the telegram girl," I said to my wife before I left the villa.' A conspiratorial laugh was slyly issued. 'I shall call you that, little Marianne. My telegram girl. Welcome to Montreux.'

'I hope my lateness hasn't been inconvenient.'

'Heavens, of course it has not! But I worried personally in case the funeral upset your travel bookings, and that the journey might be uncomfortable because of that.'

'No, it wasn't in the least.'

'A parson, your father? Dorset, if memory serves?'

'Yes.'

'Dorset is delightful. And the funeral. Not someone close, I hope?'

'An aunt. In Ireland.'

'Ah, Ireland . . .'

Whenever he spoke he perused me closely, apparently seeking my eyes. A perpetual smile was not quite hidden by his beard.

'No one dislikes Montreux,' he confided as we drove off. 'We become a family, my wife and I, with the girls who visit us. No one has ever been unhappy in our house.'

We passed by a great expanse of water, which Professor Gibb-Bachelor said was Lac Léman. All around us the Alps were capped with snow.

'A troublesome country, Ireland. You felt quite safe, Marianne?'

'Oh yes, quite safe.'

The car passed through open gates and drew up by a house with iron balconies in front of its windows, each of which was flanked by wooden shutters hooked back against a brown wall. A verandah stretched the length of this façade, containing the wide pine doors through which we now passed.

'Gervaise!' the Professor called in the hall while I waited with my luggage. He inclined his head in a way that was becoming familiar to me, sticking it out a little as he listened for his wife's reply.

'The telephone rang,' a lank girl with spectacles informed him.

'Ah, thank you, Cynthia.'

I was aware of garish colours on the walls: in the hall an excess of murals had all the appearance of being the work of the Gibb-Bachelors' charges over the years. There was a lakeland scene, and an alp, and halfway up the stairs a castle with birds.

'How d'you do, Marianne?' Firm and jaunty, much shorter than her husband, Mrs Gibb-Bachelor was suddenly there. She was neatly dressed in different shades of mauve, her salt and pepper hair permanently waved. 'Come please with me, Marianne.'

She led the way back to the room she had just emerged from.

'Please sit down,' she invited, placing herself behind a table and gesturing at a chair. There had been chairs of the same kind in the hall and in the verandah: cushionless, a loop of canvas for seat and back. Bare boards, I had noticed also, were the order of the day, with here and there a woven rug.

'I am delighted to welcome you to Montreux,' Mrs Gibb-Bachelor continued briskly, in a throaty Scottish voice. 'Culture is the byword in our villa, but otherwise we live in the local manner. Classes are given daily by our friend Mademoiselle Florence, and my husband instructs in the history of the cantons and of the country. The regime is not arduous, but we do like an early start to the day and all conversation with Mademoiselle Florence is of course conducted in French. Thank you, Marianne.'

I rose and in turn thanked Mrs Gibb-Bachelor.

'The other girl from your school . . .' Mrs Gibb-Bachelor poked through papers on her desk.

'Agnes Brontenby.'

'Ah, Agnes Brontenby. Of course. Agnes is quite delightful. We have as well, this autumn, Mavis and Cynthia.' Mrs Gibb-Bachelor paused. 'Are you quite healthy, Marianne?'

'Yes, I believe so.'

'You're a wee little creature, but you mustn't let that worry you, you know. Any disadvantage is better than gawkiness.'

I said I had become used to my diminutive size, but Mrs Gibb-Bachelor appeared not to hear me and continued with her theme.

'It doesn't mean you are unhealthy, Marianne. Your teeth look sound, eh? Well, that is excellent. Your mother will probably have told you that artificial teeth have ill-bred connotations.'

'I don't think my mother did, actually.'

'Ah, well.' Mrs Gibb-Bachelor paused again. Her head slipped a little to one side. 'In our Swiss home we do not ignore the manners of the past. You understand, Marianne?'

'Yes, Mrs Gibb-Bachelor.'

'Excellent. You will share with Mavis. She suffers a little from rashes, but I do not believe the trouble is in the least way infectious. Your time here will be happy, Marianne. No girl has ever been unhappy in our home.'

'So the Professor said.'

'I can see the Professor has taken to you already. Now that is excellent.'

Following Mrs Gibb-Bachelor, I carried my suitcases upstairs. We crossed a landing which featured further murals, and entered a cell-like chamber containing two beds, one unmade. Mrs Gibb-Bachelor gestured at the room's window, stretching to the floor and draped with net. She crossed the room to it, undid a latch and pushed the two curtained frames outwards: below us in the twilight lay Lac Léman and the twinkling lights of Montreux, towering above us the snow-peaked Alps. 'One of the finest views in Switzerland,' Mrs Gibb-Bachelor stated with confidence, and went away.

I closed the window and sat down on the edge of the bed, not yet unpacking. Ever since I had left Ireland I had found it difficult to be with other people. On the journey back to the rectory, and after we'd arrived there, I had longed to be alone, to escape from my mother's worry about leaving you, and my father's sympathetic murmur. 'We must pray for his peace of mind': more than once my father had bent his head over clasped hands, closing his eyes. When eventually I left the rectory to set out on my second journey the sense of relief made me feel ungrateful.

'Hullo,' a voice said. 'Are you Marianne? My name is Mavis.'

'Yes, I am Marianne.' I stared back at the speckled face that stared at mine. I asked about letters, but when I went to the letter-rack in the hall it was empty. I didn't know why I'd asked or had gone to look. Of course there wouldn't be a letter yet.

The bosom of Agnes Brontenby was more shapely than it had been beneath a gymslip, her beautiful blue eyes more liquid even than I remembered them at school. In the dining-room she sat across the table from me, with the bespectacled Cynthia beside her and Mavis next to me. The Gibb-Bachelors ate privately, at some different time.

Free of murals, the dining-room was on the gloomy side. Its walls were a shade of gravy, as were the velvet curtains that all but obscured the windows. The pine boards of the floor were sprinkled with French chalk.

'The food's inedible,' Cynthia informed me, and Mavis said that last year a girl had run away. But the sweetness of Agnes Brontenby already pervaded this gathering atmosphere; already, I guessed, she had stifled gossip on its utterance and discovered silver linings. She scooped up pale soup with vermicelli in it and said it was delicious. Only that afternoon Mrs Gibb-Bachelor had confided to her that the girl's running away last year had been due to a misunderstanding. 'Oh look, let's not be horrid,' she protested when Cynthia said she doubted if Mrs Gibb-Bachelor had ever told the truth in her life.

'He's *awful*,' Mavis said.

'Oh, quite beyond the pale,' Cynthia agreed. She added that Mrs Gibb-Bachelor's letter to her parents had categorically stated that each girl had a room to herself and that Mademoiselle Florence instructed in German as well as French. 'Then why are we suddenly sharing?' she demanded. 'Have they mislaid some rooms or something? And how is it that Mademoiselle Florence can miraculously teach German since she says herself she can't speak a word of it?'

'Oh, you are funny, Cynthia!' cried Agnes. 'Mislaid some rooms!'

She tinkled with laughter and then became serious. She insisted that there had clearly been another silly misunderstanding. She couldn't remember how Mrs Gibb-Bachelor had written to her own parents, but wasn't it in any case best to be cheerful?

Mavis and I did not contribute to the argument that followed. Duties in the dining-room were to be shared among us: it was mine, that evening, to clear away, and Mavis's to give us each a plate of sliced apple and cheese.

'Another thing,' said Cynthia, 'there was a distinct reference to domestic staff.'

'Oh now, the Gibb-Bachelors do do their best, you know. And actually I quite enjoy the kitchen-work course. Mrs Gibb-Bachelor's going to show me how to make toad-in-the-hole.'

'If you ask me these appalling people are doing extremely well for themselves – their house decorated, their food cooked, dusting and cleaning, early-morning tea carried to their bedside. Not to mention the way the Professor stands so close to you.'

'Oh, Cynthia, you *are* amusing! But you're missing England, aren't you, Cynthia? You'll love it here in the end, you know.'

'I wouldn't be too sure,' said Cynthia.

When we had finished, Mrs Gibb-Bachelor was waiting for us in the hall.

'Girls,' she announced, 'the Professor's lantern lecture is at nine.' She inspected each of us closely, as if for dirt. She fixed Cynthia with a stern eye. 'My dear, I have to inform you that a napkin must be opened across the knee, never tucked into a garment. And it is ill-bred to prop ourselves on our elbows when drinking a cup of tea or other beverage.'

'I'm sorry, Mrs Gibb-Bachelor.'

'These are wee little faults I have noticed during the course of today, Cynthia. You understand too, Marianne?'

'Yes, Mrs Gibb-Bachelor.'

'Then that is excellent.'

She strode jauntily away, her scent lingering behind her.

'Foul old pussy,' Cynthia said.

The Professor's magic lantern showed us pictures of English landscape and houses which he attempted to relate to literature. He quoted the poetry of James Thomson, illustrating it with slides of Hagley Park. He quoted George Eliot and Mrs Gaskell, and in particular Wordsworth. 'Here, by Nether Stowey, he walked with Dorothy. Here we see his house at Rydal Mount. *And I have felt a presence that disturbs me . . . a sense sublime . . .*' He showed us Lyme Regis, and the Temple of Apollo at Stourhead. '*I have through every Garden been,*' he solemnly intoned, '*among the red, the white, the green.*'

The reedy, academic voice came and went, as did the pictures of woods and meadows and mazes and rose-beds. I thought about you, unable not to. '*But there's a tree, of many, one,*' the Professor continued. '*A single field which I have looked upon . . .*' Trees and fields appeared on the sheet which Mavis had been requested to pin up as a screen, oak trees and beeches, Scotch pines, alders, ash and apple. The fields were shown in different seasons and there was talk of ploughing and then of mellow fruitfulness. 'Will the wretched man never cease?' Cynthia muttered beside me.

I dreamed of you that night, among the landscapes of the magic lantern show. Your warm body warmed mine, your lips were passionate, as they had been.

'*Non, non,* Marianne,' cried Mademoiselle Florence. 'You do not make the effort.'

I tried. I apologized. I did my best to speak and smile.

. . . so very busy, wrote my father, *with all the preparations for the Harvest Thanksgiving. Your mother has spent two days in bed, her nerves fallen all to pieces after the turmoil of the last few weeks, Ireland*

and then the arranging and rearranging of your journey to Montreux. My blessed child, you are in all our prayers.

In the famous castle by the lake the Professor stood by the pillar on which Lord Byron had scratched his name.

'You're troubled, little Marianne?' he sympathetically enquired while the others marvelled over the flowing signature.

'No,' I lied. 'No, not at all.'

'You may always come to me, you know. You may always tell me.'

He stepped a little closer and placed a hand on my shoulder. He was my friend, he said.

Again, that day, I looked in case there was a letter. In the early morning I had written down the Gibb-Bachelors' address in Montreux and had placed it on your dressing-table. Then I had crept away while still you slept.

'Visiting cards,' decreed Mrs Gibb-Bachelor, 'are placed on the hall salver or on some convenient table. Engraved of course, never printed.' A married lady left one, and two of her husband's. But should the lady called upon be unmarried or widowed then only one of the husband's cards might be placed on the hall-stand or the convenient table.

I prayed, listening to her voice. I asked for forgiveness. I promised that I did not seek to excuse my sin, that I would live with it and suffer for it if I might be given a little mercy now. 'Dear God,' I pleaded. 'Dear kind God, please hear me.'

Mrs Gibb-Bachelor smiled at each of us in turn.

'And do not presume that hem-stitching is beneath you. The plain girl who is acquainted with the art of caring for her garments has the advantage over the pretty girl who is slap-dash.'

That day, too, I looked in the letter-rack, although I had resolved I would not any more.

The Professor said:

'Little Marianne, you did not listen to a word of my lecture on Wordsworth's sense of rhyme.'

'Oh yes, I did indeed, Professor.'

'Ah no, my little girl.'

To my distaste, he laid a bony finger on my lips and did not take it away. His wig moved slightly as he shook his head. We were alone in the library.

'For me you are a special girl, Marianne. Your discontent is all the more distressing because of that.'

Again the finger, cold as ice, was laid across my lips. A fresh smile engaged the Professor's own, drawing them back until large teeth protruded, like pale tombstones. We stood in the alcove of a window, I with my back to it.

'Much of what I say when I speak of Wordsworth is specially for you, little Marianne.'

'Please, Professor –'

'You are labouring under stress, little girl.'

Again he came close to me, pressing me back against the window. His breath had garlic of a day or two's duration on it. His lips touched my flesh, high on my left cheek, just below the cheek-bone, and while they did so the palm of a hand slipped down my thigh, as light as the touch of a butterfly. I pushed him away, shuddering and feeling sick in my stomach. How could I tell him anything? 'We might go to Kilneagh,' you'd said. 'It would be nice to show you Kilneagh.' How could I tell him that no day in my life had been as happy? The men in the mill-yard had shaken my hand. In Lough you'd pointed out Driscoll's shop and the Church of Our Lady Queen of Heaven. In Fermoy you'd pointed out the ironmonger's and the draper's where you'd done your Friday shopping. We'd been too shy to say what really we felt, but somehow that hadn't mattered.

'Now, my dear,' Mrs Gibb-Bachelor announced breezily in her office, 'a wee little bird has told me you have fallen in love.'

'If Agnes –'

'I did not say Agnes, dear. But it isn't difficult to know when a friend's in love, now is it? There are time-honoured signals, are there not?'

'This is a private matter, Mrs Gibb-Bachelor.'

'To be sure it is. On the other hand I cannot have my girls distressed. Our monthly visitation – clockwork regular, is it? Oh no, don't look askance. I do assure you I have known love to upset girls mightily in that department. Quite topsy-turvy it all becomes.'

'I would really rather not talk about this, Mrs Gibb-Bachelor.'

'My little bird is a reliable wee creature.' Head on one side, Mrs

Gibb-Bachelor smiled, looking for a moment like a bird herself. 'There need not be a secret between us, Marianne. Other girls before you have fallen in love with the Professor, my dear.'

In astonishment I denied that charge. Repelled and outraged, I spoke as firmly as I could. 'I am not in love with your husband, Mrs Gibb-Bachelor.'

Mrs Gibb-Bachelor softly replied that love, too often, was not a matter of choice. It was understandable that girls should love her husband: the Professor was notably attractive, many girls had found him so.

'But this isn't true, Mrs Gibb-Bachelor. In no way is what you're saying true.'

'My husband is a fine and sensitive person. No one blames you, Marianne. Indeed, to tell you the very truth, I often think it denotes a fullness of the spirit in a girl –'

'I do not love the man.'

'My dear, it is ill-bred to refer to the Professor in that way. It is also ill-bred to interrupt.'

'Mrs Gibb-Bachelor –'

'Above all, it is ill-bred to raise our voices. My dear, no blame possibly attaches to you and if our monthly visitation is not quite clockwork we must not worry. Love is its own master, Marianne.'

I shrugged my shoulders and was told that that was ill-bred also. I began a further protest, then abandoned it. After all, what did any of it matter?

'It will pass,' Mrs Gibb-Bachelor promised. 'The sentiments that have seized you, Marianne, will pass. Time is the healer, my dear.'

These words dismissed me, and I did not reply.

'Look, come for a walk,' Agnes Brontenby invited, waiting for me outside Mrs Gibb-Bachelor's office.

I shook my head and tried to pass her by, but she touched my arm with a restraining gesture.

'Dear Marianne, you must be sensible. We have known each other for all these years. I always liked you at school, Marianne, and I am sure I always shall.'

'Please leave me alone, Agnes.'

'The Professor –'

'Oh, for God's sake, it has nothing to do with the wretched Professor.'

I walked away, leaving her astonished that I should use such unpleasant language. She afterwards mentioned that, but I did not say I was sorry.

Day followed day, week succeeded week. Mavis's rashes did not improve. Cynthia said she'd lost a stone because of the unappetizing food. The waiter in the Café Bon Accueil eyed Agnes Brontenby with a pleasure that was undisguised. *'Dans l'immense salle régnait une ambiance joyeuse,'* dictated Mademoiselle Florence, but I could not understand and did not wish to. *'Vous êtes très stupide,'* she shrilled at me. 'Not ever a more *stupide* girl come to Montreux.'

Each morning when I awoke everything came tumbling back at me, the lamp flickering and going out, the smell of paraffin in the darkness. I tried to write to you but could not. I wanted to say I was sorry, but at the same time longed that you would write and tell me you were glad.

'Ill-health bedevilled me as a younger man. I might have married earlier in my life if it had not been for that.'

Again I was alone with him, by the lake. He had contrived to dispose of the other girls in the Bon Accueil, hurrying them on to order our coffee and Florentines.

'It is not wrong to feel tenderly for a man who is older than your father. You have been distressed by these feelings, little Marianne, but there is no cause for it.'

I shook my head, staring over the still water of Lac Leman. I felt his arm on my shoulder, and then the coarseness of his beard on my chin and cheek, like mattress hair. His large teeth, seeking my lips, were cold.

'Please, Professor.'

I pushed at the scrawny body, as I had in the alcove of the library, the palms of my hands spread against his chest. His knees, one on either side of my left leg, grasped it strongly. He whispered that he could not live without me, and did not wish to. 'You are my little wife,' he whispered.

'Please take your hands off me, Professor.'

I broke from his embrace and stood furiously some yards away. I wanted to stamp my foot and then actually did so, my heel making a sharp staccato on the tarmacadamed path.

'I do not feel tenderly for you,' I cried, causing two women who were passing with dogs to look discomfited. 'I have no feelings of any kind whatsoever for you. I am not your wife. It is absurd to say I am.'

'My little child, I simply wish you were.'

'You have a wife already. You are a lecherous man, Professor Gibb-Bachelor. Your wife is disgraceful to encourage you.'

'Please,' he whispered. 'I cannot help my feelings for you. You are beautiful, little Marianne, more beautiful than Agnes Brontenby.'

I told him then: I said I was no longer a virgin. 'I believe you know that. I believe you've guessed, Professor Gibb-Bachelor.'

'My dear sweet child, of course you're a virgin. Do you not know the meaning of the term?'

I told him how I had left my bedroom and crossed the landing, carrying the lamp with me. I would love you for ever, I said, even if you despised me and were ashamed.

'Oh, little heart, this is not the kind of talk we like.'

I hit him then. I hit him on the side of the face with my clenchèd fist. I told him he disgusted me. Without emotion I said:

'So please in future leave me alone, Professor. Try this on with Agnes if you are tired of your wife. Try it on with Cynthia or Mavis or Mademoiselle Florence. But I would rather you kept your hands off me.'

'You must not repeat this to Mrs Gibb-Bachelor, Marianne. It is the realm of fantasy, but it may be our secret, all this you like to think about your cousin.'

'It is true. It occurred.'

'Yes, yes, of course. But Mrs Gibb-Bachelor must not ever know. My dear, she'd pack you back to England this instant minute.'

'I have no intention of informing your wife since she does not sensually attack me.'

'Please, little child, don't speak so harshly. I only love your prettiness.'

I did not reply, except to say when he addressed me again that if my sinfulness was in some way revealed in my demeanour it did not follow that I would satisfy his lust. He wiped at his cheeks with a handkerchief, pretending, I believe, to cry. But by the time we reached the Café Bon Accueil he had recovered his composure.

Conveniently he drifted into a reverie of such intensity that the scene by the lakeside might not have taken place. When later I said his attentions had become so pressing that I'd had to push him away from me and even had hit him Agnes Brontenby assured me I must have been mistaken. 'Filthy old savage,' Cynthia said, and was all for reporting the matter to Mrs Gibb-Bachelor. But I knew it wasn't going to be worth it, for I would have no more trouble with her husband.

Please don't think badly of me. Oh, Willie, I do still love you so. The words could not be written; they belonged in conversation, yet conversation was impossible. All of it was punishment, the haunting emptiness, the fear, the unknown in the years that lay ahead. The teeth and the breath of the Professor were punishment also, his knees and fingers. Of course he had smelt out my sin.

I spent that Christmas and the New Year with the Gibb-Bachelors, with Cynthia and Mavis and Agnes Brontenby. In early February all four of us prepared to return to England. 'You have benefited enormously,' Mrs Gibb-Bachelor insisted, the same remark to each of us. 'Everything about you is splendidly improved.'

I could not remain in the rectory. I knew that as soon as I returned. I walked in the gardens of Woodcombe Park, since we, its poor relations, were permitted to: by the mock-Roman summer-house, by the willows and the lakes and the stately yews: so different your Kilneagh was, a poor relation too. Like some uncharted region, fearsome and unknown, Kilneagh repelled me now, yet the pocket money I had saved in Switzerland was added to the modest amount I otherwise possessed and the journey to Ireland planned. For how could my father bless his congregation with the peace of God, knowing no peace himself because of the ugly truth with which I would soon disgrace him? How could my mother bear those cruel glances at her Mothers' Union meetings?

I fell in love with Willie, I wrote in the note I left behind for them and then I closed down shutters on my mind, unable to bear their pain as well as my own. I was pregnant with our child, I wrote.

4

The boat was several hours late arriving in Cork, slowed down by a snowstorm at sea. Exhausted and still seasick, I made my way to the house in Windsor Terrace, hoping to spend that night there before continuing my journey. But in several of the windows the blinds were drawn and there was no reply to my knock. I waited for more than an hour in the hope that Josephine might return and then, since she did not, I dragged my suitcase down the pavement steps of St Patrick's Hill, past the pawnbroker's shop at the bottom of its steep incline. I asked a woman if she knew where I might find cheap lodgings and she directed me to the Shandon Boarding House, not far away. It was a melancholy place, about which hung an odour of old food and where payment was required in advance. There was a statue of the Virgin Mary on a table in the hall and a picture of her in my room. Long lace curtains were grey with the dust that lay thickly elsewhere as well, on the sideboard in the hall, on the staircase and the windowsills, on the hall-stand with its array of letters addressed to boarders of the past. No other boarder was resident at the moment, I was told by the unprepossessing woman who ran the place, though usually, she assured me, the house was full. I lay down for a while and then returned to Windsor Terrace, but there was no reply to my knocking. I slept poorly that night, haunted by fragments of disjointed dreams in which I was endlessly pursued by my parents' weeping. In the morning I sat alone for breakfast in the airless dining-room, its tablecloth patterned with stains and crumbs.

I took the train to Fermoy and left my suitcase at the railway station. Feeling doubtful about affording a hackney car, I walked to Lough, three miles you'd said it was, and then a mile to Kilneagh. Snow had begun to fall again and somehow it seemed apt that everything should look so different. I peered through the gates of

Kilneagh at the long, whitening avenue, as beautiful now in frozen landscape as it had been that summer. I walked on to the mill, increasingly apprehensive of how you would greet me.

'Good Lord above!' exclaimed Mr Derenzy, regarding me with an astonishment he made no attempt to disguise. I expected to see you after I'd knocked on the door and his voice had called out that I should enter the office. I was determined to remain calm, not even to look at you in Mr Derenzy's presence. But you were not there.

'Willie . . .' I said.

'Willie?'

He frowned at me, grimacing just a little. I was wearing a brown fur hat which my mother and father had given me for Christmas. I took it off and placed it on a chair. I shook the snow from my coat.

'I've come to see my cousin, Mr Derenzy.'

The furrows on his forehead deepened. 'But Willie isn't here, Marianne. Willie left Kilneagh, you know. He hasn't been here for months.'

'No, I didn't know.'

'Oh yes, indeed.'

I did not say anything. I could not for a moment.

'Anyone might want to go away, Marianne, after what had happened.'

'Where is he, Mr Derenzy? Where has he gone?'

Slowly he shook his head.

'Please tell me, Mr Derenzy.'

'No one has had a line from Willie. The house in Cork is to be sold.'

A silence gathered in the small office. I stared at the leather spines of a row of ledgers and at wooden cabinets with shallow, labelled drawers. In the corner there was a pile of sacks, and in another some kind of cog-wheel. I said I had been to the house, hoping to find Josephine there. Mr Derenzy nodded, another silence began. It crept into the corners of the office, over the drawers and the ledgers and the neatly arranged papers on Mr Derenzy's desk. He offered me a pinch of snuff from a blue tin box, and when I shook my head he took some himself. A kettle on the coals in the grate began to boil. Reaching for a teapot on a shelf behind him, he said:

'I remember the day Willie was born. I've known him all his life.'

What you had called his skeleton's face looked up at me from the hearth where he was spooning tea into the teapot. No smile lit his bony features, his springy red hair was still. The teapot was well-used, its brown enamel chipped around the spout and on the lid.

'If you left a message I would put it straight into Willie's hand.' He spoke with a finality that sounded almost grim. He poured the tea and offered me a cup with roses on it, on a saucer that matched it.

'Do you think Josephine has been in touch?'

'I really don't know.'

'Where is Josephine, Mr Derenzy?'

'She is working in St Fina's. An institution in Cork, run by the nuns.'

I left the chair which he had placed close to the hearth for me, and stood by the window. The sky was grey and heavy. I watched the softly falling snow, gathering already on the roofs and the cobbles of the mill-yard. The green-faced clock gave the time as twenty past eleven. Mechanically, I remembered your saying that it was always fast, and in the same mechanical way I wondered if the snow would affect it. Would the big hand, travelling upwards after the half-hour, come to an untimely halt because of what had accumulated on it? I turned from the window, endeavouring to hold the mill manager's glance with my own but not succeeding.

'Are you keeping something back from me, Mr Derenzy? Has something happened?'

'Ah no, no, Marianne.'

There was little conviction in his voice. As if to lend it more, he shook his head, floating his hair about. I said:

'I must know where he is.'

He did not reply. He drank some tea, then very faintly sighed. I said:

'I am going to have Willie's child.'

His eyes closed, the lids dropping down as though he could not bear to look upon me. A sound came from him, like the whimper of a creature in distress.

'I cannot be at home, Mr Derenzy. I cannot disgrace my parents. That is why I've come here.'

As if I had not spoken, he said:

'It would be better to go back to England, Marianne.'

'I don't believe it would be better. Mr Derenzy, when do you imagine Willie will return?'

127

'As soon as he does he shall know immediately that you came here.'

'Do you think it terrible, what I have told you?'

'I'm the manager of this mill, Marianne. I've been a bachelor all my life. I don't know about these matters.'

'But you and Willie's aunt –'

'That is a private friendship, Marianne.'

'I'm sorry.'

He said it didn't matter. He said again it would be better to return to England.

'Mr Derenzy, Willie is not aware of my plight. He must surely have said something about where he was going. Oh, I do, I assure you, understand that he had to go away. But he must have said something, Mr Derenzy.'

'Willie left here a few days after you and your mother left, when arrangements had been made with Lanigan and O'Brien about the house in Cork. I came in one morning and Willie was not here.'

His hands, fragile on the ordered surface of his desk, were trembling, and in his eyes there was something that might have been terror. Again he closed them, as if to cloak it.

'I'd like to walk over to Kilneagh.'

His mouth was pulled down at the corners and I sensed that for a moment he could not speak. Then his eyes opened and he regarded me wildly.

'Please go back to England. Please, child, I beg you now.'

I shook my head, not knowing how to answer otherwise. I remembered the way to the house, I said, and after a pause he rose and took from a hook on the back of the door a navy-blue overcoat and drew on woollen gloves. He led the way down the wooden stairs that were like the stairs to a loft. A man with a limp, dapper in his working clothes, crossed the yard, whistling. He didn't see us; you had told me his name on our visit, but I could not remember it now.

'There,' Mr Derenzy said. 'Keep the thorn hedge on your left and then you'll see the stile. But this is no weather to go walking, Marianne. And Willie is not at the house, you know.'

'Yes, I do know that.'

I followed his directions, and the tears I had been holding back in the mill office flowed in a torrent on my cheeks. A pathetic creature,

Mr Derenzy had no doubt considered, an immoral girl who had come to make a nuisance of herself because she didn't know what to do. I thought of the rectory and the kindness it contained, the cosiness and comfort of its rooms. They did their best, my father and my mother, saving to send me to a boarding-school they could not afford, saving to send me to Montreux because they believed that would be advantageous for me. They had always done their best. They had worried when I was upset, they had put things right. Like a tumult shuddering through my body, my weeping continued, its stream of tears warm on my icy face. In the rectory it would be time for morning coffee now, with the oaten biscuits my father liked so. But they would neither of them have the heart for biscuits.

I stood still, waiting for my agitation to calm. I moved on then, passing through the wood of birch trees before the ground rose gently and afterwards more steeply. When I reached its greatest height the burnt-out house lay below me, its stark outline beautiful against the pale landscape. Slowly I descended, clambering over a stone wall and through a gate, into the jungle of rhododendrons. The house, no longer beautiful, loomed grimly above me and around me, black walls exuding such damp bleakness that involuntarily I shivered. The weeds in the hall were less green, less vigorous than they had been that summer, and snow fell in the drawing-room you'd told me had once been scarlet. Lightly it lay on the mantelpiece and on the wreck of the grand piano; lengths of rough timber were nailed across an archway. I found the kitchen, and above it rooms that were undamaged. Nothing was locked, but there was no warmth in any of the rooms, and moisture seeped up the walls.

In the garden a greenhouse had fallen to pieces, its door sagging on rusted hinges, its glass collapsed. High, withered thistles gathered snowflakes where beds for vegetables had been. You had stood here with me, recalling the old gardener, and Tim Paddy who had been in love with Josephine. It was then that the name of the limping man in the mill-yard came to me: Johnny Lacy, whom Josephine had preferred.

'Marianne!'

Bewildered, your Aunt Pansy was beside me. I took her meekly proffered hand and followed her into the orchard wing, into the chill square sitting-room where that summer we had been given mid-morning scones, where after your mother's funeral we had awkwardly stood around.

'I'm very much afraid my sister is not here,' she said. 'She and Father Kilgarriff went out early and, really, I'm alarmed because of this snow.'

Again I took off my new fur hat, but did not remove my coat.

'A cup of tea?' Aunt Pansy offered.

'I've had some tea with Mr Derenzy. Thank you.'

'I'm so surprised to see you, Marianne.'

'I didn't realize Willie had gone away.'

'Oh yes, I'm afraid so.'

Nervously playing with a cameo brooch that hung from her neck on a fine silver chain, Aunt Pansy sought to efface herself in the manner I remembered. She pressed herself against the back of the wine-coloured sofa, bundling herself into it as if she did not wish to be seen. Yet she could not prevent an expression of concern from gathering in her ageless, cherubic face. She looked away from me when she spoke.

'I'm awfully sorry, Marianne.'

'But where has he gone?'

As Mr Derenzy had, she shook her head. As before, there were several dogs in the sitting-room, on the armchairs and the sofa and sprawled along the hearthrug. Above a mantelpiece cluttered with ornaments and oddments the severe face of Gladstone was darkly framed, dominant between scenes of oxen working on a mountainside. Books were packed untidily into high, glass-fronted bookcases. A grandfather clock, inlaid with black and white marble, ticked solemnly in a corner by the door. The room smelt of soot and of the dogs. Their hairs clung to the sofa and the armchairs.

'I'm really *awfully* sorry. But, Marianne, surely you haven't come here specially?'

'Yes, I have.'

Aunt Pansy nodded, and for several moments continued to do so. I said:

'I'm in love, you see, with Willie.'

A further effusion of pink darkened Aunt Pansy's pink cheeks, a plump small hand played frantically with the cameo brooch. The silver chain was wound around one finger and then the next, the brooch itself rubbed and pressed, cast aside and then attended to again. For a moment or two it was used to trace the outline of her lips, before she opened them and spoke.

'Well, I think we guessed that. That morning Willie brought you here – yes, we rather guessed. And later Willie talked to Father Kilgarriff and Father Kilgarriff said something to my sister. And Mr Derenzy guessed, I think, and said something to myself. Everyone was pleased. Mrs Driscoll, who keeps the shop, said something to my sister because Mr Derenzy had passed it on to the Sweeneys and they had passed it on to her – or Johnny Lacy's wife had, or one of the men from the mill, I really can't remember. The rector knew, I do remember that, because one Sunday he remarked to us that of course we were all rather looking into the future when we spoke of another English wife at Kilneagh. He was thinking of your both being – well, no more than children, and Kilneagh being half a ruin now. Naturally it would be ages before it could possibly be a place to live in again. But it *did* make us happy, looking into the future like that, it really made us happy.'

Running out of breath, Aunt Pansy gasped, very pink in the face now. I said I was glad that people were happy.

'Oh, happy when we guessed, I mean. Happy *then*, I mean.'

The silver chain was tightened yet again around each finger in turn. A lightly marked Dalmatian, asleep on my feet, snored. I said:

'Before the death of Willie's mother?'

'Yes, before her death.'

The subject was unobtrusively dismissed. In the chilly sitting-room the marriage referred to was no more than speculation that had come to nothing. The looking into the future, and the contentment the gossip had inspired among the people of Lough, belonged already to the past.

'If you'd written to us, my dear, we could have told you Willie was not here. It's a very great distance to come and find . . . I mean, at the end of your journey to have to turn round again and go all that way back . . .'

'But where *is* Willie? Does Father Kilgarriff know?'

Again she shook her head. '*Please* let me get you some tea, Marianne.'

'No, thank you.'

I could not remain there. I stood up, and Aunt Pansy rose also, with an alacrity that betrayed relief.

'My sister will be disappointed. And Father Kilgarriff, of course.'

'Yes, I am sorry too.'

'The truth is we've bought a little motor-car. This morning is the first time Father Kilgarriff has driven her out in it. That is why I am alarmed because it has begun to snow.'

She didn't want to talk about you. I had been foolish, I should have written first, I was no more than a silly lovesick child; all that was in her face, although she did not wish it to be there.

'I am going to have Willie's baby,' I said.

I walked over the frozen fields, watching the birds as they poked for grubs on the riverbank, not caring where I went or how I felt. Sheep huddled beneath a hedge, cows kept close together. I envied them their drear complacency. I prayed and pleaded as I had in Switzerland, I asked for mercy. It was too much that as well as everything else you should not be here: I begged that that at least might be miraculously changed.

It was nearly five o'clock when I arrived back in the village and when I asked in the shop about the Cork train I was told I'd be too late now to catch it. In any case, since it was snowing heavily again the walk to Fermoy looked as though it would not be possible. I might have returned to Kilneagh but I did not wish to do that. I went instead to Sweeney's public house to enquire about lodgings.

A man with one arm, who warmly shook my hand when I explained to him about the train, told me he was Mr Sweeney. He had recently added to his business, he informed me also, by opening a garage on the empty premises next door to his own. With some pride he led me into it and said it was he who had sold your aunts their new motor-car.

'D'you know the two women I mean? They live over by the ruins. The motor's for Kilgarriff to drive them about in. Have you heard tell of Kilgarriff maybe?'

'Yes.'

'A benighted man, God help him. Still and all, there's many a worse one wears a bishop's ring.'

'I suppose there is.'

'I'm surprised you'd have knowledge of him. Aren't you a stranger yourself, miss?'

'I'm Willie Quinton's cousin. I came from England to see him. I didn't know he'd gone away.'

'Oh, glory be to God!'

We were still standing in the garage. The snow had melted on my hat and was running down beneath my clothes. My feet were soaking. Mr Sweeney muttered to himself, looking at me for a moment and then looking away. He passed a tongue over his lips, bringing the muttering to an end.

'Sure, I didn't know who you were,' he said. 'The wife'll eat the face off me.'

He led the way, through the bar and into a warm, low-ceilinged kitchen.

'It's Willie Quinton's cousin,' he said to a woman with a piece of meat in her hand. 'I'm after showing her the garage. Sure, she could've been anyone.'

The woman stared at me, her eyes wide, the meat still in her motionless hand. But when she spoke it was to her husband.

'Will you look at the cut of yourself?' she shouted shrilly. 'Smelling like a brewery at four o'clock in the day.'

She bustled about me then, unbuttoning my coat and making me take off my shoes. She accused her husband of stupidity for thinking I'd be interested in seeing his garage, a misjudgement that was entirely due to his having drunk a dozen bottles of stout instead of repairing a bent running-board. 'Sit down at the range,' she urged me, 'so you can thaw your little bones out. That old garage would freeze you raw.'

'Give her rum,' suggested Mr Sweeney. 'Heat up a sup of rum in a saucepan for her.' He stood by the door, pools of water forming on the stone floor by his feet. His wife ignored him.

'I'll have a room got ready for you,' she said when I explained my predicament, 'and there's a stew that'll warm you up only it isn't cooked yet. Would you like a sup of Bovril?'

'There's nothing like hot rum,' interposed Mr Sweeney. 'I have a good dark rum I can get you from the bar.'

'Will you keep out of that bar and go and wash yourself? You're the laziest man God ever put eyes in.'

There was a maid in the kitchen also, who on our entrance had ceased her task of cleaning potatoes at the sink. She was a shallow-cheeked, squinting girl, wrapped in a green overall that might once have been the property of the larger Mrs Sweeney.

'Stop loitering about,' Mrs Sweeney shrieked at her. 'Get three jars filled and put them into the spare bed.'

'I'm sorry to be such a nuisance, Mrs Sweeney.'

'Ah, girl, you're never a nuisance. It's only that it's a while since anyone laid down in that bed.'

'Is there a train from Fermoy in the mornings? To Cork, I mean.'

'There is of course. Sit down by that range now.'

I did as I was bidden and a moment later heard Mrs Sweeney upbraiding her husband in the scullery. 'Are you drunk or what,' she was expostulating in a loud, furious whisper, 'bringing that one here? Couldn't you have told her we were full up?' Mr Sweeney attempted some reply but his wife cut it short by calling him a fool. 'God knows the tale she'll carry back to England with her. Mind what you say to her now.'

I was still trying to warm myself at the range when Mr Derenzy entered the kitchen some time later. He clearly was not pleased to see me there and was unable to disguise his irritation when I said I had missed the train. Later, when I mentioned your name in the course of conversation at the supper table, he dropped his knife with a clatter. Appearing to share this uneasiness, the Sweeneys consumed their food with unnatural interest. They meticulously examined the contents of their plates and did their best to keep a desultory conversation going. There hadn't been snow in Lough for fifteen years, I was told, and to fill another silence I made a similar effort myself: I said I lived in the same town in Dorset that Anna Quinton had come from. Mr Derenzy, who was aware of that, nodded over his food. Mr Sweeney remarked that he couldn't quite place the person I was referring to, and I explained that she was the Anna Quinton of the Famine. 'Haunt Hill is called after her, Mr Sweeney. And it was she who planted the mulberry orchard at Kilneagh.'

'Would you credit that? Well, that beats Banagher!'

Since this slight interest had been shown, I described the house she had grown up in. It was interesting, I said, that your mother had been connected with the Woodcombe family too. But my voice faltered, for what I was saying suddenly seemed absurd to me. 'I didn't realize,' I said instead, 'that my cousin had left Kilneagh.'

The shallow-cheeked maid sniffed into the sleeve of her overall and was at once told to be quiet by Mrs Sweeney, who informed me that the girl had a terrible cold.

'We're destroyed with colds this winter,' Mr Sweeney affirmed, but the girl hadn't a cold. Just for a moment she had wept.

When the meal came to an end Mr Derenzy slipped away and Mr Sweeney went to serve in the bar. After they'd washed up the dishes Mrs Sweeney and the maid put on wellington boots and left the kitchen to attend to livestock in the yard. I had offered to help with the dishes and the animals, but Mrs Sweeney had been adamant that I shouldn't lift a finger. I was sitting by the range when the limping man who had passed through the mill-yard entered the kitchen, whistling the same tune he had been whistling that morning.

'I'm Johnny Lacy,' he said. 'I met you two summers ago. Would you remember?'

'Yes, of course I do.'

He placed a large glass of dark-coloured beer on the table and drew up a chair beside mine.

'I married into the Sweeneys. Did Willie tell you that, by any chance? We're two doors up. The blue-washed cottage.'

'Willie told me you'd married.'

He reached for his glass and drank a mouthful of the beer. He wiped his lips and whistled again.

'D'you know that tune?' he enquired.

'I'm afraid I don't.'

'You can dance "The Rakes of Mallow" to that tune.'

'I see.'

'Mallow's not far from here.'

He drank again. He said:

'You'll take the Cork train in the morning?'

I said I would, and he nodded approvingly. I wondered if he had come into the kitchen at the behest of Mr Derenzy or the Sweeneys, in order to ensure that I didn't decide to dawdle.

'Where d'you think Willie's gone to, Mr Lacy?'

He reached again for his glass. Instead of answering he asked if he might fetch me a drink from the bar, but I said I wasn't thirsty.

'Willie's best left,' he said.

Mrs Sweeney and the maid returned to the kitchen while he was speaking. He stood up at once, and politely insisted that it had been a privilege to meet me again. When he'd gone I asked:

'Whereabouts in Cork is St Fina's, Mrs Sweeney? Where Josephine works now?'

She was sitting down at the table, pulling off her wellington boots. Still wearing her green overall, on which a residue of snow was rapidly dissipating, the shallow-cheeked girl clattered buckets in the sink, washing them out. Instead of immediately answering my question, Mrs Sweeney said that the snow was heavier than ever. She mentioned an abandoned motor-car and said it would need to be towed home by a tractor in the morning.

'I would like to see Josephine. In case she heard from my cousin.'

'St Fina's is on the Bandon road, outside the city. The thing is, miss, I think your cousin would want to be on his own.'

'But, Mrs Sweeney —'

'There's things you wouldn't want to disturb, girl.'

The early hours of that night passed slowly by.

I lay in a bed that felt faintly damp in spite of Mrs Sweeney's hot-water bottles. I lay there in a nightdress she had lent me, but I did not sleep. I stared into the darkness, wondering what things were better left undisturbed, and what tale they feared I might carry back to England. Had Mr Derenzy told them I was to have your child? Did all of them know where you were and not wish me to know also because I would trap you into a marriage?

Dwelling upon these doubts and speculations, I wearied myself into an uneasy sleep and dreamed you were showing me the estuary at Cork again. Then suddenly it was different: I was showing you Woodcombe Park. In sunshine, by the mock-Roman summer-house, you put your arms around me, you said you loved me and always would. Among the yew trees there were people in colourful clothes: all over the lawns they were scattered, the Professor and Mrs Gibb-Bachelor, Agnes Brontenby and your friends, Ring and de Courcy. Cynthia was eating a pear and Mavis was with Hopeless Gibbon, and old Dove-White was having his burnt clothes mended by the waiter from the Café Bon Accueil. The mullioned windows of the town were beautiful, you said, and when I led you from room to room in Woodcombe Park you said that they were beautiful also.

'Lemonade!' your small headmaster cried, hurrying in the garden. 'You've never become a manufacturer of lemonade!' Your mother laughed, and so did mine; my father said our prayers had been answered. Aunt Pansy took Mr Derenzy's arm, and Father Kilgarriff said it was only in a dream he'd been unfrocked. 'That's what I'm trying to tell you,' you said. 'I'd never let you cry. It's only in a dream that you cried in the fields.' The shadows stretched out before the sun set on the horizon, the shadows of the yew trees and the people in their colourful clothes. 'It's heaven here,' you explained because the pillars and the windows of Woodcombe Park had become golden in the golden sunlight. *That's* where you'd been, you explained: wandering in the places I'd told you about, the rectory and the town and the gardens of Woodcombe Park. No point in staying in a ruin, you explained, and we stood in the mulberry orchard that Anna Quinton had copied. 'How elegant England is!' you said. 'Not frightening like Kilneagh!' Then you took my hand and we walked among the people at the party.

When I awoke, the first flickers of dawn were appearing around the curtain at the room's single window. It was a shock to find myself there after the vividness of my dream and as the realities of the day before pressed in upon me I felt tired and melancholy, and longed to sleep again, to go on dreaming. I listened to the early-morning noises and finally pulled the curtain back, spreading a weak morning twilight into the room. I washed and dressed, and at a quarter-past eight went down to the kitchen.

Mr Derenzy had already left for the mill. Mr Sweeney exuded an odour of petrol: he had been working with a tractor in an effort to haul out of a ditch the motor-car his wife had mentioned the night before. Consuming sausages and bacon, he informed me that the snow had stopped falling at five minutes past midnight. He'd been in the yard at the time, dumping crates of bottles. The wind had dropped and in no time at all a galaxy of stars had appeared in the sky.

'We'll make you up sandwiches for your journey,' Mrs Sweeney said. 'A couple of ham and a couple of jam. You'll be as right as rain for the day then.'

'You'll enjoy yourself on the train,' said Mr Sweeney. 'Aren't you the lucky girl to be going back to England?'

Later that morning I said good-bye to both of them. 'Good-bye so,' said Mr Sweeney, wiping an oily palm on his trousers. 'That's interesting what you told us about the place in England.'

'Go back on the steamer today, girl,' Mrs Sweeney urged in a low voice. She clenched my hand and seemed about to say something else, but did not do so. They would accept no money from me.

The shallow-faced maid was given the task of accompanying me to Driscoll's shop, where a lift to Fermoy on an outside car had been arranged for me. In cold sunlight, which the fallen snow reflected and intensified, we stood together outside the grocer's shop and in a moment or two a woman who introduced herself as Mrs Driscoll came out and said we'd be warmer waiting inside since the horse was still being harnessed out at the back. She offered us biscuits from a glass-topped tin, one of a number which ran in a row along the counter. She repeated what I had been told already: that there hadn't been snow in Lough for fifteen years.

The horse and cart rattled over the ice of the yard at the back of the shop, and someone shouted out that it was ready. I said good-bye to Mrs Driscoll and gave the maid a threepenny piece.

'Oh, miss, miss,' she cried, her squinting eyes watery with gratitude, and then she hurried me to the car.

'Hold on to the rail, miss,' the driver ordered. 'I don't want the old horse to go down.'

Obediently, I did as I was bidden and at a very slow pace we made the journey to Fermoy railway station.

5

The nun's eyes blinked rapidly behind spectacles. The spectacles were so embedded, so tightly held in place, that they might have been there to inflict pain. Her teeth were crowded, jutting from her mouth when she spoke.

'We don't know why you've come,' she said.

'To ask if I might talk to Josephine.'

I stood with the nun in the hall of St Fina's, a huge expanse of brown and cream tiles, freshly washed, still smelling of Jeyes' Fluid.

A wide pitchpine staircase, gleaming with linoleum, rose gently and then sharply formed an angle. This linoleum bore a pattern of greens and reds and blues, faded now to a nondescript speckling. The walls were nondescript also, an oatmeal shade that did not catch the eye. The hall was empty of furniture.

Beads jangled as the nun shifted her weight from one foot to the other. 'Better it would be,' she said, 'to write a letter.'

'There isn't time to write a letter. It's very important.'

'Excuse me then.'

She went away, her black shoes silent on the tiles. She disappeared through a door, which she softly closed behind her. Another nun descended the stairs with rags and a tin of polish in her hand. She smiled at me and said good-morning.

More than twenty minutes went by before Josephine entered the hall. She looked different in her lay sister's clothes, less pretty than in the uniform she'd worn before. Breathlessly, as if she'd been running, she spoke before I could.

'I couldn't think who it was who'd come.'

'I'm sorry. I didn't mean to alarm you.'

'Did someone tell you I was here? Are you in Cork on a visit, miss?'

'Do you know where my cousin is, Josephine?'

'Oh no, miss. No, no.' The worry in her voice was an echo of Aunt Pansy's and Mr Derenzy's. I remembered the moment when the Sweeneys' maid had wept.

'Do you think he's in Ireland, Josephine?'

'He didn't say to me, miss. He didn't say he intended to leave the mill.'

She fidgeted with a dish-cloth she held. The cloth was blue and white. It had a damp look, as if she had been drying dishes with it.

'I came here to find him, Josephine. I came all this way.'

She nodded, and then said she should not have gone to Kilneagh that day, leaving your mother alone. Abruptly she turned and hurried from the hall, and as she did so the nun with glasses descended the stairs, holding out a charity box.

'If you could help us at St Fina's,' she said.

Distractedly, I found a coin and pushed it at the slot in the box. I would have run after Josephine if the nun hadn't arrived. I still tried to, but she had already disappeared and the nun with the glasses shook her head. She opened the hall door, drawing back bolts which she had secured in place when she'd admitted me. She blinked again and smiled, the crowded teeth bursting from her face.

'Josephine's not at peace yet,' she said.

'At peace?'

There was no reply. The door closed and I walked away from the sprawling mansion that might once have been the pride of a local family and was now a convent institution. I passed down a long, straight avenue, not at all like the avenue at Kilneagh, being open to fields on either side. An elderly man, poorly dressed, emerged from a gate-lodge. It was a lovely day, he said, touching his cap. 'Thank God for that, miss.'

I returned to the Shandon Boarding House. *Willie will look after me*, I had written in the note I had left behind in the rectory. *Please do not worry*. I wrote a further letter now, as humbly as I could, requesting forgiveness and protesting repentance. But I did not give the address of the boarding house and I didn't reveal that you had not been at Kilneagh.

I walked about the streets, half hoping that I'd meet you, that suddenly you'd be there. Brooding, not knowing what to do, no longer praying, I wept and often could not cease. The weather remained cold, but it did not snow again.

In Thompson's Café, surrounded by warm-cheeked country-women and men gossiping in their sing-song city voices, I dawdled through those two afternoons, preferring to be there than in the dour boarding house. The steaminess and gaslight made the café cheerful, and sometimes I would close my eyes and pretend that you were pushing your way through the crowds to where I sat. 'John Gilbert's marvellous,' a woman at my table remarked to her companion when once I pretended so. I opened my eyes and there were bronze chrysanthemums on top of a basket of shopping and a cherry falling from the cake the other woman ate. It was extraordinary that people did not guess at my misery, that the punishment I suffered did not show in my face.

No children played in the playground, but a light shone from the two schoolroom windows. I pushed open the door and walked down a passage. 'Yes?' Miss Halliwell called out while my knuckles were still raised to rap on the panels of the door to the schoolroom.

Among the maps and charts, the table she sat at stacked with exercise-books, the schoolteacher was younger than I had imagined. You had given me the impression of a woman in middle age: Miss Halliwell was not yet that.

'Oh yes, I do so very well remember Willie. Please sit down.'

I sat on the edge of a battered desk. I explained how I had come from England only to find that you had disappeared, that all I could think to do was to ask people you had mentioned if they had news of you.

'Willie's no longer at his mill?'

'No.'

'Ah . . .'

The exhalation was soft. Behind the pile of exercise-books there was a daydream in Miss Halliwell's eyes.

'I only wondered,' I began, 'if perhaps you'd heard something here in Cork. Willie pointed out this schoolroom once. There was just a chance you might have heard something.'

'Ah, no.' Miss Halliwell smiled distantly. She ran a thin fore-finger around the edge of a text-book, at the same time turning her head away and keeping it quite still, as if posing for a portrait.

'I used to feel sick at heart,' she said, 'when I thought about what had happened to that boy. It made me sick at heart, that fearful tragedy and all it left behind.'

'Miss Halliwell, is there anyone else you can think of who might know?'

'His mother was a drunkard. Every day the child would walk home to that. No matter how well he had recovered there was always his mother's selfishness to remind him.'

'I feel that no one is telling me the truth. I feel there's something being hidden. Even Josephine —'

'Josephine?'

'The housemaid the Quintons had.'

'Oh yes, a housemaid brought him up.' She spoke bitterly, the dreaminess gone from her face. It had been horrible, she said, a child alone with a mother who was given up to drink, with only a housemaid to look after him. 'Can you blame him for going away?

Can you blame him for leaving this miserable country and starting life afresh? Perhaps we should all do that.'

I stood up. Miss Halliwell had no idea what I was talking about when I said that something was being hidden. She knew nothing about your whereabouts; I apologized for disturbing her.

'Is there some reason why you should communicate so urgently with your cousin?'

'Yes, there is.'

'You haven't told me.'

'It doesn't matter now. I've been a nuisance to you. I'm sorry, Miss Halliwell.'

'I loved him, I dearly loved him. That isn't easy, you know.'

I didn't know that; you hadn't told me; perhaps you hadn't known yourself. Miss Halliwell said:

'I met your cousin on the street one day. I invited him to tea, but he did not wish to come. No, don't go yet.' Again there was the soft exhalation of her breath. 'Of course that boy must start afresh. This country has fallen to pieces since they had their revolution. Gunmen run it now.'

'I don't know what to do, Miss Halliwell. I am going to have Willie's baby.'

'Gunmen,' Miss Halliwell repeated, and then abruptly stopped.

'That's why I came back,' I said.

A horse and cart went by in Mercier Street. A contortion twisted the features that you had once likened to a wilted flower.

'Willie's baby,' I repeated.

'My God . . .'

'If Josephine had still been in the house in Windsor Terrace I might have stayed there and waited for him.'

'What on earth are you talking about?'

'I have very little money, Miss Halliwell. I have lodgings in a place where they make me pay every morning before I leave the house. Soon I shall be destitute.'

'How dare you come here in this manner.'

'I know I shouldn't have. I'm sorry.'

'You come here to beg, a child I have never seen before, saying you are Willie Quinton's cousin –'

'I am his cousin. And I am not begging.'

'It's a lie, what you say about a baby.' Her hand reached out and grasped my wrist. 'You speak of other people's lies but you are telling lies yourself.'

'No, it isn't a lie, Miss Halliwell.'

The grip on my wrist tightened. In her faded face the school-teacher's lips were drawn back in distaste, and when she spoke a fine mist of saliva moistened my forehead.

'I've seen boys in this schoolroom growing into sniggering louts. Willie was never like that. He was a special child, who was led astray.'

'Please let me go, Miss Halliwell.'

She withdrew her hand from my wrist. The anger had ebbed from her face, leaving it white and puckered. She looked away, and for a moment held her head quite still, as she had before. I left her, crossing the wooden floor to the door.

'I hope you suffer,' Miss Halliwell said. 'For all your life you deserve to suffer.'

I passed the shop windows we had passed together, the Turkish delight shop, the façade of the Victoria Hotel, brightly lit. I remembered the beggarwoman you had so harshly turned away, and the seagulls above our heads. By the river it was bitterly cold. In the sunshine of that summer we'd watched the men painting the ironwork of their cargo vessels. We'd lingered on all our walks.

Darkly the river slurped now, an oily sheen gleaming in the moonlight. Had I been absurd, when that summer was over, to imagine in the rectory and at school that we might be married? I had imagined so very clearly your mother and your aunts in the church, my father guiding us through the service, my wedding dress with a shade of yellow in it. We would sing Psalm 23, I'd thought, and afterwards we would be together for ever.

Slowly I walked along the quay. What courage your mother had possessed to draw a sleeve back and expose those vulnerable arteries throbbing beneath the skin, to take the blade from the coloured paper that wrapped it, to bear the pain, the sliver of metal slipping home. In a month or so the condition of my body would be apparent to everyone who saw me; I could not melt away as you and Josephine had. I wished you might know that I stood above the cold river, but I knew I would not be granted even that. And then I wished I had your mother's courage.

I turned and began the journey back to the boarding house. A man almost as small as a dwarf paid me some attention which I shook off, telling him to go away. But he was beside me again before I reached the front door, bobbing his head at me, not quite plucking at the sleeve of my coat, although his fingers made a plucking motion in the air. His eyes were eager, darting over my features.

'Please go away,' I repeated, and it was only then that I noticed he was attempting to give me an envelope. I took it from him. The note it contained read:

Mr Lanigan of Lanigan & O'Brien, Solicitors and Commissioners for Oaths, would ask you to call upon him at eleven o'clock tomorrow morning. There followed the address of Lanigan and O'Brien's offices and brief directions as to how to reach them.

'I'm sorry I spoke like that,' I said, wearily, to the man. The invitation he brought me in no way raised my hopes or expectations; it seemed impossible that anything good would happen now. 'I'm sorry,' I said again.

The man did not reply.

6

'That was Declan O'Dwyer, Marianne. Without the gift of speech. Willie may perhaps have told you.'

'Do you know where Willie is, Mr Lanigan?'

'No, Marianne, I do not.'

A brown suit draped the shape that had reminded you of a pyramid. A fresh, polka-dotted bow-tie was like a butterfly poised on the incline of Mr Lanigan's neck. He smiled invitingly, offering me refreshment.

'No, no,' I said. 'No, really, Mr Lanigan.'

'We have a fine fruit cordial, or sherry if you should prefer it. Declan O'Dwyer would be honoured to bring us in a tray.'

An ebony ruler, raised to strike the wall as a summons for Declan O'Dwyer, was delicately returned to the solicitor's blotting-pad.

The blotting paper, as yet hardly marked with ink, was blue. There was sealing-wax on the desk also, long sticks in red and black and green, and rubber bands in a brass container.

'Dear Marianne, I am glad you did not elude us. You mentioned your boarding house to the good Mrs Sweeney, otherwise we might have had a mischief finding you.'

His tone was sympathetic. His tiny, twinkling eyes moved sympathetically over my features. He was the only person who appeared to like me, or at least to welcome me, since I had made my ill-fated journey back to Ireland. His sympathy, and the concern in his face, caused me to weep. I turned my head away to dry my tears and when I could speak I told him how I had visited Josephine in her convent institution, and Miss Halliwell in her school. No one would talk about you, I said; no one had helped me. I spoke of the rectory and the calamity it would be if I gave birth to a baby among my father's parishioners. I even told him about how miserable I had been in Switzerland, my unhappiness increased by the Professor's lecherous pursuit of me. As I finished he rapped on the wall with his ruler and briskly ordered coffee and toasted crumpets when his mute clerk entered the office.

'You have upset yourself considerably,' he softly chided me when the man had gone. 'Dear child, you look exceedingly ill.'

'I am not ill.'

He nodded ponderously. His smile had faded a little.

'I have to tell you, Marianne, that a wire has been received in Kilneagh from your parents. They are naturally most concerned.'

Declan O'Dwyer returned with the coffee and the toasted crumpets. Mr Lanigan's eyes were beadily contemplative, a neat hand still gripped the ebony ruler. When the door had closed behind his clerk he spoke again. He questioned me closely, wishing to know if I could be certain beyond all doubt that my condition was as I had stated; if I had visited a doctor, which I had not; if I had calculated when the child would be born; if I was sure I did not feel unwell.

Impatiently, I brushed all this aside.

'People are keeping something from me. I know they are and so do you, Mr Lanigan.'

He did not reply. He sipped his coffee and divided a crumpet into quarters. When he spoke he ignored what I had said.

'A wire has been sent back to the rectory to say you have safely arrived here. Please let me send another to say you are forthwith returning, Marianne. And please do drink that coffee.'

He smiled coaxingly at me, two rows of teeth like pearls decorating his face. I said:

'I have written them a letter. They will receive that also, in a day or two. I cannot return there.'

I stirred the skin that had formed on the coffee's surface. I tried to eat part of my crumpet. I felt more confused than I had before our conversation had begun.

'I do not belong there now,' I said.

The crumpet had made my fingers sticky. I wiped them on a handkerchief. Mr Lanigan continued to smile at me.

'Belong, Marianne?'

'I do not belong in Woodcombe Rectory any more.'

The smile began to fade again, but his voice had not ceased to be concerned and friendly. He said:

'I have summoned you here so that you may hear a proposition, but before you do so I most earnestly entreat you to return to Woodcombe Rectory. Of course it will be painful for your mother and your father. Of course it will be hard for them to hold their heads up, but even so I would beg you to return to England.'

'I would like to hear your proposition, Mr Lanigan.'

The smile went completely. The coffee tray was pushed to one side. Mr Lanigan, too, wiped his fingers on a handkerchief. Quietly he said he was disappointed, then drawing a sustaining breath continued:

'I am an intermediary in what follows, Marianne. I am passing on to you what I have been bidden to pass on. I do not approve the wisdom of this message. You understand, Marianne?'

'Yes.'

'Well then.' He paused again. 'Well then indeed, Marianne.' He pursed his lips, reluctant to continue, meticulously observing me for any sign that might betray a change of mind. He sighed. 'Well then, Marianne, I am to say that if you should remain adamant in the position you have adopted, and provided there is no legal objection on the part of your father – who has every right so to object – then without prejudice, and the arrangement being in no way binding, and on the understanding that it may be terminated by your benefactress at will, your cousin's Aunt Fitzeustace will take you in. I mention his Aunt Fitzeustace since it is she who has communicated with me and who is, I believe, generally in charge in that household at Kilneagh. Neither she nor her sister condones; that is to be made clear. And you would be expected to make a fair contribution, in so far as your condition permits, to the labour involved in various household tasks.'

I did not say anything. I could not because it was during this long speech of the solicitor's, without warning or relevance to what he was saying, that the truth crept into my mind. With startling abruptness I shared with him, and with Mr Derenzy and the Sweeneys, with Johnny Lacy and Josephine and Aunt Pansy, what they sought to keep from me. Of all the people who knew you only Miss Halliwell and I had been outside that circle and now Miss Halliwell was alone. Until someone told her, you would be the same in her eyes as you had always been: in mine, in a matter of seconds, you had acquired a different identity.

'So you see, Marianne,' Mr Lanigan finished up.

I should have been afraid but was not. I should have wept but I had wept enough already. I felt calm, without the desire to exclaim or to make any comment whatsoever. Nor did I seek to question Mr Lanigan: there was no need for that. I was aware only of sensing that my reason for refusing to return to the rectory was not that I would bring disgrace with me. A different reality hung like a weight in the solicitor's office, and I understood perfectly that for my sake you had sought, as best you could, to destroy our love. I had not permitted you to, but I did not believe you blamed me for that now. Our love was still there, wherever either of us might be. I could feel it all around me in that office, part of the truth that made everything different.

'Now, there is another matter, Marianne.'

The sharp little eyes again scrutinized my features, perhaps even penetrated these thoughts.

'It is simply this, Marianne. Your cousin visited me before he went away. Certain documents were drawn up which may or may not have led me to deduce that your cousin intended to be absent from this country for more than a little time. I must, without comment, place the deduction before you. I must also, since such is my duty, reveal to you that should you find yourself in need – and I quote that form of words, Marianne – should find yourself in need, certain monies will be made available to you.'

There was a pause, and further scrutiny.

'Your cousin made provision for an eventuality of which I myself remained in ignorance. It is clear to me now that he had the possibility of your present circumstances in mind. I am authorized, Marianne, to implement the agreed form of words, and it would seem I must decree that you do clearly find yourself in need.'

Mr Lanigan went on talking. He made a final effort to persuade me to return to England, but after a time I heard no more than the sound of his voice, a rush of words without comprehension. More than ever, Kilneagh was a fearsome place and yet there was nowhere else I wished to be. No matter how grim that half-ruined house was, no matter how much nobody there wanted me, it was where I belonged because you had belonged there also. Every detail of my existence, every vein in my body, every mark, every intimate part of me, loved you with a tenderness that made me want to close my eyes and faint. Every second of my twenty years of life had to do with you, and I thanked God for the anxiety of our grandparents in India when they had worried so about your mother. Their anxiety had given us our summer and our love; it had given us our child. At Kilneagh I would wait for you. I would exist in whatever limbo fate intended, while you wandered the face of the earth. Solitude claimed you: I understood that.

'I did not read of what occurred,' I said to Mr Lanigan, surprising him with an interruption unrelated to what he was saying. 'Because of course I was in Switzerland.'

He nodded slowly, his flow of words abruptly halted, not taken up again. In the rectory that occurrence would have been read about in the newspaper, my father shaking his head over the mystery of it, my mother failing to connect one name with another. 'Rudkin,' you had said, and had described the man, a hand cupped round the cigarette he lit, his genial salute as he stood at the street corner.

IMELDA

I

Beside the ruins a picnic was spread out on a tablecloth. There were Marmite sandwiches and strawberry-and-cream cake and little iced scones decorated with hundreds and thousands. A fire had been made to boil the tea kettle, and there was milk in a corked bottle that had to be kept in the shade. There was lemonade which Imelda had helped Father Kilgarriff to make from yellow crystals that morning. Her mother wore her new flowery dress. It was Imelda's ninth birthday.

Aunt Fitzeustace had given her a dragon brooch with a broken pin, which had been in the Quinton family for donkey's years, so she said; and Aunt Pansy had given her two bars of Fry's chocolate, each composed of brightly coloured creams of different flavours. Mr Derenzy, who had walked over to the ruins from his office in the mill, had given her sixpence, and Father Kilgarriff a green wooden top.

When the picnic was over the remains of the cake and the iced scones were left on the tablecloth and everyone stood around, endeavouring to fly the kite that had been the gift of Imelda's mother. It was Father Kilgarriff who eventually got it to catch in the wind, running with it above his head while Aunt Pansy paid out the string from the short stick it was wound around. The red and blue triangle rose high above the trees and the ruins, swooping and diving in the sky while Father Kilgarriff showed Imelda how to jerk the string and keep it taut. The pull of the wind was like something alive between her fingers.

Two of the spaniels lazed on the grass, displaying no interest in the excitement engendered by the flying of the kite. The other dogs had preferred to remain in the cool of the old dairy. Strictly speaking, there had been no need to make a fire to boil the kettle on since the teapot could easily have been carried from the orchard wing, but Imelda had specially asked for it. Picnics always had fires, she'd said, and milk in a corked bottle instead of a milk jug. No one had disagreed.

In a whispering, private voice Mr Derenzy spoke to Aunt Pansy about some trouble he was experiencing with the new young traveller from Midleton Sacks. 'Insolent,' he reported. 'And soil enough behind his fingernails to grow potatoes in.' Aunt Fitzeustace delved into her commodious handbag, searching for her cigarettes.

The kite lost height. The string that had been pulling so excitingly through Imelda's grasp slackened and went limp. Father Kilgarriff took the white stick from Aunt Pansy and as swiftly as he could wound the string on to it. He tried to jerk the kite this way and that, but it wouldn't obey him. It drooped and plunged. It fell into a tree.

'Will it be broken?' Imelda asked. 'It's only made of little rods.'

'Ah, no, no.'

Nor was it. When Father Kilgarriff had coaxed it down they could find no damage of any kind, and when it flew again it soared so far away that soon it was hardly even a dot in the sky. Mr Derenzy and Aunt Pansy took a turn at guiding it and feeling the tug of the wind through the string, and then Imelda's mother ran with it, her new dress pretty in the sunlight, her hair tidy in its bun. 'No, I'll not bother, dear,' Aunt Fitzeustace said.

'A kite's probably the nicest thing a person can have,' Imelda said when the string was wound up for the last time.

She drank more lemonade and the others drank more tea. She had woken up in the early morning and found the kite, wrapped in brown paper, at the foot of her bed. She hadn't guessed what it was because it was just a long, bundly parcel, none of the parts put together yet. It was Father Kilgarriff who had done that, after breakfast at the kitchen table.

As she drank her lemonade, Imelda could still see the kite vividly in her mind's eye, its sudden swirling movement, and the faces gazing up at it, hands slanting as a shade against the sun. The fuzzy grey-red hair of Mr Derenzy, Father Kilgarriff's anxious eyes as he guided the string, her mother's tiny figure in her flowery dress: together with the faraway kite and the clear blue sky they made a picture, with Aunt Fitzeustace and the spaniels as still as ornaments.

They sat in the dwindling heat of the day telling stories, which Imelda loved, and it was nearly seven o'clock before everything was gathered up. 'You're a big girl now,' Mr Derenzy said, a form of leave-taking. Mr O'Mara the postman had said the same thing when he'd come into the kitchen with the *Cork Examiner* and the *Irish Times* that morning; and Father Kilgarriff had said it, and so had Philomena, Aunt Fitzeustace's and Aunt Pansy's maid, who had forgotten what age she was herself but guessed it might be seventy-eight. 'It's nice to be nine,' Aunt Pansy had said. 'I remember it was nice being nine.'

Imelda said good-bye to Mr Derenzy and thanked him for coming to her birthday. Then she returned with her mother and the others to the orchard wing, each of them carrying something from the picnic, the spaniels trailing behind. They did not pass through the ruins but made a semicircle around them, arriving in the cobbled yard through the archway at the back. Immediately a commotion began: barking and snarling, the dogs rushed from the old dairy; hens scurried out of their path, geese screeched. Father Kilgarriff beat the dogs off and made his way to the orchard to drive in for milking the household's single cow. 'Oh, do behave yourselves!' cried Aunt Fitzeustace, beating at the dogs also, with her handbag. 'Do tell them to behave themselves, Pansy.' Aunt Pansy did as she was bidden, mildly addressing the obstreperous animals, telling them they were terrible.

'I wish it could have lasted for ever,' Imelda said a little later in her bedroom, after she'd repeated the Lord's Prayer to her mother. 'It was a lovely day.'

'Yes, it was.'

Her mother bent to kiss her, and then pulled the curtains to, excluding the evening light.

'It's nice having a birthday in summertime,' Imelda said. She searched for other things to say, not wanting the conversation to cease. Sometimes her mother told her about the time before the fire, what the house and the garden had been like then, even though she'd never known it herself. She spoke of a scarlet drawing-room and the scent of sweet-peas wafting into it in summer, and of the portraits of a man and his wife, Quintons who belonged to the past. But tonight her mother did not seem inclined to linger.

'You go to sleep now,' she urged, and kissed her again.

Lying with her eyes open, Imelda wondered about the portraits for a moment, trying to imagine them. Then she thought about the two pictures of Venice in the dining-room, the faded green gondola drawn up by a quayside, the domed church near a bridge. It was Aunt Pansy who had told her the boat was called a gondola, and Father Kilgarriff had explained that Venice had canals instead of streets. 'I'd love to go there,' she'd said, and he had said who knows, one day she might.

She thought about the bowl of wax fruit on the sideboard, and the silver teapots that did not gleam, the empty decanters, the nutcrackers that were used at Christmas. There were eleven mahogany chairs in the dining-room, with tapestry on them that was as worn as the carpet. The pattern on the wallpaper had disappeared but if you very slightly pushed to one side the little picture by the door you could see that the pattern had been of lilies, bunches tied with ribbon. There was a mirror, too heavy to push, between the windows, and another picture, of a waterfall. There were yellow vases, and plates and candlesticks; the clock on the mantelpiece had always been stopped at five to six. On the staircase wall the pictures were all uninteresting, none of them coloured; the stuffed peacock in the hall should have been thrown out years ago, Aunt Fitzeustace said.

Sleep did not come. 'Count the dogs,' was Aunt Fitzeustace's advice. 'That's what I do.' Dandy and Rifleman, Brigid the blind setter, Ginger and Pickles the spaniels, Murphy the greyhound, Achilles, Clonakilty, Blackguard and Sam and Maisie Jane. Murphy had been left in Lough by the tinkers, the priest who'd owned Maisie Jane had died, Clonakilty was the name of a town. In the past there'd been others: a Pomeranian and a Kerry Blue, terriers called Spratts and Bee, and Ludwig, a three-legged elkhound. Imelda counted them all, and then the fourteen hens, and the geese.

A week ago, when it had thundered, the dogs had barked in fear but the hens hadn't seemed to mind, objecting only to the rain. Philomena had sought refuge from the lightning beneath her bed. Father Kilgarriff had attempted to calm the dogs and Aunt Pansy had several times crawled in to where the maid had hidden herself, with cups of milky tea. 'You go, Imelda,' she'd said the last time.

It was because of the lingering excitement of her birthday that she could not sleep: at suppertime Aunt Fitzeustace had said she was still excited, and Father Kilgarriff that that was only to be expected. Aunt Pansy had added she'd never been able to sleep herself on Christmas Eve. They would all be in the sitting-room now, a fire lit because no matter what time of year it was Aunt Fitzeustace said the orchard wing was draughty. Aunt Pansy would be pressing flowers, Father Kilgarriff reading. Imelda's mother, still in her new dress, would be making an entry in her diary, something about the picnic. Aunt Fitzeustace would be smoking cigarette after cigarette and throwing the burnt-out matches into the fire. Sometimes Aunt Fitzeustace read a seed catalogue but usually she just smoked. In the twilight of the gaunt sitting-room the whiskered countenance of William Gladstone would seem grimmer than it did by day, and the ticking of the grandfather clock more solemn.

'Well then, count the mulberry trees,' Aunt Fitzeustace had also adjured. 'Start in the west corner, close your eyes and each tree will come into your mind.' But Aunt Pansy advised that the best thing was just to think of something nice. Aunt Pansy and Aunt Fitzeustace were so different that when she was younger Imelda had not guessed they were sisters: it was her mother who had explained to her that they were. Aunt Pansy was forever passing the jam and butter to Father Kilgarriff or to Imelda's mother or to her sister. She was forever slipping away from the dining-table to pick up Philomena's frilled cap when it fell to the floor or on to the roast meat on the sideboard. Aunt Fitzeustace never noticed such things. Her lips were tobacco-stained, her dog's head tie-pin was often upside down, and the grey hair beneath her old tweed hat was untidily grasped together. She cut the grass and manured the shrubs, and had a passion for looking after the motor-car, hosing it down or polishing the upholstery and the paintwork.

'Thirteen,' Imelda said, and could not continue. There was the mulberry tree that was shaped like a crow and the lopsided one and the one that never bore fruit. There was the one with its roots coming out of the ground and the one with sour berries; there was the ragged one, like something tattered in the wind, and the nine that were all the same, in a row down the side of the orchard. But it was too difficult to try to see the others.

Imelda Quinton is my name, Ireland is my nation. A burnt house is my dwelling place, Heaven's my destination. At the new convent in

Lough, a cement building with a white statue of the Virgin Mary in front of it, there had been a craze for the rhyme. She had written it on the inside of the cover of her transcription book, the words sloping neatly on the orange surface. 'Heaven?' Teresa Shea had said. 'You'll not be going to heaven, Imelda Quinton. How could you?' Teresa Shea was big and awkward and stupid, well known at the convent for the tartness of her tongue: Sister Mulcahy said to take no notice.

Imelda tried not to think about Teresa Shea. Successfully, she pushed the girl's face out of her mind and saw instead the kite soaring in the sky and everyone gazing up at it. In time she slept.

She had a nightmare and her mother came to comfort her. It was the same nightmare as always, the children and the flames. 'Now, now, now, Imelda,' her mother comforted. 'Shh now, pet.'

Long multiplication was taught. Imelda found it difficult and was grateful when the bell rang. The lay teacher, Miss Garvey, hooked up her skirt, for in search of relief it was her habit to loosen it at the beginning of each lesson. Chattering began in the classroom, and fell away to nothing as the girls strapped their satchels and left the convent. Eating liquorice outside Mrs Driscoll's shop when school was over, Teresa Shea remarked:

'There's people says you shouldn't be at the convent, Imelda.'

'Don't be unpleasant, Teresa,' another girl said.

'I'm not being unpleasant.'

'Why shouldn't I be in the convent?' Imelda asked.

'Because you're not a Catholic. Imelda Quinton! God, the nerve of that!'

Teresa Shea laughed and went away, banging her satchel against her legs. The worst thing she'd ever said was to tell little Maevie Cullen that her mother had died on the way to America, where she'd gone to visit an uncle. In fact, it had been true.

'Take no notice of her,' the girl who'd called her unpleasant said.

But as Imelda walked through the village the difficulties with her long multiplication homework, which she'd been anticipating all day, were overshadowed by what had been said. She loved going to the convent and hated it when anything spoiled it for her. She had watched the convent being built, and she had always known she would go there because the Protestant school in the village no longer

156

existed. Everyone was kind to her, the Reverend Mother and Sister Mulcahy and Sister Hennessy, Miss Garvey and the lay sisters. During prayers and Catechism she practised the piano or watched Sister Rowan making bread in the kitchen. Nobody except Teresa Shea minded that she was different because she wasn't a Catholic.

She didn't mind being different herself, not having a First Communion dress, nor rosary beads, not being able to walk in the Corpus Christi procession in Fermoy. She asked forgiveness if she stepped on a snail because Sister Mulcahy had once explained that a snail was just as much God's creature as anything else was. But Imelda knew that a Protestant asking forgiveness, and never being required to say Hail Marys as a penance, was different also. 'Proddy-woddy green-guts,' Teresa Shea had whispered on Imelda's first day at the convent, and once she'd muttered beneath a laugh that Aunt Fitzeustace was peculiar, and had muttered something also about Father Kilgarriff. Imelda knew that strictly speaking he should not be called Father Kilgarriff since he had not been a priest for ages. But that didn't seem important and she didn't consider Aunt Fitzeustace peculiar. 'Heretics,' Teresa Shea muttered beneath her laugh. 'Crowd of bloody heretics.'

Her mother tried to explain. She said that for ever so long, for centuries, the Catholics had been prevented from practising their faith: no wonder there were people like Teresa Shea now. Father Kilgarriff told her about Daniel O'Connell, who had achieved religious freedom for the Catholics without resort to the gun or the sword. Her mother talked about the Mitchelstown Martyrs and the skirmish there had been at Cappoquin in 1915. Once when they were all out for a drive in the car they passed the place where a famous revolutionary had been shot in an ambush: Michael Collins he'd been called. When they went to the seaside at Youghal her mother told her about the priest who had been executed there in 1602 for refusing to renounce his faith. She told her about the English major who had wished to rest his horses at Kilneagh but had been ordered to go away. Her mother said that the revolutionary who'd been killed in the ambush used to visit Kilneagh and that the Quintons had given him money for his revolutionary cause. Her mother had shown her the tree the other man had been hanged from, the man whose tongue was cut out because of his traitorous talk. It was good to see the ivy growing over imperial Ireland, her mother used to say, and on their drives would point at ivied ruins like Kilneagh's and sometimes at houses that were still intact but had become training schools for priests or insane asylums. The pacific Daniel O'Connell was not her mother's hero: she spoke instead of Ireland's fighting men, of the Earls of Tyrone and Tyrconnell who centuries ago had fled into exile, as the survivors of Ireland's lost battles had always fled. Imelda's own father had to remain in a foreign country, unable to return to his mill, and often Imelda tried to imagine him, wondering if he was like the Earls of Tyrone and Tyrconnell. The nuns at the convent spoke of him as a hero, even as somebody from a legend, Finn Mac Cool or the warrior Cuchulainn. 'You're my special Imelda,' Sister Rowan had announced when Imelda first watched her making bread, and she knew that had been said because of her father. 'He will never be forgotten,' Sister Mulcahy had assured her. 'Your father will never be forgotten, Imelda, in Lough or in Fermoy, in all County Cork. He is every day in our prayers. Our Lady will intercede.'

There was a photograph of her father in her mother's bedroom, standing among rows of other boys. It was hard to make out what he looked like, except that his hair was light-coloured, as her own was. He was smiling a little in the photograph, but when she tried to look more closely at his face it became misty. 'Teresa Shea's only jealous,' a girl at the convent had said. 'A father like you have.'

Imelda picked mulberries in the orchard, thinking about a poem Miss Garvey had read out, *The Lake Isle of Innisfree*. It was beautiful, just as beautiful as the lines Father Kilgarriff sometimes quoted from William Shakespeare. *Dropping from the veils of the morning to where the cricket sings*. Softly she repeated the words to herself. *There midnight's all a glimmer, and noon a purple glow*.

In the mulberry orchard the midges began to bite. Fallen apples from the single apple tree lay among the long grass, green cooking apples, too bitter to eat. Was it Jerusalem Sister Mulcahy had said the Earls of Tyrone and Tyrconnell had gone to? Was it Cuchulainn who had sent the headless bodies galloping to his enemy's camp in chariots?

She'd become curious about her father because everyone made such a fuss, Sister Rowan saying Our Lady would intercede and Teresa Shea being jealous. He had very blue eyes, her mother said, and sometimes, just for fun, Imelda pretended he stepped off the bus at Driscoll's shop and she ran up to him because she recognized him. All the girls outside Driscoll's, eating liquorice or Rainbow toffees, went silent. Then Mr Sweeney came out of his garage and Mrs Sweeney appeared at the door of the public house. They waved delightedly, and Imelda walked with her father along the road to Kilneagh and he told her about the places he had travelled to.

He was a hero because his courage and his honour insisted that he should do what he had done: her mother had explained all that. No one, not even Teresa Shea, said it was wrong to get revenge on the Black and Tan who had burnt down Kilneagh. It was not even the beginning of a crime, her mother explained, not when you thought of the massacres and the martyrs, and the cold-blooded murder of the Quintons in the middle of the night.

Because she was curious Imelda went often to her mother's bedroom to look at the photograph. She examined the eyes that were apparently very blue. She wondered what he'd been smiling at. 'Oh, he was the most ordinary little boy when he was your age,' Aunt Fitzeustace said, and Father Kilgarriff remembered that he'd been bad at Latin.

Imelda closed her eyes. Pictures slipped about. The flames devoured the flesh of the children's faces and the flesh of their arms and of their legs, of their stomachs and their backs. Trapped in her bedroom, fat Mrs Flynn wept in panic; smoke filled her lungs, her eyes streamed. The man in the teddy-bear dressing-gown carried his wife down the burning stairs and went in search of his children. Frightened in case they'd been recognized, the soldiers returned. In the yard the gardeners who had come from the gate-lodge quickly died, and then the labradors died and then the stray dogs. The empty gate-lodge became a furnace also. The sound of the motor-car engine died away.

Imelda watched while the wheels of the motor-car were taken off and the car itself placed on wooden blocks in the old dairy. Mr Sweeney had come to do it and stayed all morning in the kitchen talking to Philomena. He said he had lost his arm near the Somme in 1916. 'This time round it's up to Russia,' he predicted. 'You'll never subject the might of Russia, Philomena, whichever side she comes down on.'

She watched while Father Kilgarriff and a man from Fermoy put up an aerial for the wireless Aunt Fitzeustace had bought. It had to be attached to a chimney, and the earth wire had to be attached to a metal rod which the man from Fermoy sank into the ground outside the French windows of the sitting-room. The man explained to Father Kilgarriff about the wet battery and the dry battery and how the wet battery would have to be charged, maybe once a week.

On Sunday evenings there were the national anthems on the wireless and Mr Derenzy remained to hear them after he had taken Aunt Pansy for her Sunday-afternoon walk. Imelda was allowed to stay up to hear them also, but she noticed that her mother didn't take the same interest in the European war as the others did. Aunt Pansy and Mr Derenzy sat in the window alcove and Father Kilgarriff beside the wireless in case it began to crackle or fade. Aunt Fitzeustace, in her usual position among the dogs on the sofa, smoked and beat time with her hand. *Flow gently, Sweet Afton*, it said on her brown and cream-coloured cigarette packets.

'Were you here in the times before the fire, Philomena?' Imelda asked, and Philomena said she had been. Previous to that she'd been Canon Connolly's housekeeper, and when Canon Connolly had died and she'd nowhere to go Aunt Fitzeustace and Aunt Pansy had taken her in. Imelda listened. She'd never heard of Canon Connolly before, and Philomena told her that he had liked to eat an apple in bed and couldn't bear to wear vests. Philomena had a way of laughing whenever she spoke, throwing her head back and displaying her almost toothless mouth.

'Do you remember my father, Philomena?'

'Ah of course I do, child.'

'Did he shoot the Black and Tan? Was that how it was done?'

Philomena inappropriately laughed. She didn't know anything about things like that, she said. She crossed herself.

'Did you know it was Liverpool where the man was, Philomena? It's a harbour town up in the North of England. Ships come in there from all over the world.'

'What's that, child?' Busy with a cabbage, washing it beneath the kitchen tap, Philomena laughed again. She poked a grub out of the cabbage. You wouldn't want to find yourself eating a creature the like of that, she said.

'I think maybe that was how it was done,' Imelda said.

Again Philomena crossed herself. The fire had been terrible, she said. All over Co. Cork people knew about the fire there'd been at Kilneagh, come to that, all over Ireland. She'd heard about it herself the next morning, staying with her sister at Rathcormack.

'No better than ruffians, half them Tans was. Sure, wasn't it an extraordinary thing, that no one took a knife to that scoundrel before?'

'A *knife*? Was the Black and Tan killed with a knife?'

Philomena was vague in her reply, still rinsing the cabbage leaves. The face from the photograph came into Imelda's mind again. She wondered if it had been a knife like the one on the draining-board, Philomena's favourite because it was so sharp, her 'little brown knife' as she called it because of its discoloured handle. Yet it didn't seem quite the right implement because the end of its blade was rounded, not pointed the way it would have to be if you were planning to stick it in someone. It would go into the heart, she supposed, the way you'd aim for the heart with a bullet. But the revolutionary leader who used to visit Kilneagh had been shot through the skull. She could remember her mother saying that.

'Oh, there's a pretty little party,' Mr Lanigan said, arriving in the orchard wing with business to conduct. Whenever he visited Kilneagh Aunt Pansy packed jars of mulberry jam into a cardboard box for him to take back to his family in Cork, and wrapped eggs in newspaper before placing them in the squares of the egg-box. The eggs were for Declan O'Dwyer, his deaf and dumb clerk who Aunt Fitzeustace said was an angel, causing Imelda to imagine a creature with wings. 'And isn't Imelda a most beautiful name?' Mr Lanigan always said. 'Aren't you glad to've been given it?'

According to Father Kilgarriff, she shared the day with the Blessed Imelda Lambertini of Bologna, May 13th. She'd been born more than a month before she was expected and so apparently had the saintly child of Bologna. While not yet twelve years old the Blessed Imelda had experienced a Sacred Host hovering above her head while she knelt in prayer in a Dominican convent. And as that miracle occurred so had her death.

'The income would not cease,' Mr Lanigan was saying when Imelda listened at the sitting-room door, 'if you returned to England, Marianne.'

Her mother said something strange: that when you looked at the map Ireland and England seemed like lovers. 'Don't you think so, Mr Lanigan? Does the map remind you curiously of an embrace? A most extraordinary embrace to throw up all this.'

'Embrace?'

'You think I'm extravagant in my Irish fancies? Father Kilgarriff thinks so, and the others too. Yet I am part of all this now. I cannot help my fervour.'

Imelda moved away from the sitting-room door. In the kitchen she drank some water and played for a moment with the terriers and a sheepdog. She thought of the Blessed Imelda because Mr Lanigan had put her in mind of her namesake. She had told Sister Rowan about the miracle of the Sacred Host and Sister Rowan had listened attentively but had revealed in the end that every Irish nun was familiar with the details of the marvel. In the kitchen Imelda imagined the Host as a wispy outline, no more than a shred of mist. Then she forgot about it and copied out a headline: *Insects have neither lungs nor gills*. Just as she'd finished she heard the voices of Mr Lanigan and her mother in the hall.

'A town called Puntarenas,' Mr Lanigan said, but later when Imelda looked in her atlas for somewhere that sounded like that she was not successful. She knew the conversation had turned to the subject of her father and guessed this town was where he lived. 'I'd say the old Jerries have given him the works by now,' Teresa Shea had ages ago suggested, with a smirk. Imelda had wondered about that, but now she wondered about the town that had been mentioned. She didn't want to ask her mother because her mother would know she'd been listening. She asked Aunt Pansy and Philomena but they said they'd never heard of anywhere that sounded like that. So in the end she did ask her mother, ready to explain that she had overheard by accident, which in a way was true. Her mother didn't reply. Instead she suggested a walk, and at the end of it she pointed at the tree the man had been hanged from, as though her answer lay in that.

'Just an ordinary tree, Imelda. You could pass it by and not know a thing.'

After the hanging there had been the fire and years later, Imelda's mother had explained, there had been the woman who had taken her life in Cork. Imelda had once been shown the house, at the top of the very steep hill. A dentist lived there now: a brass plate outside the hall door said so.

'You can pass by anything and not know, Imelda. I never knew when I walked in the gardens of that great house in England that a girl had gone from there to Kilneagh. She pleaded with her family, but what was it to them that ignorant peasants were dying in another country? There has been too much wretched death in Ireland.'

They walked across the fields together and climbed up Haunt Hill, and her mother told her about how she'd come to Ireland with a single suitcase and stayed in a boarding house she'd been told about by a woman on the street. On another occasion, climbing the hill, her mother said:

'Your father and I never had a chance to get married. That is something you must know, Imelda.'

Her mother went on talking, about a scene that had taken place in the sitting-room of the orchard wing: how her parents had come to take her back to England. 'Arrangements had been made for you to be born in a house in Clapham, which is a place in London where a cousin of my father lived. You would have been born and then left with this woman and her husband, and I would have returned to Woodcombe Rectory, as though nothing much had happened.'

Imelda frowned, in bewilderment and surprise. 'I would not be at Kilneagh?'

'These people in Clapham would have brought you up as their daughter.'

Imelda thought about this visit to Kilneagh of her mother's parents, and the fruitless persuading that had taken place in the gaunt, square sitting-room. A light rain had been falling, she imagined, and outside the French windows the hens had been pecking among the gnarled trees of the mulberry orchard. 'We have made firm arrangements,' the clergyman announced, 'for the child to be born in Clapham.' And Imelda's mother replied by speaking of Irish martyrs and Irish battles, and of the Easter Rising that years ago had taken place. Aunt Fitzeustace and Aunt Pansy passed by the windows, bringing the dogs back from their afternoon walk. And then Philomena was in the orchard with a waterproof coat thrown over her head, calling out to the hens. 'No one could live here!' the clergyman's wife cried in Imelda's imagination. 'This is a terrible place.'

Imelda smiled although her face remained serious. She was aware that her mother's voice was continuing about something else: she did not listen. 'Now, time for tea,' she made Aunt Fitzeustace say on that rainy afternoon, entering the sitting-room with a sponge-cake on a plate, with Aunt Pansy and Father Kilgarriff and all the dogs behind her.

'An old colonel he was,' her mother's voice was saying. 'In India.'

They had reached the shale near the summit of the hill. They scrambled over it, conversation difficult for a while. At the top Imelda said:

'India?'

'If those two old sticks hadn't been anxious my mother and I wouldn't ever have come to Ireland. If they hadn't written that letter your father and I would never have met, and neither you nor I would be in Kilneagh now.'

'Was he nice, the colonel?'

'He was very tall, straight as a die. Oh yes, I always think of them as nice.'

Imelda imagined the tall old colonel sitting down in the Indian heat, in a little Indian pavilion, to write the anxious letter.

'What I mean, Imelda, is that's how things happen. The most important things of all happen by chance.'

Imelda nodded. 'Say we are distinctly worried,' she made the tall man's wife say. 'Tell them to go forthwith to Cork.' Aunt Pansy sometimes said she was distinctly worried. 'I'll do that forthwith,' Mr Derenzy had promised last Sunday, assuring Aunt Fitzeustace about the sharpening of the blades of her mowing machine. In the pavilion a turbaned Indian waved a palm over the two old people to keep them cool and to drive away the mosquitoes.

'No, I must say it, Marianne,' Father Kilgarriff insisted quietly, but with some anger in his voice.

Imelda's mother did not reply. They were in the sitting-room with one of the French windows open. In the mulberry orchard Imelda listened, which was a habit she'd got into.

'She's my child after all, Father.'

'There is bitterness in what you say to her.'

'How could there not be bitterness? I cannot be good like you are, Father. You forgive that bishop who deprived you of your vocation. You forgive that man who came here with his thugs and his petrol cans.'

'That man is dead. In his lifetime I did not forgive him.'

'And do you forgive Willie, Father?'

'That is the saddest thing in all my life.'

'Do you know, my parents have not written me a single word since the day they came here? They have turned their back on me, and do not wish ever even to think of me.'

'You broke your parents' hearts, Marianne. There is that too, you know.'

'I loved my parents, Father.'

'I know, Marianne. And was there anyone, in this house or outside it, who did not urge you to return to England with them?'

'To have my child brought up as someone else's? To have forgotten her existence? To have waited in that rectory until some widower should come along and have me as his housekeeper? I would rather have ended in a work-house.'

'It isn't easy for Imelda to be here. But since you have chosen it, Marianne, don't make it more difficult still. That's all I'm asking.'

There was a silence in the sitting-room. Then Imelda's mother said:

'Destruction casts shadows which are always there: surely you see that, Father? We will never escape the shadows of destruction that pervade Kilneagh.'

'I only wish that, even now, you would take Imelda away from them.'

Her mother replied in a low voice which Imelda couldn't hear. Then she became cross and shouted:

'For God's sake, what kind of an existence do you think he has? In one Godforsaken town after another?'

'There's not much left in anyone's life after murder has been committed. God insists upon that, you know.'

Her mother's anger abated: again she spoke in a voice so low that Imelda could hear only the end of what she said.

'You've been in pain yourself, ever since that night. You could have killed yourself, running with that kite.'

There was something else which Imelda could not hear, and then she crept away. She went to a distant corner of the mulberry orchard and sat down in the warmth, with her back to the trunk of a tree. She watched a bee investigating a rotten berry and then humming busily off, in pursuit of something else. She couldn't understand how Father Kilgarriff might have killed himself flying her kite that day. Again she imagined the boy in the photograph, in one town after another.

'Oh, just writing,' Aunt Fitzeustace said one winter's afternoon, seated at her writing-desk. The grandfather clock wheezed and stuttered before chiming the half-hour. The murky face of Gladstone looked unwell.

'I wrote a letter to my love,' Imelda said.

Aunt Fitzeustace laughed. 'Well, I have no love now.'

'Once you had. Philomena says –'

'Oh, don't listen to Philomena.'

'Philomena says you were married once.'

'Yes, I was married for a very short time.'

'Father Kilgarriff had a love.'

'Did Philomena tell you that too?'

'Teresa Shea did.'

'Well, it doesn't concern Teresa Shea.'

'Wouldn't it be nice if Mr Derenzy married Aunt Pansy?'

'People have said so.'

'Then why doesn't he?'

'Mr Derenzy is governed by his sense of order.'

Aunt Fitzeustace rose and left the sitting-room with a stamped envelope in her hand, ready for Mr O'Mara to collect when he came with the newspapers the next morning. Imelda crossed to the writing-desk and stood by it for a moment, listening to Aunt Fitzeustace's footsteps in the hall. She heard her voice addressing Aunt Pansy and then the sound of the kitchen door closing. She pulled out the two little props that Aunt Fitzeustace had just pushed in. She eased down the heavy mahogany flap and rested it on them. There was a mass of drawers in the desk, horizontal drawers and perpendicular ones, little fluted pillars, and hinged inkwells. There were secret drawers: Imelda had heard Aunt Fitzeustace asking Aunt Pansy to put keys in the one on the right. She had watched, but had not been able to see how it opened.

She pulled out a drawer full of bills, and another with darning cards in it. She read a letter from a shop in Cork, which said the coats had come in, and another from Mr Lanigan, thanking for the hospitality and the mulberry jam, which all his family had enjoyed. Then there was a letter which interested her greatly. Dated many years ago, it was signed *A. M. Halliwell*, and Imelda knew who that was because her mother had often mentioned the name. *What I have heard cannot be true. I did not know until a week today. I am a stranger writing to you, but I ask for assurance that none of it is so. If it is true, it is my duty to tell you that this child should not be given life. In such a child there is the continuation of the tragedy that made the child's father what he is. This is the most evil thing I have ever known of.*

3

Aunt Pansy knitted Balaclava helmets and sent them to the Red Cross. Aunt Fitzeustace said that Mr Lanigan had reported German spies in Cork, people called Winkelmann who ran the glove factory. Father Kilgarriff read aloud from the *Irish Times* of the fall of France. Imelda, in secret moments, continued to listen.

'Sometimes I wish I could be more like him,' her mother said. 'Every breath he draws is painful, yet he resents nothing.'

'He's a man who's made like that,' Aunt Fitzeustace replied. 'I've known him a long time. Before he came to live here someone wrote to me and said he'd been unfrocked, and to tell you the truth I wasn't in the least surprised. It seemed like part of his nature that he should fall foul of some powerful man whose daughter he'd befriended. I remember him as a boy, you know. He used to come out from Lough and do odd jobs for me in the garden. He hated to see anything hurt, even an insect. It was quite natural that he should come back to Kilneagh when everything fell to pieces for him.'

'I wish he didn't think I should have gone away. Or indeed still should go.'

'He can't help believing that in England you would have a better life ahead of you.'

'And you?'

There was the sound of a match scraping on the sandpaper of Aunt Fitzeustace's match-box, and then Aunt Fitzeustace's sigh of satisfaction as she inhaled the smoke. Imelda imagined it billowing from her mouth and nostrils, one leathery hand stroking the head of a dog, the blind setter it would be since the blind setter was her favourite.

'I have to agree, my dear,' the old woman said at length. 'There has been nothing nicer since the tragedy than having you and the child with us in Kilneagh, but I must be honest, Marianne.'

'He will come back, you know. One day Willie will come back.'

Hearing that, Imelda drifted into a familiar reverie: her father again stepped off the bus at Driscoll's, dressed in a suit that was as light-coloured as his hair. 'In tropical countries a nun wears white,' Sister Mulcahy had said in a geography class. *Puntarenas is a seaside town in Costa Rica*, Imelda had read in one of her mother's diaries. *The Bank of Ireland has been transferring money there, but now he's gone to somewhere else.* Imelda thought of a seaside promenade like the one in Youghal, and of an artist composing pictures on the sand with coloured powders. 'Jays, will you look at the cut of Quinton?' Teresa Shea sniggered in the convent whenever Imelda slipped into a reverie, but Imelda couldn't help herself. More and more her reveries claimed her in the classroom or when she wandered about

168

the fields or during the Sunday-evening anthems, or in bed. It was a habit she'd got into, like reading her mother's diaries, and listening. 'Whatever are you doing there, Imelda?' Aunt Pansy said, coming upon her among the bushes of the old shrubbery as she and Mr Derenzy were setting off down the avenue on their Sunday walk. Mr Derenzy had been talking about something at the mill, nothing of any interest.

Her mother's diaries were kept in a cupboard in her bedroom, a stack of jotters the same as the ones Imelda did her rough work in at the convent. The pencilled entries on the rough, lined paper were faded now, almost indecipherable. *I had never even heard of the Battle of the Yellow Ford until Father Kilgarriff told me. And now he wishes he hadn't. The furious Elizabeth cleverly transformed the defeat of Sir Henry Bagenal into victory, ensuring that her Irish battlefield might continue for as long as it was profitable: Father Kilgarriff had told you too, in the scarlet drawing-room with the school-books laid out between you. Just another Irish story it had seemed to you and perhaps, if ever you think of it, it still does. But the battlefield continuing is part of the pattern I see everywhere around me, as your exile is also. How could we in the end have pretended? How could we have rebuilt Kilneagh and watched our children playing among the shadows of destruction? The battlefield has never quietened.*

Tidily, Imelda returned the jotter to its place. For some reason a line of the poem she liked came into her head and she carried it with her to the fields and down to the river. *I hear lake water lapping with low sounds by the shore.* She knew the poem by heart now. She was the best at poetry, Miss Garvey had said, and had told Teresa Shea to leave the room because she smirked. '*I hear it in the deep heart's core,*' Imelda said aloud, lying down among the daisies on the river bank. She wondered what it had been like for the Blessed Imelda to experience the Sacred Host hovering above her while she knelt in prayer. She'd once asked Sister Rowan, who'd said that no ordinary mortal could know a thing like that. But it interested Imelda and she was curious.

She jumped from one stepping stone to another, crossing the water when it was shallow. She walked by the river for a while and then returned to the cobbled yard between the ruins and the orchard wing. Two geese wandered off towards the ruins and Imelda followed them. She told them they'd find no food among the stones and undergrowth. She shooed them back into the yard and then she ran into the kitchen.

Her mother was angry.

'It's horrible, Imelda. Eavesdropping's horrible. No one likes that kind of thing.'

'It's only when there's nothing to do.'

'You can bring the dogs for a walk. I often see you going for a walk.'

'I go to the mill. Or down to the river.'

'Well, then.'

'Sometimes it's boring.'

'I don't want you ever, ever again to listen at doors. Promise me now, Imelda.'

Imelda promised, since promises were easy. They were in the dining-room because Philomena was in the kitchen and Aunt Pansy and Aunt Fitzeustace in the sitting-room. The door was closed.

'You like it at the convent, don't you, Imelda? Teresa Shea can't help herself and after all everyone else is nice to you. All the nuns are, aren't they?'

Imelda did not speak. She watched a fly on the wax fruit in the centre of the table. How disappointed it would be, she thought, when it discovered that the fruit had no juice. Yes, everyone was nice to her, she agreed.

'And everyone at Kilneagh's nice to you. No one could be nicer than Aunt Pansy. And so's Aunt Fitzeustace and Philomena, and Father Kilgarriff. So is Mr Derenzy when he comes.'

The fly left the fruit and circled the glass of the lamp on the sideboard. It settled on the stopper of a decanter where another fly already was. The stopper of the decanter was cracked, a deep, discoloured fissure that spoilt its appearance.

'Yes,' Imelda said.

'Would you rather not live at Kilneagh, Imelda?'

Both flies ceased their interest in the decanter. One disappeared into the shadows of the ceiling, the other crept along the mahogany surface of the sideboard. The gondola in the green picture of Venice seemed, just for an instant, to give the slightest of shivers, as if about to begin its journey. But the figures outside the church by the bridge remained motionless. Imelda said, not looking at her mother:

'Is he really going to come back?'

'One day he will.'

'Sometimes I think it could be all a mistake about what happened. Sometimes I think maybe everyone is wrong.'

'Mistake?'

'Like it mightn't be true that Cuchulainn sent the bodies in a chariot to his enemy. Like it mightn't be true about the Mitchelstown Martyrs or that priest in Youghal.'

'But it is true, Imelda,' her mother said gently. 'We mustn't pretend it isn't.'

Again it seemed to Imelda that the gondola moved very slightly and this time she could have sworn that one of the figures outside the church raised a hand.

'That lady thought I shouldn't have been given life.'

'What lady? What on earth are you talking about, Imelda?'

'You told me about her: Miss Halliwell.'

'But I never said anything about –'

'There is a letter in Aunt Fitzeustace's writing-desk.'

'You mean you opened that writing-desk? Imelda, you shouldn't have done that. Don't you see you shouldn't? It's like listening at doors. It's horrible. It's a dreadful thing to read other people's letters.'

'I know.'

Philomena's voice called from the back door, attracting the attention of the hens. It reminded Imelda of how, listening to her mother telling her about the time her parents had come to Kilneagh to persuade her to return to England, she had imagined Philomena passing by the French windows with a raincoat thrown over her head. She repeated that to her mother now, hoping to please her because she was still angry, but her mother regarded her with surprise. As far as she could remember, she said, Philomena had not passed by the windows on that occasion.

'Oh, I think she did,' Imelda contradicted. 'I'm sure she did.'

Greater bewilderment gathered in her mother's face. Imelda said that Aunt Fitzeustace and Aunt Pansy had come in from their afternoon outing with the dogs, Aunt Fitzeustace with a sponge-cake on a plate. Father Kilgarriff had entered the sitting-room also.

'He put a bit of turf on the fire and blew it with the bellows. He said a day like that would drive the damp into your bones.'

She smiled at her mother, her smile suggesting that there had been no difficulty in the conversation they'd had. It was nicer if they could agree that there had been no difficulty, if they could forget any awkwardness. But her mother didn't appear to be aware of that. She continued to frown for a moment and then went on with the conversation as it had been. Imelda had to promise all over again that she would not eavesdrop and would not go poking in Aunt Fitzeustace's writing-desk. She was glad at least that the conversation had not obliged her to reveal that she'd also read the jotter diaries.

In bed that night Imelda thought about the conversation, wishing it had ended in a different manner. She didn't quite know how it might have ended, only that everything would not have been quite such a jumble. Then she thought about the scarlet drawing-room and the school-books laid out upon the table, and the fair-haired boy, just the same age as she was, being bad at Latin. The scent of sweet-peas wafted in from the garden and the next thing was she was in the garden herself, watching Tim Paddy while he raked the gravel.

It is considered that a butcher's knife was most likely to have been the type of weapon employed.
Imelda replaced the neatly cut-out piece of paper in the secret drawer and snapped the drawer back into place. In the end it hadn't really turned out to be very secret: all you had to do was to run your fingers along the little pillar.

Soundlessly she closed the flap of the writing-desk and pushed in the two little supports. *The head was partially hacked from the neck, the body stabbed in seventeen places.*

'The head,' Imelda said aloud, standing with her back to the writing-desk and leaning against it. She imagined the head, its weight tearing the flesh that still attached it to the body. She imagined the eyes and the mouth, and the body twitching the way she'd seen a turkey's once, for nearly a minute after death.

'Hullo, Imelda,' Mr Derenzy said.

'Hullo, Imelda,' Johnny Lacy said.

She wondered if she liked the mill. She wondered if she liked the green-faced clock or the sound of water, or the autumn russet of the creeper that covered the stone. She thought she didn't. Abruptly she thought that none of it was nice.

'We're busy today, Imelda,' Johnny Lacy said. 'Or else I'd tell you a story.'

'Hurry up now, Johnny,' Mr Derenzy called.

She sat for a while on the cobbles of the yard, her thin legs stuck out in front of her. 'Thin shanks,' Teresa Shea called them. Teresa Shea said they'd never stop getting longer, but Aunt Pansy dismissed that as nonsense. 'You'll grow up beautiful, Imelda,' she'd promised. 'There's no doubt about that.'

Funny the way her mother said it so often: one day he will, they only had to wait. Funny the way she wrote things down in an old jotter so's you could hardly read it. Imelda clambered to her feet and went to talk to Mr Derenzy in the office.

'Do you like the mill?' she asked him. 'D'you think it's nice?'

'Oh, I dare say I'm well enough used to the place.'

'Will it always be here, Mr Derenzy?'

'I'd say it would be.'

She walked through the birch wood and the fields. It was best to go up to the tree and lean against it like she had the day before yesterday. Best to put her arms around it because it wasn't its fault; horrid to blame a poor old oak tree, silly being frightened of it. 'Silly-billy Quinton,' Teresa Shea used to say, but she hadn't said it for ages now.

She sat down and closed her eyes and when he stepped off the bus at Driscoll's she felt like she did when she made herself lean against

173

the tree. 'Imelda,' he said. 'What a lovely name!' And she told him about the Blessed Imelda and how the Host had come to her. He smiled and stroked her hair.

She jumped up and ran by the edge of the field she was in. Sometimes when she ran what she imagined fell to pieces, shattering into fragments. But this time that didn't happen. He went on stroking her hair and he told her how he'd stood in a shop where there was dust everywhere, a shop like the pawnbroker's at the bottom of the steep hill in Cork. An old woman with bad eyes lifted three knives tied together from the shop window, and he undid the hairy string. He had to go to a place like that, he explained: he was no more than a shadow for all the half-blind old woman knew.

Imelda climbed a stone wall and lay on the grass on the other side of it, too breathless to go on running. On the deck of the ship there were people who had been at a wedding, people singing, with confetti on their clothes. A child in white satin had chocolate marks around her mouth, two men danced and drank from bottles. All the time on the journey he kept feeling the blade of the knife in his pocket.

'And evening,' Imelda whispered to herself, running again through the fields, 'full of the linnet's wings.' Sometimes it helped when she said the poetry. She crouched in a corner of the ruins, hidden by the nettles that had grown. 'And noon a purple glow,' she whispered.

Water dripped beside her, and Imelda watched it falling on to stones and plaster. She searched in her mind for the poetry but she could not remember the order of the words. She closed her eyes and in the room above the vegetable shop blood spurted in a torrent, splashing on to the wallpaper that was torn and hung loosely down. The blood was sticky, running over the backs of her hands and splashing on to her hair. It soaked through her clothes, warm when it reached her skin.

Imelda pressed her face into the nettles and did not feel their stinging. She pressed her fists into her ears. She closed her eyes as tightly as she could.

But nothing went away.

The screaming of the children began, and the torment of the flames on their flesh. The dogs were laid out dead in the yard, and the body of the man in the teddy-bear dressing-gown lay smouldering on the stairs. The blood kept running on her hands, and was tacky in her hair.

In the classroom Miss Garvey began to hook up her skirt, for the lesson was almost over. 'On Thursday we'll take a look at "The Ballad of Father Gilligan",' she said.

She asked for the blackboard to be cleaned and then, to her astonishment, she saw that Imelda Quinton had raised both her arms in front of her and was slowly moving away from the desk she shared with Lottie Reilly, as if walking in her sleep. With hesitant steps, occasionally stumbling, the child walked to a corner of the classroom. She huddled herself into it, crouching on the floor, pressed hard against the two walls that met there. She made a whimpering sound and then was silent.

WILLIE

I received a telegram which simply said, *Josephine is dying. Hospital of St Bernadette*, it was signed. The nun who sent the message must have known it wouldn't be necessary to be more precise, and she was right: when I tried to recall Josephine's other name I could not.

I went immediately when the telegram came. I packed a small white suitcase and from Sansepolcro, where I lived at that time, I took the Arezzo bus, not even pausing to look up the trains from Arezzo to Pisa. 'This is Josephine': my mother had stepped ahead of her through the French windows of the morning-room, on to the grass.

The bus moved slowly through sunshine and the soft spring landscape of Umbria. The first green shoots decorated the vines on either side of the road; new growth freshened the olive branches. It seemed preposterous to be leaving behind my Canary roses, my irises and wistaria, I who was so lost in the world of Bellini and Ghirlandaio. Yet even more urgently as I progressed on it I wanted to make the journey.

At Pisa the airport was on strike. I took the Rome Express to Paris and on it ate *pasta in brodo* and *scallopine*, staring out at orange-tiled roofs and ochre walls. I drank a litre of Brolio and ordered grappa with my coffee. She would be humble in old age, I thought, and felt ashamed that I did not know her other name. I knew nothing of her life since last I'd seen her, so very long ago, how she had spent it, where she had been. I had not said good-bye, which perhaps was why I so determinedly made the journey now.

On the plane the pretty stewardess was attentive, smart in her green uniform. Her voice reminded me of Ireland. 'Yes please,' I said. 'Yes, I think a little whiskey.' She smiled a soothing, airline smile. 'Jameson?' she murmured, caressing me with the familiar name.

In Cork there was a wait before a taxi was available. I drank more whiskey, for how could I soberly arrive at a strange hospital, in this city again after so long?

'Ah, the traffic's shocking these days,' the taxi-driver said. 'Shocking altogether.' I had asked him to be as quick about the journey as he could. 'I understand,' he replied, and I could feel him guessing what was at stake, since we were going to a hospital. Involuntarily he crossed himself.

'I haven't been to Cork for forty years,' I said.

'You'd find it changed, sir.'

'I used to live here.'

'Is that so, sir? You don't sound like a Corkman. I took you for a stranger, sir.'

'I've become a stranger.'

'It wasn't much of a place, I'd say, forty years ago?'

'I remember it as thriving. The docks were always busy.'

'It's thriving now all right. The Yanks love Cork.'

'I can imagine that.'

'There's a few, sir, put off by the trouble up in the North. There's a confusion that we might be affected down here. But there's not so many like that.'

'I've read about the trouble.'

'Where're you living now, sir?'

'In a town called Sansepolcro. In Italy.'

'I was never in Italy.'

The hospital was of grey, unpainted concrete, dominated by a white cross. In a car-park grotto there was a statue of the Virgin, with flowers in jam-jars on a ledge by her feet. An old woman knelt in prayer.

'Good luck so, sir,' the taxi-driver said as I paid him, and I carried my white suitcase through swing-doors and spoke to a nun at a reception desk. The surface beneath my feet was highly polished parquet that stretched away to other swing-doors and beyond them, becoming a corridor. The reception area was enormous, with chairs against cream-coloured walls, and a cross on the wall above the nun's desk.

'Please wait a moment,' she said, smiling with practised, hospital sensitivity: a consoling or a joyful smile, you could take it as circumstances dictated. 'Take a seat now till I find out.'

I sat among other people, all of them silent, men and women of different ages, two small children. The nun spoke into a telephone but I couldn't hear what she said. The man beside me took a packet of cigarettes from his pocket and then remembered there were signs requesting you not to smoke.

'Please come with me,' another nun said, and I followed her through the second set of doors, down the long corridor.

'I'm not too late, Sister?'

'No, you're not too late.'

Josephine was in a dusky room with rosary beads on the table close to her. She was propped up on pillows with her eyes closed, a crucifix on the wall above her. A young nun sat by her bed.

'I'll leave you with Sister Power,' the nun who'd brought me whispered, and Sister Power rose from the bedside. Without making a sound except for the rustle of her habit she crossed the room to where I was standing and led me out into the corridor again. We stood a foot or two from the door, speaking in murmurs.

'She was brought in a week ago,' she said. 'They thought at St Fina's she might have pneumonia and would need our care.'

'And has she?'

'No, just a little cold. But she's sinking all the time. I'm sorry,' she said, 'but I'm going to ask you to do something. It could upset her when she wakes up if you smell of drink. I'm going to ask you to take a mouth-wash.'

She returned to her duty at the bedside, and I accompanied another nun to a small room where medicines were kept. 'Don't mind,' she said, as if what was happening was quite usual.

I washed my mouth out and spat into a basin, and then drank some water. When Josephine came into the dining-room at Kilneagh to clear away the dinner dishes no one stopped talking, no matter what was being said. First thing every morning she lit the range. After that there was the fire in the drawing-room and then the one in the breakfast-room.

'Thank you,' the nun said, and led me back to where Josephine was propped up. I sat down and for the first time I examined her face. All the prettiness had gone. It was a thin face, thinner and more wrinkled than my own, lifeless because her eyes were still closed. The grey hair was scanty, brown blotches marked the skin of the forehead. But on the white candlewick bedspread her hands were not as I remembered them: the skin was marked with elderly freckles also, but the rawness caused by work had gone.

'Well,' she said, her eyes abruptly opening. 'Well.'

Behind a glaze of weariness the same softness lurked in the depths of them. Her fingers twitched on the candlewick, her lips slightly parted.

'You have a visitor, Josephine.'

The eyes closed, and after a moment opened again. They stared ahead of her, between the nun and myself, at the blank wall opposite her bed.

'A visitor,' Sister Power repeated, making her nun's gesture in my direction.

'Kilneagh,' Josephine said. Tears oozed from the corners of her eyes. 'Dear Mary, console them,' she whispered.

Sister Power placed the rosary beads between the bent fingers, but Josephine didn't notice. 'Console them everywhere,' she said. 'Console them.'

Her eyes closed again.

'She's asleep,' Sister Power said.

She pressed a bell beside the bed and after a minute or so another nun came in. Sister Power asked her to take her place by the bedside and then nodded to me. I followed her down the corridor to an office that had another crucifix in it, small and black, hanging between two windows. There was a picture of the Sacred Heart as well, and a plaster image of the Virgin.

'I'm going to have some coffee myself,' Sister Power said, plugging in an electric kettle. 'I hope we did right with that telegram?'

'Yes, of course.'

'Would you like some coffee yourself?'

'Yes, I would please.'

She opened a cupboard and took a tin containing biscuits from it. She placed blue cups and saucers on the desk, among papers and wire trays. She found sugar and a tin of instant milk in the cupboard also.

'We didn't know to send for you or not. She mentioned you repeatedly one day, all day long, and then they discovered your address from the solicitors. Italy must be lovely, is it?'

'I'm fond of it.'

'I don't think she was unhappy at St Fina's. They speak of

her with great affection. They ring up every day now that she's here.'

'St Fina's?'

'The place she worked. An institution for old nuns.'

The kettle boiled. In silence Sister Power made the instant coffee. She didn't seem to mind these silences that occurred. She said:

'She hardly ever ceased to pray towards the end. She asks the same thing all the time: that the survivors may be comforted in their mourning. She requests God's word in Ireland.'

I did not say anything. I was offered another biscuit but did not accept one. Sister Power rose and I followed her back to the room where the old woman was dying.

'Josephine,' I said, as softly as I could.

'"Bring out a drink to those men," your father said. He never forgot the needs of anyone.'

'Yes, he was kind.'

'"I want a blackness," your mother said. All the wallpaper I put up for her she didn't care about. The new house meant nothing to her.'

Her eyes closed and opened at once again. 'Imelda,' she said. 'The Blessed Imelda.' She died just after she spoke, the rosary beads idle in her hands.

A stout grey-haired priest murmured the burial words with a display of feeling, and I guessed he must have known Josephine and have felt affection for her humility and her piety. Nuns from St Fina's stood in a bunch, their lips moving in a whisper when they were required to. As soon as the little crowd eventually began to disperse two gravediggers appeared with shovels.

'Excuse me,' the priest said, behind me somewhere. I turned and waited for him. 'I know who you are,' he said. 'You've come from Italy.'

'Yes.'

'She's at peace now.'

'Yes, she is.'

He walked with me. The wind blew his surplice about. It was bitterly cold that day.

'You could safely remain in Ireland, sir. Enough years have passed.'

'Is that why she sent for me?'

'No one would bother with you now. If you'll forgive me, Mr Quinton, for saying that.'

I returned to Italy, to my world of Ghirlandaio, to my Canary roses and my irises, to the saints that Italy honours so: the Blessed Imelda of Bologna whom Josephine mentioned, whose day my daughter shared; St Clare who saved the city of Assisi; St Catherine who cut her hair off so that no one would wish to marry her. St Crispin was a shoemaker. St Paul made tents. A spring gushed in the desert when St Euthymius prayed. The dead body of St Zenobius revived a withered tree. Late in my life I had grown to admire the saints.

At the railway station in Florence a mass of azaleas bloomed in huge terracotta pots, marvellous elaborations of brilliant flowers, reds and yellows and creams, elegantly grouped: I travelled by way of Florence especially to see them. 'If you study the lives of the saints,' the nun in the hospital had said after Josephine had mentioned the Blessed Imelda, 'you'll find that it is horror and tragedy that make them what they are. Reflecting the life of Our Lord.' Josephine was a go-between, a servant even as she died. At Kilneagh my daughter was insane, yet Josephine had wished me to return: in Ireland it happens sometimes that the insane are taken to be saints of a kind. Legends in Ireland are born almost every day.

MARIANNE

April 4th 1971

In the cemetery he did not see me, nor even look around for me. Have all of them been right: should I have years ago returned to Dorset, to that pretty town? Have I been nonsensical and silly, all this talk about a battlefield continuing?

Time stopped instead. The child, the priest, the faces of the aunts, the hands of the clock recording time that has no meaning. Days, hours, months, years: a jumble while I wait.

In the darkness I come downstairs, I cannot sleep. The letters we might have written would not communicate: I understand, of course I understand.

January 12th 1976

I close my eyes and I am safe again in Woodcombe Rectory. A tiredness floats away from me, and then returns.

She might be married and have children. She might, somewhere in Wiltshire or Somerset, in London or Southampton, be a doctor's wife or an architect's wife. She might be a doctor or an architect herself. How very strange that seems!

June 22nd 1979

Father Kilgarriff died today, no trouble in his great old age. He was right when he said that there's not much left in a life when murder has been committed. That moment when I guessed the truth in Mr Lanigan's office; that moment when she opened the secret drawer; that moment when he stood at his mother's bedroom door and saw her dead. After each brief moment there was as little chance for any one of us as there was for Kilneagh after the soldiers' wrath. Truncated lives, creatures of the shadows. Fools of fortune, as his father would have said; ghosts we became.

August 6th 1982

Today he has returned.

IMELDA

Murmuring to one another, the elderly couple rise and make their way outside, into the warmth of an autumn mid-day. Her tininess is wizened by old age. Pleasanter to be here, he reflects, than seeing out his days in the Ospedale Geriatrico. Blotches freckle his forehead, matching in colour the tweed of his suit. The skin of his hairless head feels tight, like a shell: limping old crab, he calls himself, since his walk is assisted by a gold-capped cane. There is a slight, anchor-shaped scar near his right cheek-bone, a reminder of Puntarenas, one of the many towns where he has lived. A tram there knocked him down in 1942: he has had the scar since.

They walk beneath the mulberry trees. A favourite wonder is again mulled over: that anxiety in India should have brought them together. Fingers touch. One hand grasps another, awkwardly in elderliness. She tells of the dream she had once, when so many people from their lives congregated in sunshine on a lawn. They wonder if Mavis still has rashes, if Cynthia is still alive. They wonder about Ring and de Courcy and Agnes Brontenby. Somewhere he'd heard that de Courcy had not become an actor but had taken over a laundry in Singapore. Could it be true, the rumour there was, that Miss Halliwell had married a man in a bank and had blossomed in contentment?

They say the mulberries should soon be picked, a bumper crop this year. Odd that the summer's drought should have urged the fruit on so.

They do not speak of other matters.

Imelda does not speak at all, nor ever wishes to. Her smooth blonde hair has a burnished look where the sunlight catches it; in her middle age she is both elegant and beautiful, her face meticulously made up. She walks by the river and the derelict mill. She imagines the bones of Father Kilgarriff resting gently in the cemetery, and the bones of the Quintons in the Protestant churchyard, at the other end of the village. The children of the fire flank their father, their mother is a yard away. Anna Quinton and her dog-faced husband are close again, Aunt Pansy lies far from Mr Derenzy, Aunt Fitzeustace is alone. The family as it was is reflected in the arrangement of the Quintons' bones; tranquillity is there, no matter how death came. 'O Lord, now lettest Thou Thy servant,' intones the voice on Sundays and it is pleasant then in the musty church, no matter what the season.

Imelda is gifted, so the local people say, and bring the afflicted to her. A woman has been rid of dementia, a man cured of a cataract. Her happiness is like a shroud miraculously about her, its source mysterious except to her. No one but Imelda knows that in the scarlet drawing-room wood blazes in the fireplace while the man of the brass log-box reaches behind him for the hand of the serving girl. Within globes like onions, lights dimly gleam, and carved on the marble of the mantelpiece the clustered leaves are as delicate as the flicker of the flames. No one knows that she is happiest of all when she stands in the centre of the Chinese carpet, able to see in the same moment the garden and the furniture of the room, and to sense that yet another evening is full of the linnet's wings.

They sit, all three of them, in the kitchen of the orchard wing. A meal has been cooked, a stew of chicken and vegetables which the local people brought. In a day or two the local people will come again with groceries. Even Teresa Shea, married to Driscoll of the shop, sees to it that milk for the Quintons is not forgotten.

'We cannot wait beyond tomorrow,' he says. 'We must pick the mulberries tomorrow.'

He smiles the smile of the photograph, and in the band of her straw hat the girl he loves wears an artificial rose. They are aware that they exist so in the idyll of their daughter's crazy thought. They are aware that there is a miracle in this end, as remarkable as the Host which hung above the head of the child in Bologna. They are grateful for what they have been allowed, and for the mercy of their daughter's quiet world, in which there is no ugliness.

'No, we must not wait beyond tomorrow,' he repeats, and Imelda listens while there is talk of how chip baskets will be put ready tonight, and a chair to stand on brought to the orchard in the early morning. Almost a week it will take to pick the fruit, longer if rain interrupts.